Airmed

The Eight

Book One

I0677007

by

Sharilyn Skye

Copyright 2019 by Sharilyn Skye
All Rights Reserved
Paperback ISBN 9780960015993
First Edition: June 2019
Revision: March 2021
Cover Design: Dark Horse Publishing
Cover Photo: Depositphoto

Dark Horse Publishing

Morgantown, WV

To Dawn, Your inspiration and experience are invaluable. You know what I mean... Believe me, there will be piercings and more tattoos soon enough.

Chapter One

Ari

I dropped my bags on the floor of the house with a huff, blowing out a breath to get the stupid curls out of my face. It was not a bad house. In fact, it was quite lovely, a huge step up from what I was used to. The floors were a pretty, gray, smooth polished stone, and the walls were white painted wood. It was clean, fresh-smelling, and flowers sat in vases on almost every surface. Books lined the shelves in the living room, and the place was free of dust. There was a water source somewhere, seeing as aqueducts had been built into it, and there was actual plumbing in the kitchen. Despite the damp chill of the day, the room was warm and dry as hearth fires burned. These are luxuries few have at this time. The living and kitchen areas were open, and five closed doors faced the center of the home.

For that was what this place was meant to be, regardless of what I wanted. My mother gave me to the four men that live here, and if I did not try to produce a child with one of them, we would all be punished in some horrible fashion, knowing her as I do. That is her decree. Long live the Queen and all. She says that I should be honored. She says that I should be grateful. She has chosen these men personally, and they are the finest in the land. I feel neither honored nor grateful.

My name is Airmed, but my friends call me Ari. My mother calls me daughter and nothing more unless angered into remembering I have a name. I am the last of a generation of children born to the once powerful and now rotting Daoine Sidhe, the final of the twenty or so purebloods to be popped out not that long ago. I think I am aged thirty winters or so but cannot be sure, for no one counts the years since our birth. Of those twenty children that survived their childhood, twelve were boys leaving eight girls. The boys have since vanished as they were worthless in my mother's broodmare program. I hate that bitch.

She whisks in behind me as if the world should stop simply because she is in it and seems disappointed that no one is waiting to greet her. She is wearing one of her damn dresses. This one is sky blue and woven with silver thread. It makes her dark, blood-red hair pretty. She has worn it down, and it softens her face. It's almost as if she is hoping all the male attention will be on her instead of her daughter. She can have the men; I don't want them, I will go back to my bakery.

I'm wearing soft doeskin pants, a habit she hates. I dress like a hunter even though I can't hunt to save my life. I mean, I took the classes, but it wasn't my thing. I am certainly the most educated and polished breeding sow in the land; all eight of us are. We are trained in the arts and sciences. Even the boring ones, like the art of pleasuring a man, although our virginities are intact by order of the Queen. Goddess forbid we bear a child whose lineage is not accounted for. I can hold a sword, speak several Fae languages, read and recite poetry, play many instruments, and dance with the best of them. Yet there I was, waiting to meet four men that were going to try to impregnate me, regardless of the fact that I am highly skilled in higher math, astronomy, engineering, and many other things. Failing to try will result in their death. It is all spelled out clearly in their contract with her. The contract in which I had no say.

Things were not always this way. Once upon a time, Talamh na Sithe flourished. There were enough Fae that there were separate courts and many branches of royalty, but that has all changed. Everything changed. No one speaks of this, and most of the old histories have conveniently disappeared. Still, there are a few old books in the great library that tell the tale of a time when things were different.

Suddenly, the doors open, and the four men step out, dropping to one knee at the sight of their Queen. I groaned loudly, rolling my eyes before walking over to the lounge and flopping down on it in disgust. If anyone graded my eye rolls, this one would certainly be a solid A-plus.

"Stand up and meet your mates, Daughter." She growled at me.

"I'm good. Hi, boys. I am Airmed. My friends call me Ari. I am not your friend, so you need call me nothing," I sighed. Aramea walked to me and jerked me up by the arm. I stood facing her toe to toe and let my power build. I had quite a lot of it for my age but couldn't dream of taking her in a fair fight. At least not yet, but I knew something she didn't; she wouldn't hurt a hair on my head. Not one. She needs me. Well, she needs my girl parts to try to fix the disaster her and the other ancient ones caused by punishing one of Goddess's favorites. No one will confirm this, but all know it to be true. It is whispered about so often they may as well announce it from the Great Fae Hall. Which, by the way, is falling apart and still smells like his blood.

When he died, it is said the fires of Talamh na Sithe died too, and now we suffer. Although the nightmare fairy tales say she did not kill him properly and that now he hunts us to extinction. If something can be cocked up, my mother will do it. If everything they say is true, I don't blame him a bit. I'm only saddened that he didn't start his rampage with her. If he had, maybe things would be different.

The men's eyes snapped to me as they watched this exchange with fear, not fear of me and certainly not fear for me, just simple fear. I understood it, but long ago gave up caring about fear. When you have been raised as I have, you find there are only two paths to travel, live in fear of what life holds and never live at all, or be fearless and face every day fighting, caring not when it may end. Guess which path I chose.

"You don't need your power to be laid like the lamb you are, little girl, be cautious, or I will strip it from you. Now do your job." She sneered at me. It didn't matter that she was taller than me and built like an ogre; I would not back down. She knows this. It wasn't our first argument. Most of them end in fire or bloodshed, but it was for show. Mostly. Turning to the men, she added, "Use whatever means necessary to temper her attitude; you have my permission. In fact, I encourage it." She looked at me once more then walked out the door, leaving me alone with them. The room was so silent, I thought they had vanished, but they stayed on their knees and said nothing. Smart.

"Don't worry about her, I insist." I rose and began walking around, trailing my fingers off the spines of the books, noting their titles. "Here's how this is going to go, gentlemen. I know my job. I know that you will all face grave punishment should you not make me malleable or some such. I will not be malleable, but I will also not cause your deaths. Know this. I have no small amount of power, so do not try to force yourselves on me; it will end badly for you. I will do my job, as my mother so eloquently puts it, but I will do it at my own pace. Other than pastries and cakes that I make for my bakery, I will not cook for you, so do not expect it. I will continue to make my normal deliveries and sell my goods at the bakery. I will not clean up your messes, for I am not your beloved wife or your maid, and even if I was, I would tell you to stuff it and clean up after yourselves. I don't know what you did to get this crap assignment, but it must have been horrible. My condolences." I stopped, turning to face them, and caught the looks of shocked horror they gave me. "Now, I would like a tour of this place, and then you will show me your horses, for that is the only way to judge a man." They said nothing, just looked at one another with impossibly wide eyes, their bodies frozen in place.

"Very well." I picked up my bags and went to the only room that the door was still closed to, assuming it was mine.

The room was lovely, if I am honest, and you can't always trust me to be, despite my Fae blood, but I am truthful in this. It was designed with my favorite colors in mind. The walls were a pale turquoise and white, soft animal hide rugs covered the stone floor, and the covers on the bed matched the rest. The room had its own water closet, which was a luxury I did not expect. I hoped beyond hope that the wood fires outside heated water for my bath. Maybe this would work out, despite my hag of a mother. Calling her that isn't fair to the hags though, they aren't nearly as bad as she is. I threw my bags on the bed and began to unpack. I heard a throat clear from the doorway. I turned to find all four men, watching from beyond the threshold with varying looks of concern and possibly a few thoughts about self-preservation showing in their multifaceted, brilliant eyes.

We will show you our horses, my Lady," the darkest one said.

I turned my assessing gaze to them; they were indeed handsome. Dark, light, and in between. Faemen are known for their beauty, but usually, their attitudes take away from the overall pleasure one gets from looking at them. They are difficult and cocksure.

Hopefully, the tone had been set with these four, and their egos would not overcome their loveliness. I dropped my clothes onto the bed in a rumpled mess and moved to follow them. I watched their backs and wondered why these supposed warriors would turn them to me. They were missing something big, but I would not let them know that. Let them underestimate me. It would work in my favor.

They were tall, all of them, as Fae typically are. In fact, they towered above me, my head would hit the upper third of the shortest ones back. I was not the usual Fae. Instead, I was a throwback to some time when, as a people, we lived in the mortal realm. My hair was the wrong shade of red, and my skin a tad too pale. Freckles dotted my nose, and I had never seen another Fae with those in my life. My emerald green multifaceted eyes were the only thing that looked like a proper Fae should.

I know the man claiming to be my father, and I look nothing like him. He makes my mother look like a cuddly bear. I wondered what these faemen had done to get the runt of the litter;

my mother must be punishing them for something. It made me feel almost bad for them.

Almost.

Maybe they didn't know what they were getting into; maybe they did. Who can say?

They did not show me their rooms but instead started in the kitchen. It was a lovely place. Pans of all sizes hung from a holder on the ceiling. Multiple baking ovens with separate heating fires stood waiting for cakes and cookies of all kinds. A sink large enough to wash pots in had its own water source and a huge table sat to the side that would be perfect for rolling cookies or icing cakes on. They were wise to show me this room first.

The tallest male, with silver blond hair grazing his shoulders, led the way outside. Warm sunlight spilled into the treeless back garden, and stone benches near water fountains invited one to find peace. A sheltered area with full-grown herbs ready to harvest was set to the side, and another filled with budding fruits and vegetables was set to the other. A stone wall as tall as a man surrounded the space, but a little gateway led to the woods beyond.

At least I was not trapped here. I closed my eyes and breathed in the scent of rosemary, sage, and thyme. My soul settled, and I felt my anger slip away. A wind chime tinkled merrily in the faint breeze. They were kind enough that they had thought to make me comfortable. The men had to apply and were tested to receive the gift of one of The Eight. These men had done their homework. I suppose that was something in their favor.

"This way." My eyes flew to the face of the darkest one in the bunch. His eyes were so brown as to be almost black, and dark mahogany hair curled and twisted around his face. I had never seen a Fae as dark as he. His skin was a deep brown and had a creamy look about it, like black tea with a hint of milk. His eyes sparked wickedly as he led the way from the garden, and I wondered what trouble I could be in now.

"Our horses, my Lady, you wished to see our horses," he said when we reached a small field next to the house.

Good Faerie horses roam freely but come when asked. It is an equal relationship by all parties, but only good men have free horses, for bad men must tie and fence theirs. Horses are smart creatures and the best judges of character; they should never be doubted. The men whistled in unison. It sounded like a chorus of different chords as they called.

In a blink, four horses came running through the field, stopping short of us, looking at us with kind, curious eyes. They were beautiful, their feet round and well cared for, their manes brushed to a shine, and their coats glossy. They were not of the Goddess, but then few are. There was not a fence in sight.

"May I?" I asked permission before I approached them, and all four heads nodded yes.

"Well, hello there, beautiful ones. Aren't you lovely?" I petted each in turn, breathing into their nostrils. They were fat and glossy beasts, black and white, brown and white, blue and white and red and white, as tradition goes. They were small but stout spotted horses that had feathering of hair down their legs, falling to cover most of their hooves. Their manes brushed their shoulders, and they were, no doubt, envied by many. My plain horse would pale in comparison. I turned back to the men who stood watching the exchange expectantly. "Now, you may tell me your names and title if you please," I said, providing them with a deep, proper curtsy.

The one with the silver hair stepped to me. His gray eyes met mine, and I startled at the look of him. He was lovely. Gray eyes are rare, and they matched his hair beautifully. His face was clean, and his features perfect. His skin was fair, not as fair as mine, more like soft, pale moonlight. He was lean with muscles defining his bare arms, but he was not muscle-bound. Every movement he made was delicate and graceful. It was possible I might be in trouble with this one.

"I am Saige, Captain of the Archers, and I am pleased to have you in our home," he said, bowing to me. I rolled my eyes as quietly as possible, only a B plus effort. I just bet he was pleased. Female Fae are difficult to find.

I am Lann, Captain of the Swordsmen." The dark one stepped forward, meeting my green eyes with his nearly black ones. They twinkled merrily like this was the most fun he had in ages. It almost made me feel pity for him since this would be no fun at all. He was more muscular than the first one, but his movements no less graceful. Charm oozed off him, and I wondered if it was part of his magic. He would bear watching. Goddess, was he beautiful.

"I am Seal, Master Huntsman." His hair was a light brown or dark blond depending on how the sunlight hit it, with nearly white highlights here and there like the sun-kissed those spots every day. His eyes were the color of fall leaves, brown, tan, and a hint of gold mixed in them; they glittered with intelligence and mistrust. He had a bit of scruff on his face, softening his otherwise hard features. Without a doubt, this one was a predator; he screamed danger to the very core of me. His color combination was also odd and not seen among Fae I have met, but he was no less striking for it. His predatory eyes brought the package to another level. I was beginning to see a theme among them.

The final one moved to stand next to his peers, shoulder to shoulder. "I am Laith Dearg; my friends call me Laith. You may call me whatever you like, my Lady. I am Master Blacksmith and sword maker for the land." I quirked a smile at his play on my words. His auburn hair and green eyes looked at me from a face of pure perfection. His arms were thick with muscles and his back wide from his work, yet he narrowed at the hips despite his size. He was what Faemen were supposed to look like traditionally. It was obvious my mother had tried to make them as different and as lovely as possible. Two Captains and two Masters. Perfect.

There would be no egos here.

None.

"Well met, gentleman." Thank you for the tour, now I would like to settle. I whistled for my horse, and she came running, undoubtedly following me from my mother's house to this one even though it was nearly an hour by carriage. She rarely let me out of her sight.

She was an odd thing. A throwback, like myself, to some other breed or time. She was pure white with the blackest eyes you ever saw. So much intelligence shone from them that it made up for the fact that she was plain. She had no feathering, and her legs were clean to the hoof. Her mane was shorter, her face refined, and her tail thick and fat to the point it could not be braided.

She was uncommon and beautiful to me because of it. She ran to my side, brushed her head on my belly, and begged me to scratch her ear. I did. She trotted over to the other horses, touching noses before turning her back and kicking at them solidly with a squeal. Good Mare. Why should we be any different? A low chuckle sounded from the men, and they turned to leave. I followed behind and went into my room, shutting the door behind me.

Chapter Two

Saige

"What have we done?" I said to the others, scrubbing my face with my hands when the little spitfire shut the door to her rooms. "This is not at all how I thought this would go. I thought the wretched girl would feel honored. Maybe even appreciative."

"Did you see the way she spoke to the Queen? Did you know this when you made an application for us to get her?" Seal said, pacing the floor of the living room.

"I did not know. I heard she was difficult, but no one spoke of her being this difficult," I said, easing myself onto a chair.

"Just go in there and have a go at her," Laith laughed from the kitchen where he was more likely than not making a stiff drink. I needed one too, but it would have to wait until this was settled.

"You have a go at her, Laith. I like my bollocks. I may not use them often, but I don't want to lose them forever." A small surprised laugh sounded from behind her door, and I lowered my voice.

"She said she will not be malleable," Lann said, from where he leaned facing the wall like a child in trouble.

"I am not inclined to believe she knows the definition of the word malleable," I said to him, scrubbing my hands down my face again. "What have I done?"

"Well, it is too late to undo it; we must simply see how it shakes out. She is a beauty. She is the Queen's daughter. It will work for us in the end," Seal whisper yelled, ripping the drink from Laith's hands and downing it.

"The Queen knew what she was doing when she accepted us. I am certain of that. If any can handle her, it is we four," I said, lacking any real confidence in the statement. We are friends. We have fought many a battle on many a front. This is just another one." I sighed, rising to make my own drink.

She stomped out of her rooms then, wearing an apron the color of the sun over her man pants and boots. She moved into the kitchen and began to set fires in the ovens. She tossed pans and ingredients around, making naught but a mess. She grumbled under her breath about sterile, dried up old men and delicate young broodmares. I dared not say anything. I took my drink and sat with my brothers to watch her.

"Do you have any fucking eggs," she asked, glaring at the four of us like we had kidnapped and brought her here ourselves. Lann rose cautiously, pretending not to be shocked by her language, and pointed to the only counter she had yet to destroy, then sat back down, speechless. I have never seen Lann speechless. Of all us, he is usually the one to woo and charm the rare lass we come across.

Her hair flew about her in a perfect mess, flour dotted her face, and her eyes sparked in the light of the torches she lit as the sun set, catching her red hair ablaze. When she was done, she was calmer, her curses fewer, and the tears she tried to hide gone from her eyes.

She brought three loaves of bread, a tray of cookies, and the most perfect cake I have ever seen, leaving them on the table before going back into her room, shutting the door quietly. Her shoulders had eased, and her body relaxed.

"Never let us run out of flour or eggs, Laith, never," I said, walking hesitantly to the table, taking a cookie. I half expected her to open the door and throw something at me, but she did not.

"Aye, Captain," he said. The four of us surrounded the table and filled ourselves to the point of gluttony on the best baked goods we had ever enjoyed in our lives. I have no doubt the moans of our pleasure at eating them reached her behind her door. Lann even cleaned the kitchen, putting out her fires and washing and hanging her bowls.

I made soup with the rabbit Seal brought home for dinner. It was a good soup; we used the last of her bread to soak up the remaining broth. After a vicious argument involving insults to our mothers, I was elected to take her a bowl when we finished.

We had seen her eat nothing since her arrival, and that was many hours ago.

Her rooms were dark when I entered, and there was no torch or hearth fire lit. Clothes were strewn all over the floor, and the bed and space around it was a mess. I had thought she came to unpack, but she was not there.

I peered around the corner carefully and found her in the bathing tub. She slept curled up in water that had long ago turned cold. Goosebumps raised on her blueish flesh, but she did seem to mind. Flour still dotted her face. The curve of her arms cradled her small breasts, and her round backside faced me. Goddess, but she was beautiful, her face unguarded and young.

I had forgotten when all this started how young The Eight still were. They are barely old enough to be finished growing and be ready for the attention of a man, but they had been raised fast from the beginning for one purpose alone. It made me sad for her, but Faerie was dying, and no one wanted to see it fade away completely. We would all do our jobs to the best of our ability.

I, for one, hoped to enjoy it, for she was finer than any female I had seen before. So different than the few women I encountered with her tiny size and blaze red hair. I would wait for her to settle in, but then we must get to work.

Chapter Three

Laith

Her horse is as magnificent as she is. Well-groomed and uncommonly stunning. It made me think better of her, but not by much. She is of horrible temperament. The girl, not the horse. How had I gotten dragged into this? Friendship. Friendship and a desire to settle down. A need to find our center.

We had all been together a long time, in as many ways as one can be, but we had no center. She was supposed to be that. I should have rounded up sheep instead, as the others did, but I find that habit disgusting. What to do about Airmed, don't call me Ari, you may call me nothing?

That thought stilled my soul. She had been raised as nothing. A vessel for a man's child. She was the Queen's daughter, but there was not a spot of warmth in the Queen. Not one. It made me think more kindly of her.

Just a little.

Then she baked us cakes and cookies. One cannot have a bad soul and bake like that. I liked her just fine after tasting her baked goods.

I took Seal to bed that night and held him close. We did not make love; we just held each other. We needed to be grounded after the chaos of the day. Saige braved checking on the Lady, and Lann went to bed alone. It would work out or not. We had each other and many years of friendship. I was hoping our wish to be settled would not get us killed.

Chapter Four

Ari

I awoke on my bed, covers piled on top of me and my hearth fire burning, despite the heat. I had fallen asleep in the tub. That was the last thing I remembered, yet here I was, warm and covered in blankets. I wondered which poor soul had gotten roped into that. Stretching, I bumped into a familiar warm body.

My cat, Isa, lay at my feet, the cat my mother had refused to allow me to bring. The cat disregarded a direct order from the Queen and followed me anyway. Poor dear. I petted her soft black fur and nosed her face. She stretched and rolled over, giving me her belly. I rubbed it for a moment before dressing. I pulled a simple shift to cover my nakedness and went out to make tea. Jumping off the bed, she followed me, exploring our new home.

Hearth fires burned in all the rooms, and it made the damp air cozy. Isa jumped onto the big table and lay down to watch as I made medicine from the herbs I collected in the garden. I brewed tea and baked bread that would sell in my bakery today. I would bake the cookies and cakes there, so they would suffer no damage from the long ride into town. I drank my tea and made peace with my surroundings. It was a nice home. I could have gotten worse. There are horrors in Talamh na Sithe that would have loved to have one of The Eight. These men, whatever their faults, were not horrors. I put on a pot of eggs to go with the bread and added tea to brew for them. It was a small concession. Someone had cleaned my mess from last night, and I should be thankful. I left my medicines on the counter to strengthen and went to dress. It was hours before dawn. I would get to the bakery early and have plenty of time to set up.

I called my horse to me, and she came despite the dark. She is used to baker's hours. I loaded my bread onto her saddle and prepared to mount when strong hands gripped me from the back, tossing me onto the horse. I squealed, grabbed the small knife I kept in my pants, and readied my power to fight back.

"Steady, Lady. Aren't you quick with a knife," Seal chuckled, silhouetted in the night, his dark golden blonde hair practically glowed against his olive skin. I have an early hunt. Thank you for breakfast and tea."

"You are welcome," I said, putting my knife away and pressing my horse forward.

"I will accompany you into town," he said, whistling for his horse.

"I don't need a babysitter, my Lord," I said formally, moving to pass him.

"Humor me, Lady." The Dire wolves are not yet asleep.

"Dire wolves?" I screeched.

"Yes, my Lady. The Dire wolves roam free here in the countryside."

"Good to know, Sir." I kicked my mare more aggressively and headed toward town. On horseback, the trip would be much faster than by carriage, possibly less than a half-hour if I kept a brisk pace. Seal mounted bareback and trotted up beside me. Solas pinned her ears and bared her teeth at the stallion beside her. She is a smart girl.

"My Lady."

"Oh, for the Goddess's sake, call me Ari. Please. I am no one's lady," I interrupted with a sigh.

"You are our Lady now, Ari," he said, glancing at me from the corner of his eyes.

"By decree of the Queen," I whispered.

"We are honored. We have been friends for a long time. You are the one thing we have always wanted that will make our friendship complete."

"Not me personally, surely, any girl would do." I sneered. He sighed, pinching the bridge of his nose.

We rode in silence for the rest of the way. Dawn began to break as I stopped in front of the bakery and pulled the saddle off Solas, letting her roam.

Seal brought the loaves of bread, set them on the counter, and then lit the walls' torches. It was nice. Familiar even though it had no right to be. I set fires in the ovens and began to pull out ingredients.

He came to me then, brushing his lips against mine. They were soft, and he smelled of my bread and tea. I had never been kissed before and did not expect his lips to feel so good when his eyes were so hard. It was such a shock that I did not have time to hit him or kiss him back. I was also unsure which of those things I wanted to do. He pulled away before I could gather my strength, but he left me with a tingle my sex class called desire. I didn't like it.

He was gone before I could think of a thing to say.

I baked bread and cookies with abandon that day and made more profit than I had in weeks.

Chapter Five

Lann

"Why is there a fucking cat on our table?" I growled, arms crossed and staring at the black beast coiled up and pretending to be sweet and uninterested in the large men scowling at it. The damn thing purred loud enough to wake the dead.

"I assume it is hers. It was here when we got up, sitting with the breakfast she said we could shove up our collective asses because she would never cook it," Laith said, his arms mirroring mine.

"Where is Seal?" I asked, looking around.

"Early hunt, he probably rode with her into town."

"Of course, he did."

"Better him than Dire wolves for an escort."

"I think they are likely afraid of her."

"It's quite possible."

"Do you think she will notice if we kill it?" I asked, rubbing my hands together.

"The cat is off-limits." A low groan came from Saige as he joined us at the table, arms crossed and staring at the feline that lay in a spot of sun on our table. "She made breakfast?"

"Tea, bread, and eggs. The tea is tolerable, but I wouldn't touch the eggs if I were you. She added a bit of herbs to them. She is looking to poison us, I'm certain," Laith argued, eyeing the eggs like they might start a fight.

"She is but a lass. Surely she is not so hard as that."

"Have you met her mother?"

We stood in silence, watching the cat.

We had all met her mother.

"Seal ate her breakfast. His plate is on the rack."

"And he may be dead in a ditch for it too."

I pulled my plate and piled it with food, filling my cup with hot tea. I had never been made breakfast by a woman before. I wanted to see what it was about. I took the first bite with care. It was not bad. Not as good as her cookies, but I did not feel poisoned after eating it. Then I began to wonder if one feels poisoned or simply gets poisoned and dies. I have no experience with poison. Swords, yes. Maces, yes. Knives, yes. Bows, yes. Poisons, no. I considered it while I chewed. Airmed's profile said she was skilled with herbs and medicines. I assume that also means poisons. I ate her breakfast anyway.

"We should check in at the bakery. One of us should escort her home. The Dire wolves and all".

"Dire wolves, dragons, electric eels, large birds of prey likely will not hazard a run-in with her," Saige said, picking at his plate of bread and eggs. "They don't taste poisoned. I like the hint of garlic in them."

"We should check the ditches on the way to town to see if Seal is in one."

"Good idea."

We called our horses and rode into town. I noticed we all took a little extra care with our clothes today. We did not find Seal dead in a ditch. We felt a bit more confident at that.

Chapter Six

Ari

The Queen stopped in before closing time; she made the air heavy just by darkening my door. I sighed. Tossing down my cleaning rag, I readied myself for the battle I knew was coming.

"Oh, Daughter, I had hoped you would not come in today." She sighed, taking in my messy attire and flour-covered hair. "You have more important duties; someone else can take the bakery."

"No, Mother. The bakery is mine, and regardless of my other duties, I will work it," I said, wishing I could be anywhere else.

"Surely, there are other things you can do," she said, strolling the line of baked goods and gathering a few things in a basket.

"I can't lay on my back all day, Mother; the men have jobs. No one is lying about, and neither shall I. This bakery is mine, and I will see to it.

"Did you bed any of them?" she asked, eyeing me over the loaves in her basket.

"Mother." I glared.

"It is a simple question," she asked, feigning interest in a pie.

"No, I did not. I just learned their names. I will not bed them until I am ready." I sighed again, pinching the bridge of my nose with my fingers to keep my brains from leaking out.

"It does not matter what their names are, Daughter. They are good men. They wanted you enough to build a home just for you so that you would be comfortable. I understand you find this distasteful…"

"Distasteful?" I shouted, interrupting her grand lecture. "Distasteful? You have got to be kidding me. Distasteful is sitting through hours of sex master class. Distasteful is learning to do one's hair in a manner that is pleasing to the male eye. What you have set me up for goes beyond distasteful. Not only am I to be your broodmare, but I am to be your broodmare on your schedule. Which would you like me to bed first, Mother? Should I allow them to have a go all at once? Is there a particular position to induce pregnancy that you recommend? I missed that part of sex class."

"You insolent brat," she said, lobbing a ball of magic at me. I ducked to miss. Living with her from time to time had made my reflexes quite sharp. I fired back my own and hit her square in the chest. It was just a tap, but she bellowed with rage anyway. "You will do as I say, Child."

"I never said I wouldn't," I screamed at her, "but I sure as shit am not doing it on day one. You want to hear the details of their juicy sex lives, then approach them yourself and have a go at them. You killed all the boys who might be young enough to be virile and left us with aging sperm. The lack of children in Faerie is not the fault of the children born into it. The fault goes way, way back to before any of The Eight were shot from the dried-up old ball sacks of Faerie men." I shot another volley at her and dove under the counter as she fired back, hitting one of my precious ovens.

"You will not speak of a thing you know nothing about, Airmed." Oh, now I was in trouble. She used my real name.

"Everyone knows about it, Aramea. Everyone. It's the worst kept secret in the land." I glared, peeping above the counter to see her face shrouded in thought. "You should go now. I need to clean up and go home."

"You will do my bidding, or it will mean death to those men," she yelled, pulling the door open and slamming it behind her.

"I don't care if they die, mother, how can I? I don't even know them, but I won't have it be my fault," I told the emptiness around me as I began to clean up from our fight. This one was tame by our standards. The last time we got into it, we burnt down an entire wing of her castle.

Chapter Seven

Saige

"What are they doing?" Laith asked, watching from the stone wall upon which the four of us sat.

"Trying to kill each other," I said matter of factly. "She will die by her mother's hand before we can even call her by her given name, let alone the name her 'friends' call her," I said, making air quotes around the word friends.

"She told me to call her Ari this morning." Seal smirked from his spot on the wall. His horse stood behind him with a stag draped across it.

Arrogant prick.

"They are going to set the bakery on fire," Laith said, absently watching the two women shoot fireballs at one another. "What manner of girl shoots fireballs at the Queen?"

"One we should be cautious with," Seal answered.

"Said the man allowed to call her Ari. Do you feel poisoned?" Laith asked, looking the Huntsman over.

"She did not poison us with breakfast."

"We thought we would find you dead in a ditch," Lann stated, deadpan as if it would be no great loss. Seal ran his hands back through his hair, making a mess of it. Blood from the stag covered his pants; he dropped from the wall, mounting his horse.

"I will go and cut the meat for dinner. Do not let the Queen kill our mate before we have a chance to mate with her," he said over his shoulder as he rode away.

"I'm not stepping in the middle of that," I shouted at him as another fireball hit the wall of the bakery, shaking the glass door.

"The four bravest men in the land are afraid to break up a fight between women." He laughed, kicking his horse faster.

"Says the guy riding away," I yelled back. I jumped from the wall and mounted my horse to follow him, leaving Laith and Lann to fight over who had to escort the 'Lady' around appropriately terrified Dire wolves.

Lann lost the fight because Laith soon joined me on the road. We cantered our horses home, feeding them and turning them loose before going about the nightly chores of filling the wood stoves and lighting hearth fires. It was Spring in Faerie, and though the days were warm, the nights could be wickedly cold.

Airmed's room was still a disaster. I went about setting it right, hanging clothes in her closets, marveling at the fact that she owned very little. How could the Queen's daughter come into our lives with so few items? This was to be her home, and yet she had nothing here. Her damn cat perched upon her bed and watched as I worked, narrowing its feline eyes if I got close to it.

She had mostly pants and shirts in the style men wear, but she did have a few dresses and softer shifts in which to sleep. The other men and I would need to see to her wants as soon as possible. I set her hearth fire ablaze and then saw to my room before she and Lann could get home.

Chapter Eight

Lann

I waited in the dark, allowing my horse to roam while she cleaned up her bakery and got the ovens ready for tomorrow. Even though the rougher side of Talamh na Sithe shows itself only at night, she had no fear.

She cleaned up the mess the fight with her mother caused and made the bakery pristine by the light of her torches. Her rooms in our house should look so tidy. She hung her apron on a hook and shook out her hair.

She was glorious. Her long, wavy red hair draped the curve of her hip even in a ponytail. She stretched and rubbed soreness out of the small of her back before closing the shop, locking it behind her. I whistled for my horse as she whistled for hers.

They came together from the woods where they waited, knowing the time was close. Her mare was lovely by the moonlight; she looked like a pale wraith all in white. She would be an easy target for the massive wolves that hunt at night. I saddled her mare as she watched warily.

"I can do that myself." She told me, placing her hand on her hip and jutting it out angrily.

"I know you can, my Lady, but you have had a long day. Allow me to help you."

"I am no one's lady; you may call me Ari," she said, throwing her leg over the mare when I was done. I said nothing for a bit as we settled into the ride home.

"You are my Lady, Ari," I whispered into the darkness between us.

She was a skilled rider and sat a horse like a natural. Many women did not take the time to learn to ride, preferring instead to take a carriage. Ari looked at home on the back of her mare.

"I appreciate the sentiment, Lann. You are very kind. Perhaps you did choose me and did not have me foisted upon you by the Queen," she said, with no small amount of bitterness in her voice. Still, the bitterness hid a deeper sadness I'm sure she did not intend to show.

"You were foisted upon no one. We wanted you to join us very much. Our life together is quite lonely," I said, reining the horse with one hand and reaching through the space between us for hers. She allowed her fingers to graze mine but said nothing.

At the sound of the wolves howling, she screeched and kicked her horse into a canter. Laughing, I followed but kept my hand on my sword just in case.

Once home, she jumped down and smacked into my chest in her rush to get into the house. I put my arms around her and pulled her to me. Her body fit so nicely with mine, I found it surprising. She stood on her tiptoes and grazed my lips with hers, smelling of flour, vanilla, and sugar. I allowed her to control the kiss, but she broke it off, jumping around me and heading into the house with a squeal. I stood for a minute in our garden and thought about the funny feeling in my stomach. Perhaps, I'd been poisoned after all.

Chapter Nine

Ari

Lann has soft lips, too. I don't like it.

I went into the house to find the men waiting for me. Dinner was laid on the table, and Isa was sprawled in front of a roaring hearth fire. Something twittered inside of me. This was what a home was. Warm fires and hot meals. I picked Isa up and put my nose on hers.

She had adopted me at our dorm, and I turned the once feral cat into a sweet lump of fur. She had been with me ever since and refused to leave, no matter how many fireballs my mother threw at her.

I washed my hands and moved to sit with the men. I said nothing as they laughed and talked of their day. Lann and his troops had fought a group of Orcs, Saige had patrolled the woods to the north of town looking for a troublesome Fae who was poaching the Queen's golden rams, and Laith had worked in his smith all day.

Seal had done what he always does; he hunted. I am not sure what he hunts, but I know the meat house in their yard is full of salted, hanging meats.

I listened as they chatted, lulled by their warm sense of fraternity. The meal was good, and I ate what I could, which was not much. Not all Fae houses have as much food as this one, and The Eight were trained to eat very little. Sadly, I was still round as a robin for some unknown reason.

I got up and gave the rest of my meat to Isa before washing my dish. The fight with my mother had left me unsettled, despite the fact that I was asleep on my feet. The men sat talking as I made cupcakes and then bread.

Still not at ease, I went out into the darkness and pulled the few ready apples from the fruit trees and made them into pies. The men got quiet when I walked out the door. They probably hoped I would just keep going.

I picked up their plates on the way back in and fed Isa until she was full from their leftovers before heading back to my ovens. I watched from the window as they stripped off their shirts and pulled their swords.

They fought each other in the torchlight. It did not appear to be practice. They were quick and generous with their blades, making small marks and drawing blood. The muscles of their bare chests flowed and moved in the most beautiful ways. I couldn't look away.

Saige had tattoos that ran the length of both arms and skirted across his back. Arrows met at the base of his neck and crossed one another to the other side. They were gorgeous. Down one bicep was his full name, 'Saighdeoir,' and down the other the word 'family.' They stood in stark contrast to his silver hair and pale skin. I had seen tattooed Fae before, but never up close.

I wanted to trace the lines of them with my finger to see if they were raised or not. Despite what I told my mother, I wasn't unwilling to do my job here, not unwilling at all. I just wanted to have some say in the matter.

Seal had tattoos too, only his were different, darker, heavier, and more ancient-looking. An old Celtic design from our Homeland went from his neck to his spine's base in seductive swirls and dark knots. I wondered if he was alive when we lived there. That would make him ancient.

I learned that I like tattoos very much that night. They danced and moved like a sentient creature on their bodies. The light from the torches showed off the hard planes of their muscles. Goddess, they were gorgeous. I held my breath, wondering what type of game they played.

They laughed and joked before moving on to kicking and punching one another. Like brothers, they ruffled each other's hair when one would get in a good punch. A touch would linger too long here and a gaze longer than necessary there. Okay, so maybe not like brothers. Women are rare in Talamh na Sithe, and most men are comfortable together. I went back to my pies.

The kitchen was clean, and the table was covered with cupcakes, pies, and bread. I took off my apron, tired and at peace at last. The men were scattered around the living room, drinking a mug of ale, shirts off, their bloody wounds unnoticed. I took a small bottle from the windowsill and handed it to Laith, who seemed to have taken the brunt of it.

"Put this on those before they get infected," I said before turning to my room.

"Do not sleep in the bathtub, My Lady," Saige shouted as the door snicked closed.

Chapter Ten

Laith

"She's asleep in the fucking bathtub," I said, almost running from her rooms. Earlier, we had fought over who would check on her tonight.

I lost. Fabulously.

"Her rooms are freezing, and she is all blue and covered in chill bumps."

"So, pick her up and dump her on the bed," Saige said, emboldened because he did not get stabbed last night with the pointy knife Seal said she carries and is quick with.

"She is naked," I yelled in a whisper so as not to wake her.

"Are you afraid of a short, naked woman one-third your size? If so, this was a bad decision for you," Seal said, laughing at me.

"Have you seen the size of her fireballs? They are very large," I snarled at him.

"I have seen her fireballs. They seem to be more bark than bite," he replied, his stupid eyes glittering in the light of the stupid fire.

"I will come to stoke her fires and protect you should she try to kill you with her nakedness," Saige sighed, rising to follow me as I tiptoed back into her rooms.

She was beautiful in the tub, her round hip out of its shallow depths. Her red hair floated around her, and she had pressed herself as close to the edge as she could. One arm was flung over the side, her soft breasts smashed against it. Chill bumps dotted her flesh, yet she looked almost content with a soft smile on her face. I grabbed a towel from her closet and scooped her up as gently as I could, trying not to wake her. She moaned and shivered in my arms, curling into me, making me harden against my pants. Stupid dick. Everything was stupid right now.

Saige had her fire going, and her covers turned back. I dumped her on her bed and made to run.

"No," she said, reaching her arm to me. Her eyes were closed, and still, she shivered from cold, her teeth chattering softly despite her clenched jaw. I looked at Saige in complete horror. "Stay," she said. Her breathing was soft, and I wasn't sure she was awake. Saige smirked at my terror and moved to sit on the side of the bed. I noticed he sat as close to the edge as he could so as to be ready to run, and I smirked back.

"The dorms are freezing at night, and we would wear all the clothes we owned and pile together to stay warm. I am unaccustomed to being quite so warm and having so much space to sleep in, so I like your tub. It makes me feel at home. Will you stay? Just for a bit?" she whispered, never opening her eyes. I looked at Saige meeting his eyes. His brows knit together in a scowl. I moved to join him on the bed, and carefully we eased in next to her.

"Where were your dorms, my Lady." He asked.

"The barracks. The old Archer barracks," she said, shivering against me. I pulled the covers over the three of us, even though the room was now warm. She faced Saige on her left side, and I moved into her from behind.

"Those barracks are falling apart, there are barely any walls, and the roof is missing in places. There are no fires to heat the space," Saige said with an edge of steel to his voice.

"I am well aware, my Lord," she said, sighing as she settled herself comfortably between us.

"How long did you live there?" I asked.

"My whole life, except the odd weekend, my mother would need to show off the fact that she had borne a child."

Saige's eyes glinted murderously in the light of the fireplace, the bedroom door was open, and I could hear the sharp intakes of breath from the other room.

"You may call me Ari," she said. Her chest rose and fell evenly, and I knew she was asleep.

She shivered against us for a long while, sleeping through it like it was natural. Which for her, I suppose it was. Winter is brutal in Talamh na Sithe, and she had had nothing but seven frail girls and barely enough clothes to keep her warm.

Saige and I curled around her, our arms enclosing her in our warmth, holding us all together. She rubbed her face on his chest like a cat, and I felt myself harden at the sight of it.

I pulled my hips away from her so she wouldn't feel it, but she settled back against me again, making me moan. At some point, we slept. I had not intended to stay all night.

She makes me nervous in ways I don't understand, but the sight of her blue and freezing in the tub and hearing the reason as to why made me fear her less and want to protect her more. Stupid feelings.

Chapter Eleven

Ari

I awoke naked and smothered in fully clothed men. Laith snored softly, his breath against my hair. Saige gripped me to him so tightly his knuckles were white. I pulled my magic to me and sent a calming sphere of blue into him. He sighed and let me go, dropping deeper into sleep.

I rose from them, looking back as they slid together, each dropping their arms over the other. I watched for a minute, a small smile on my face. I had not meant to tell them my secrets, but exhaustion had made my lips loose. I dressed quietly. It was hours before the sun would rise, but I needed to get an early start. I had deliveries to make.

The living room was quiet, the fires burned low, and I added wood to them so that the men would be warm when they awoke. Soon they would not be needed, and the oppressive heat of summer would set in, but for now, the fires were welcome. I went to the windowsill and popped the cork off the big green bottle, drinking it down with a sigh.

Why would I want a child? I have no responsibility to repopulate Fairy. None. If I have a boy, they will kill him. If I have a girl, she will be contracted for and traded like any other tool. Their job is not to get me pregnant but to try.

Others have tried for decades and failed. Why should we be different? Why should my child suffer the life I have? I packed seven vials in a soft cloth and moved to leave before anyone could ask questions I was unwilling to answer. I called Solas to me, mounted bareback, and rode off into the dark.

The Eight were scattered about the capital, myself being the furthest out. I heard the wolves howl and trusted Solas to keep us away from them. She skirted the main road, traveling some of the lesser paths.

It wasn't long until I reached the house where Arlie lived. It was a small place, much smaller than mine, but it was tidy and neat. The soft glow of fires came through the window, but the house was otherwise dark. I left her vial in the red flower pot as I said I would.

All the girls have red flower pots. They can take it or not as they wish, but they will never tell of our plot. It would mean my death for certain, regardless of the land's need for girl parts. I moved on.

Next, I came to Keena's house, which was a monstrous empty-looking thing. Her fires burned as well, lending some warmth to the starkness of the place. I made my delivery and kept going.

House by house I went, being as quick as possible. I had promised them I would continue as long as I could. Once a month,

I would make this delivery unless they asked me to stop, in which case I would. Some wanted children, and some never did. We had not been given a choice in this life, but I gave them one now.

I got off my horse at Keelin's house, creeping around to where her pot was on her back garden wall. I paused outside of her windows when I heard a low moan. On my tiptoes I went, looking through.

Her hearth fire burned, silhouetting the naked bodies of two stunningly handsome men. They had her pinned in place on her knees, one taking her from the front and one from behind. Her face was ecstatic, her skin flushed red, and her mismatched eyes closed in pleasure. Her long brown hair flowed down her back, and her head tilted upwards toward the man in front of her.

They moved in tandem, timing their thrusts so that they filled her. Her nipples were rock hard against the man's chest, and their legs were shiny with her pleasure.

I watched, fascinated, as she came, shuddering against them. It looked painful, but she sank into it and groaned like it was pure pleasure. The man in front of her stilled, and I was close enough to see his seed drip out of her flesh.

He leaned down and feathered her face with kisses, easing her onto his partner, urging her to take him deeper, even though no child can come from that. She bucked against him, crying out once more. His cries met hers, and they sagged together against the other man, who wrapped them both in his arms and eased them to the bed.

They looked sated and happy. I grinned for her, glad she was tolerating the hardship of her contract so well. Her red pot was gone.

I accepted her choice. As the first to be placed, she had been with her mates the longest. She was a bit older than I and had been in her home for a few months. I was happy for her. I was. I hoped someday I would find that happiness, too.

I went to Ravena's home last, as it was closest to the bakery. The sun would be up soon, and already the horizon was lightening. Her red pot was broken on the ground, a dead plant listing to the side.

Ravena could grow anything, and I was shocked at the sight of it. I stuffed the vial into the leaves and moved to leave until I heard the loud slapping of flesh on flesh and the sound of her sobs through the walls.

She grunted and cried out, but not in pleasure. It must be painful for her to make a sound because we had been taught to stay silent in the face of pain. The sound of an open hand slapping her sent rage through me.

I knew nothing of Ravena's men. I had not seen her since she was placed, but she was the one most like a sister to me. She had been in this home only a few days longer than I and was already suffering. It made me feel guilty for my soft life.

I listened a moment longer, letting the rage build in me until I heard him come with a disgusting grunt. The soft sound of her sniffles reached me through the stone.

"Clean up, Ravena; Lochlann gets it next." The mattress creaked as he rose, and a door slammed shut. Fury ripped through me, but I could do nothing for my friend. We had no recourse. None.

A hand gripped me from behind, pinning my arms to my side and covering my mouth. I was dragged out of the yard. I began kicking, trying to bite the strong hand of the man pulling me away. I pulled my power to me, ready to fight.

"Be still, little Faerie," Seal whispered in my ear as he pulled me away from the house. I stilled in his arms, but he did not remove his hand. "This is no place for you to be found." He carried me into the bakery, shutting and locking the door behind him before setting me down on my feet.

"What are you thinking? Rowan is a dangerous man," he said, his brows clenched in anger.

"I...I wanted to see Ravena before I opened the bakery. Someone was hurting her," I hissed through my teeth at him, not letting go of my power. It sparked and rippled over me in angry waves, making my hair blow around my face in the still air.

"Rowan is not a kind man, Ari. If he found you, you would no doubt suffer the same fate," he said, scrubbing a hand across his face, sighing.

I sank into a stool in front of the counter, letting my power go, saying nothing.

"Why did you take such a twisted route to get here, my Lady, and why did you leave so early? It is not safe. You went to all seven homes. Why?" he asked, his anger clear. He crossed his arms and waited for an answer.

I didn't give him one; it was none of his business. Rising, I went to light the ovens and pulled out ingredients for cakes. He waited, unmoving.

"They are my family. I was just checking in," I said in a huff.

"That is a lie. I can smell it on you," he growled.

"I take them healing potions and check on them, that is all," I said through clenched teeth, meeting his angry eyes with mine. "How did you follow me?"

"I am a tracker, my Lady, a Huntsman. It is my magic, and you would do well to remember that. There is nothing I set to track that I cannot find," he snarled, stalking to me.

He pushed me into the wall and covered my mouth with his, taking complete possession of it. He kissed me hard, pushing his tongue to mine and tasting every part of me until I felt the tension leave his body.

His hands kept mine pinned to my sides. He did not move to touch me. I sagged into him, deepening the kiss. I was stupid. Stupid to think I had control of this situation. Any part of it. My lips were puffy when he finally pulled away.

"I was worried for you, Ari; it is not safe to be out alone in the dark. We are your family now, do not make us fear for you," he said, softening.

"I'm not afraid of what is out there," I snarled at him, not ready to let it go. The sound of my sister's sobs too fresh in my mind. "I have no fear, for there are things far worse than death, and most of them are not caused by the creatures that roam the night," I finished, putting my dark thoughts into words.

"We would never hurt you, Ari. Never." He came to me then, wrapping me in his arms with a huff of his breath.

"You can't promise me that, Seal. There is no safety here. Not with this Queen. You don't know me, and you owe me nothing. I do apologize for worrying you." I laid my head on his chest and relaxed into him. "I'm sorry."

He kissed me again, softly this time. His eyes were still hard and angry. "We have known you since you were a child. The application process is long, and we wanted you from the first time we saw you, learning to ride a different horse with the other girls. We watched you laugh with them and knew you were the one for us.

"We changed our lives for you, and even though you don't understand that, it doesn't make it any less true. You are very wanted and have been for over a decade," he said, pushing away from me. "We can't change your past, and we can't change the reasons why you are with us, but we can find peace together, Ari.

It doesn't have to be awful for you. That was never our intention. We all want to love you and find some bit of happiness in a harsh life." He sighed, moving to the door. "Don't forget we have the Consummation ball tonight."

"What? No," I breathed the word. "Can't we skip it?"

"You know we can't." I stared at him hard, then nodded once, dropping my eyes and waiting for him to leave. He watched me through narrowed eyes and then left. I had twelve cakes, twenty loaves of bread, and dozens of cookies baked before noon.

Chapter Twelve

Seal

The sight of her lurking in Rowan's yard sent me into a rage. What was she doing there? I know I have an issue with my temper, but Rowan makes me look mild-mannered and sweet.

I have no idea how he and his brothers got Ravena, but they did, and Ari would be wise to stay far away from them. I met the others at the center of town before picking Ari up from the bakery and told them what happened. They were quiet when I was done. Each deep in thought.

"Is she delivering poison?" Laith asked.

"You are obsessed with poison. You slept with her in your arms last night, Laith. Let the poison go," I growled at him. We were the four most dangerous men in Talamh na Sithe, with the possible exception of Rowan. Still, then there is a difference between dangerous and cruel. None of us would ever be cruel.

"What have they turned her into? She prefers to sleep in frigid water surrounded by cold metal because she does not like her bed's warmth.

"She walks unafraid through Dire wolves and the worst Fae that roam at night. I smelled them all along her route; they were stalking her. She knows no fear of her mother or anything else. She can lie smoothly like no Fae can. What manner of creature is she?" Saige said, hands on his hips and angry.

"They let them know no simple comforts, they gave them nothing to live for, and now they aren't afraid to die. At least she isn't; maybe the others broke, I can't say, but she did not break," I said, angry for more reasons than I could name.

"No, she didn't break, but her fearlessness will get her killed," Lann sighed, breaking his silence.

"We won't let that happen," I said, feeling like this was going to be the most difficult job I've ever had. "She has us now, even if she doesn't realize it."

We walked to the bakery in silence, our thoughts heavy. We wanted Ari so badly, all of us, even me, I admit it. I was tired of being alone and never knowing what the soft body of a woman felt like curled next to me in sleep.

I had fucked women; we all had. There are places where you can pay for that, but I wanted something more.

Ari was soft, warm, and fierce. I wanted her more than I could say. I knew she didn't like me; I could tell by the looks she gave me, and I would not force myself on her, but hoped in time she would change her mind.

The way she leaned into me at the bakery had lit a fire in my soul. It made me dangerous, and if someone tried to harm her, it might also make me cruel.

Chapter Thirteen

Lann

The Queen waited for us at home. She had made herself comfortable in our living room and ate one of Ari's cupcakes when we walked in. I didn't like it.

"Hello, daughter," she said, rising to greet us.

"Hello, mother," Ari sighed, moving into the room.

"It is good to see you all together. I take it your bonding is going well, Saige?"

"As expected, my Lady," he answered, then stilled in mid bow, shooting a glance at Ari. I knew what he was thinking because I was thinking it too. Ari didn't like to be called that, probably because it reminded her of her mother.

"Have you bedded her yet?" she asked, looking us all over.

"Mother. I am right here." Ari sighed. "I bedded Laith and Saige last night," she snarled, waving a hand in dismissal at the Queen, making me want to take a step back.

"I want to see your sheets, little Liar," Aramea snarled back.

"I burned them this morning as they were," Ari looked lost for a word before settling on saying, "Beyond repair."

"I don't believe you, and if it is not true, I will see to it you are moved," she said, taking a step toward her daughter. "If these men are too timid, there are others who will not dally."

"It is true, my Queen," Saige said, lowering his eyes to her. I have never seen him lie, never, but then I guess this was a half-truth. Ari was changing us all. In his defense, he did sleep with her last night.

"Ah, very good. I am impressed with you, child. Two at once, I imagined you would have to work up to that. I am proud." Her words disgusted me, and I wanted to strike her foul mouth. Not that two of us having Ari was disgusting, but that her mother would speak of it.

"I'm glad my sex life makes you proud, mother. Now, if you would please go so we could get ready for your ball tonight, that would be great," Ari said, meeting the Queen's eyes and glaring.

"Why the rush, my Queen, if I may ask. Not that we aren't thrilled to have Ari in our beds, but surely some of the houses need more time to adjust and get to know one another before they begin the task of creating heirs," Laith asked.

"My reasons are my own, but suffice it to say that the land is out of time, and I am out of patience. The People have supported The Eight for long enough. The girls will be moved if their matchings are not consummated within the time frame outlined in your contracts. It's all very clear," she said, narrowing her eyes at him. I don't remember there being a time frame outlined in that damned contract. I would have to hunt it down and find out.

"Well, we certainly don't have that problem," Saige said, smacking Ari lightly on the ass. If she'd had a knife in her hand, I've no doubt he'd be dead now. She turned her head from the Queen, so the flash in her eyes wouldn't give her away.

"Very well, Saige, I hope your union will be fruitful," she said, turning to Ari. "I brought you a dress, daughter. I don't imagine you have anything decent to wear." The Queen looked at Ari with disapproval.

"Actually, Your Grace, we bought Ari a dress," I said, stepping between Ari and her mother, interrupting their stare off. I did not want their fireballs marring our living room.

"My daughter has enticed my Blade into buying her a dress; you must want to be next. These young virgins are so enticing. Are they not?" she sneered, and I hated her for it.

"Very well, I will see you tonight. I am glad that I currently do not have to make other arrangements for my daughter, but I would hate to have my captains dissatisfied with my gift to them," she said, moving to leave.

"We are quite happy," Seal said, moving to wrap Ari in his arms; she snuggled back into him gratefully."

"Perfect, you should know, daughter, that Seal carries the taint of human blood in him. If he breeds you, your child will be tainted as well." She glared at Seal, and I realized then what a real bitch she is. Seal barely has any human blood, it was generations ago, and everyone knows about it. It's not a big deal, but she was using it against him anyway.

"That's okay, mother, Seal's cock is so large that it more than makes up for the human part." Ari tilted her hips back against him, causing him to moan. Perhaps tonight is his turn," she said before giving her mother the most vicious grin I have seen on a woman's face. It brought me joy and made me a little hard to watch her hips grinding against his. Aramea nodded her head in acceptance of this statement then walked out. Ari waited for her to go and then walked directly to her room, slamming the door.

"What was that?" Saige asked. "Why would she lie?"

"She doesn't want to leave," I said. "I think that she likes it here." We all sighed at the thought. Except for Seal, his hard dick poking out of his pants made us laugh at him, and he looked more than a little frustrated. The funny thing was, his cock might be large enough, but it wasn't the largest of the four and was further proof that Ari hadn't seen any of us naked.

"You'll have to take care of that later, brother. Now we must get ready to go. We slapped him on the back in sympathy and went to dress.

Chapter Fourteen

Ari

The dress was beautiful. It was a soft cream color with tiny pearls sewn onto it. It was full length, tight in the top, but fell soft and straight at the bust line. The pearls were sewn into the bodice and would glint and glitter in the light of the torches. The skirt was a filmy material that was soft and flowing.

It was incandescent in the light of the fire and was nothing like the gown I am sure my mother had chosen, which means it was perfect. I walked forward, half afraid to touch it. Never had I seen anything so fine. I backed away, pulling my curling irons out and setting them near the fire to warm.

I drew a bath, and this time did not fall asleep. The water was warm, and I soaked just long enough to get the flour from my hair and washed it with scented soap before toweling off and rubbing vanilla oil on my skin until it shined. I darkened my lashes with paint, lined my eyes with kohl, and tinted my lips red.

I never wore makeup, but tonight was important. I did not want to be moved from this place, and I had to be careful to give the impression that I was bonded with my mates.

Soon, I would have to do the thing, but tonight it was more important to make everyone believe it was true. I curled my wavy hair tighter, wrapping the thick individual pieces in the irons until the curls were exaggerated, then I pulled them out and let them fall to the curve of my waist. When I was done, I stepped into the dress.

Taking a big breath, I turned and faced the mirror. I knew that I was not the most beautiful Fae; my hair was too red, not the norm for Fae, my stature too short, and my bottom too round and ample. I had a tiny waist a man could circle his hands around, so that wasn't bad.

Fae were tall willowy creatures, not at all like me, but tonight I looked pretty. I would make the men proud to be on my arm; it would give them a small amount of pride at their choice.

Sighing, I opened the door. The men rose as one when I came out and froze in place, staring. I looked behind me to see if there was something I missed.

"Ari, you are stunning. You make us speechless," Laith said, walking to me. He brought his hand up as if to touch my face and then dropped it to his side. I reached for it and gave it a squeeze.

"You are too kind; you are the ones that look amazing."

And they did. They wore matching tuxedos, each with a tie the color of my dress. We looked like a matched set, understated and beautiful.

Laith with his auburn hair loose about his face, Seal with his dark blonde curls tied at the nape of his neck, Saige with his silver-white hair that ran down his back, and Lann, who was my darkest knight, with his black curls tight and pulled in a tail on the top of his head. He had shaved the sides close, and the look was wicked on him.

Goddess, but they were beautiful; my breath caught in my throat when I took them in. I couldn't help but smile my approval.

"We have gifts for you," Saige said, stepping to me with a small box in his hand.

"Saige, I don't need anything. The dress is more than enough.

"Please, it would make us happy if you took them," Laith said, stepping forward with another box.

My heart sped up. I wasn't used to getting gifts, and tonight they just kept giving them. I took the box Saige held and opened it. Inside was the most beautiful necklace made of diamonds and pearls that I had ever seen. It matched the dress perfectly. Stepping behind me, he put it around my neck, kissing the side of it when he was done, his hands lingering just a minute. My body tightened at the kiss, and I felt myself soften.

I took the box Lann handed me, opening it. Inside was a bracelet that matched the necklace. I had never owned jewelry, not like this, and I was stunned to silence. Lann placed the bracelet on my wrist, placing a kiss on my pulse as he did so. My breath started coming heavy as I was overwhelmed by emotion.

Seal came forward next, almost reluctantly. I blushed when I remembered what I told my mother about him, not meeting his eyes. He handed me his box. Inside was a knife, smaller and more finely made than the one I already owned.

He got on his knees and put his hands up my skirt, drawing a gasp from me. He took my old knife out and placed the new one in the sheath he had known I would wear, regardless of the dress. His eyes never left my face, and I felt the heat spread out from my center as I watched him, and I wondered if he could smell my arousal at his intimate gesture.

Laith came last, placing the smallest box in my hands. I opened it, already overwhelmed, and I moved to sit when I saw what it held. I covered my mouth with my hand and watched them watch me. Inside was a ring. It was simple and round, bearing no gems. It had four different bands of colored metals combined into one: black gold, platinum, rose gold, and yellow gold. My eyes snapped to his.

"I forged it for you, Ari. Will you accept it?" He brought his hand out and picked up the ring; on his finger was a rose gold ring. Then, I looked at the men, and each one wore a simple band upon the fourth digit of their left hand.

My chest tightened, and I didn't know what to say, so I said nothing. He reached for my hand, placed a chaste kiss upon it, then placed the ring on my finger. A single tear escaped before I could wipe it away. I pulled him to me and brushed his lips with mine.

"Thank you, Laith. It is lovely. I don't know what to say." I stared at the ring in shock. They did not have to do this; I had been given to them already, they did not have to give themselves to me, but that is exactly what they had done.

At that moment, I knew there was truly something between us and not just a contract. Had there been no growing bond, a huge debt would have opened between us at my words that I would have had difficulty repaying. But there is no debt among lovers, and so our scales were balanced.

I couldn't speak.

"Ari, you being here has made this place a home, and we wanted to show you how much that means," Saige said, coming to my side.

"Thank you," I whispered, not taking my eyes from the ring, feeling guilty. I had given them nothing to make them happy and had generally made a mess of things.

"We should go; we don't want to be late." Lann stepped forward. I reached for his hand, and together we walked out.

I had been worried about how I would sit on Solas in this dress, but that thought vanished when I saw the carriage that waited. Saige handed me into the thing, settling himself beside me, and the others followed, arranging themselves for comfort. The carriage would take longer, but I would enjoy the quiet moment before we got to my mother's stupid ball.

I laid my head on Laith's shoulder, letting it rest there. I had been up since after midnight and was exhausted from the long day. Seal and Lann sat across from us. Saige took my hand in his, giving it a squeeze. Lann spoke softly about something that happened during training, causing the others to laugh softly.

Seal watched me like a hawk, his face devoid of expression. I leaned into Laith and closed my eyes, lulled by their voices. I must have dozed because the trip was over in a blink. The horses slowed and came to a stop, waking me up.

Carriages and horses lined the lane to the Great Fae Hall. I hated this place. Something about it always felt wrong, like darkness lived there that no amount of light would drive away. It was soaked in fear and pain, and I always swore a hint of blood lingered in the air, regardless of how many scented candles burned.

Rumors about what happened here floated through the generations, each one adding a detail that was likely not true. No one knew exactly what happened, but everyone knew this place was cursed.

Tonight, it was lit up by a thousand candles and torches. Laughter and music drifted to us as we climbed down from our carriage. I would rather have been cornered by a pack of Dire wolves backed up by angry bears than be here, but we had no choice.

The men flanked me on both sides as we walked in. Seal and Lann reached for my hands, holding them lightly. I shook my shoulders out and forced myself to relax. This was a party. A party to celebrate The Eight being matched to households and what was supposed to be the rebirth of Faerie, no pun intended. I think anyway.

The moment we walked into the door, I was set upon by squealing girls.

Chapter Fifteen

Saige

Ari was attacked by seven squealing girls when we walked into the room. Our grand entrance was marred by chiffon and silks in every color imaginable, and Ari was swept away in their wake.

I would have been offended at their assault, except her smile was the most beautiful thing I have ever seen. She tilted her head back and laughed in pure happiness as they exchanged hugs and whispers.

Ari had never smiled this way before, not for us. Not that we had seen. Already she was the most beautiful woman in the room, but with that smile on her face, no eye did not notice her, including Rowan and his brothers. They looked over our group in a calculating manner.

Ravena hung back; she wore a solid black dress that hugged her curves and showed off the perfect pallor of her bluish skin. Her black hair was piled on top of her head, and her blue eyes were sad as she hugged Ari. Ari gripped her arms and spoke feverishly in her ear until the other girls whisked them away to tables laden with food. With nothing else to do but shrug our shoulders, we joined some of our friends.

"They are all happy to see each other; each girl has piled on the next one that comes in. They have laid in wait for your Airmed for quite a while." Cory, one of my guardsmen, chuckled, sipping his drink. They are all so pretty, each one in their way. Of course, I think Keena is the finest of them all." He smiled as he found his silver-haired, blue-eyed mate across the room. "Has she made you a happy man yet, Captain?"

"She has made us all very happy, Cory; you'll get nothing more from me than that." I clapped him on the back and moved to intercept Ari. She grabbed my hands in hers when I got close enough to her, smiling into my face with the excitement of an innocent.

"Saige, these are my friends: Aileen, Keelin, Ravena, Finley, Teagan, Keena, and Arlie, but then you know that since you petitioned for one of us. This is Saige, and those handsome men over there skulking close, but not too close, are Laith, Seal, and Lann; she smiled at them with a proud look on her face. Laith wrinkled his brow in confusion, and Lann's grin lit his face. Seal's eyes narrowed in suspicion. He thought she was up to something, and Laith was always going on about poison. We had found Ari's stash of 'medicines,' but I didn't think she meant us any ill will.

"I do know their names, Ari, but we only petitioned for you, love. I kissed her hair and went to fill a plate. She looked at me with a shocked expression on her face before turning to the chorus of voices all vying for her attention.

"Oooooh, are they all allowed to call you Ari, Ari? I know your rules," the blonde one chuckled, elbowing Ari in the ribs and dragging her away.

I stepped to Lann, giving the girls their space. They were the only family each other had over the last many years, and even though everyone in the room could probably hear them, no one broke their spell. They were a joy to watch except for Ravena, who eyed the Rowan brothers occasionally. Watching where they were in the room and every movement they made.

"Which one is your favorite, Ari?" Teagan asked in a whisper.

"It's too early to tell," she answered in a low chuckle and gave the girl a smile. "They all have something to adore, and their talents run deep and varied," Ari said with a cute barking laugh and a naughty wink, causing all our eyebrows to hit our hairlines.

Music played, and one by one, we danced with Ari in our arms. She is an excellent dancer, quick and light on her feet, and a pleasure to watch. When I asked her about it, she simply said she got an A in her dance classes. I imagine that she did.

She laughed and smiled at each of us in turn, and to any watching, there would be no doubt that our bonding was a success. The ring on her finger glinted in the torchlight, and it did not go unnoticed.

The other matchings danced too, even the Rowans, for we all knew we were being judged. For the most part, the girls did not look miserable, just Ravena. They smiled and danced with their partners, some awkwardly and some not.

None looked happier than Ari did, and for that, I was glad. No one could fake the lightness and joy she glowed with. It made me happy and satisfied on a visceral level I had not known existed. We had waited so long and wanted her so badly. Just her. Never the others. Not that they weren't desirable. There had just always been a special quality about her that we felt was for us alone, or I did. The others took some convincing, but not much except for Seal. He was a jerk and trusted no one but we three.

The Queen watched from the balcony, surrounded by her court, but they did not approach us, and I was glad about that. She would upset Ari, and if the two of them fought in public, it would not be good, but she watched Ari like a raptor, and I wondered about their relationship. She did not stay long, and before the evening was half over, she left.

Once she was gone, the room took a collective deep breath, and ties were loosened, and jackets were taken off. The girls had settled at a table, huddled together and whispering about Goddess only knows what. Sometimes looking at their men with a glare or a chuckle.

The other matchings had been introduced, and we mixed about, talking and drinking. All in all, it was not a bad night and had gone much better than I hoped. Laith called the carriage, and we were hoping to be on our way soon. There was no work tomorrow for any of us, as the Queen had declared a day of celebration. Each of us had planned to take Ari to do something personal with her so she could get to know us a little better.

Ari and Ravena had moved off to themselves and were huddled in serious conversation. She was trying to block Ravena's face from the Rowans and keep their voices low, but I saw his face darken, and he headed for their table. We were across the room and further from them than he was, but we moved as one to intercept him.

He reached them before we could, jerking Ravena up by her arm. Ari stood to say something, and he backhanded her across the face, causing her to nearly fall from the force. Four swords were drawn as one and at his throat. Seal swept Ari behind his back before anyone but Rowan could see the glowing knife she had drawn on him faster than I have ever seen a knife drawn in my life. Our blades glowed with Fae magic, too. Forged by Laith himself, the last of a long line of true blacksmiths. Rowan stepped back, dragging Ravena with him.

"Rowan, mind your manners and your heavy hand with the girls, or you will lose your commission, do you understand?" Lann said. "If you so much as look at Ari again, I will take your head; the only reason I do not is that the Queen is not here to sanction it." His voice sounded calm, but his eyes blazed with fire.

"Yes, Captain," Rowan snarled before his group left the room, taking his brothers and Ravena with him.

Chapter Sixteen

Ari

"Ravena, if you want to be rid of him, let me know. You don't even need to ask, and I will make it happen," I whispered low in her ear.

"How?"

"We talked about it before we got separated. The green bottles are for you and the black for them. I will get you a black bottle or four. You tell me, sister, for my gift is yours to use." I gripped her trembling hands in mine. Her makeup did not hide the bruises under her eyes.

"Alright. The black one. Just one. The others aren't so bad, just him. I think they will be better with him gone," she said, looking over my shoulder at the biggest Rowan brother.

"Put it in his drink in a few days, so it doesn't look suspicious and then take him immediately to bed. I'm sorry, that is the only way. It will drop his blood pressure so low that he dies and does not come back. I swear it, but it must be in reaction to pleasure or pain. Tell no one, and if one of the brothers watches you with him, that's even better, so the blame is not on you." I saw her eyes shift and knew he was coming. I straightened and plastered a fake smile on my face.

He jerked her up by her arm, and I jumped to my feet to step between them. He hit me hard, rocking me back. My hand flew to my lip, and I tasted blood. I had my knife from under my skirts and was moving to his throat before I could think. I was surprised to see four glowing blades beat my blade to the hollow of his neck. Silver, gold, blue, and orange light pulsed from my men's swords as they stood between Rowan and me.

Seal's arm pulled me behind him, and I could smell his anger. I hid my blade under my dress before anyone could see it. I would have been happy to slice Rowan's throat, but it would have caused a problem for sure.

Lann, who is normally the loosest of the four, showed why he was Captain of the Swordsman when he threatened Rowan's commission if he hurt Ravena again, his blade notched in the hollow of the other man's throat, his stance threatening.

I would deal with that personally, I thought. These girls are my sisters and Ravena, a favorite; I made just enough black bottles to protect us all should it come to that and could always make more.

We were in the carriage and driving down the road before they sheathed their swords. I kept my eyes lowered.

Saige pressed a handkerchief against my lip and held it there. Taking it from him, I wiped the blood away.

"It will heal; it is nothing to bother with, my Lord," I told him. "I have medicine for it at home. I only got a C in the beatings class, though, which is why I have a potion for that. I am sorry if I embarrassed you," I finished, keeping my eyes down.

"Beatings class? Surely, you're kidding." Laith said.

"There is a class for everything, my Lord," I said in all seriousness. I heard Laith's sharp intake of breath.

Seal knelt in front of me, gripping my face in his hand. "Look at me, Ari," He hissed through his teeth.

I raised my eyes to his as ordered and stiffened my spine.

"My guess is you also got an A in the hiding your murderous intentions through downcast eyes class," he said, his voice softening.

"An A minus, my Lord," I answered.

"Did you also get an A in the being formal when you don't have to be class?" Saige asked, watching me as I stared his brother down.

"Don't apologize, Ari, and don't hide from us. We are not the Rowan brothers. We like your spirit, even if the quick draw of your knife makes me a little nervous." Lann said, smiling at me. I nodded once to let him know I understood. Seal let go of my face and moved back to his seat, saying nothing.

"Why do your swords glow?" I asked, looking at my hands.

"When the holder's intent is true, a blade made by my family will always glow with their aura; it is part of my magic. I forged all our blades personally," he said with pride.

"And we are honored by them, Laith," Lann said. "They are the finest blades in the land, except maybe the one you made for our little murderess." Lann pulled me to him in a hug and gave me a wink. You and I are going to practice some knife skills, my Lady, especially if you plan on drawing it on very large men," he laughed; I let the slur go as he didn't mean it that way.

"I got a B plus in swordsmanship, my Lord. That is the only warning I will give you." I laughed, raising my eyes to his and giving him a wink.

"Look out, Lann, she'll get the jump on you with her B plus skills," Laith teased, and the dark moment passed.

They had stepped in front of me with Rowan, and their blades glowed, proof that they were serious about not allowing him to hurt me. I knew what I needed to do, and despite the fact that it was going to suck, I steeled myself to do it anyway.

The driver pushed the horses, and we made the trip home much faster than the trip away. Once there, we piled out of the carriage and went inside.

Going straight to the kitchen, I pulled a bottle from my stash and dipped my finger in, rubbing the medicine on my lip; it would heal in minutes. That was part of my magic.

"Thank you all for a wonderful evening," I said, facing them. I knew my lip was healing and that they watched. None of us had been very open about what magics we could do, I was letting them see just a little bit of mine, and they knew it. I would heal by the morning anyway; the medicine would just help it along.

I went into my room and closed the door. I heard them talking but couldn't make out the words. I took the dress off and hung it, removing the knife and all the other jewelry. I left the ring on.

One of the men had unpacked my bags, and I riffled through what I had until I found what I was looking for. It was a simple dressing gown that tied around the waist. It was off-white, and the material was slick and soft. I went to the door and opened it, stepping back to my window and looking out.

"Seal, would you care to stay with me tonight?" I asked, my voice low. The room went still, and I thought maybe they didn't hear me. I waited for them to acknowledge my request.

Chapter Seventeen

Seal

We all froze in place when she said my name. Her door was open, but she wasn't standing there. We had been talking about the night and our plans for tomorrow; we had just begun to argue about who was going to get her out of her damned bathtub when she fell asleep in it. That argument wasn't settled when her door creaked open, and she whispered my name. No one expected such a thing- least of all me.

Laith, Goddess love him, looked grateful it wasn't his name she called. He was terrified of her. Smitten but terrified. Laith was the only one of us that wasn't a fighter at heart. He makes the best swords the land has ever seen and will kill a man if needed, but he is not the fighter we are.

I rose to my feet, shrugging my shoulders and raising my hand in question. I was her least favorite. What could she possibly want from me?

"Shut the door, if you please," she said, keeping the royal tone she used when she was not comfortable. She stood with her back to me, one hand on the window looking out. Her hair hung long and curled down her back.

She wore a soft white robe that showed her muscular calves, her bottom's roundness, and the curve of her ridiculously tiny waist. Her room smelled like sugar and vanilla. I shut the door with a plaintive look back at my brothers, silently asking for help. They turned from me.

Some brothers.

"I want to make you a deal," she started, turning to face me. She looked gorgeous in the light of her fire. She hadn't lit any torches, and the soft glow of the hearth sparked off the red in her hair while shadowing her in ways that made her look even more amazing.

Her lip had healed, and there was no bruise or swelling left. We had seen her use magic, and she seemed to have a wide variety. Wider than most for one so young.

I could track anything and manipulate the weather. Laith could infuse a thing with the aura of the bearer and his own, plus grow anything from nothing, Saige could do small-scale healings, and Lann could throw a blade and never miss. His hits were deadly, even to the mostly immortal Fae. Saige could pull warmth from the things around him and light fires while Lann could speak to animals, but that was all.

We had seen Airmed throw fireballs at her mother and absorb those thrown at her. We had seen her heal herself and Laith with her potions, and we suspected her cakes were magicked to make the taster want more of them, although that may not be true. Her cakes could be that good on their own. She is young to have so much power and such a wide variety of skills. Our lives together could prove interesting.

"I don't make deals, Ari. Deals among the Fae are not wise," I said, watching her face.

"It's less of a deal and more of a binding promise." She came forward until she was toe to toe with me. I looked down at the top of her head as she refused to look at me, sending my alert level higher.

"Ask," I snarled, not knowing where she was going with this, not yet.

"I want you to lie with me tonight, to be the first to do so, but you must promise me that you will see it through to your, um, completion and not mine. That is all I ask," she finished, meeting my eyes.

"Ari, why me? I don't think you like me all that much," I said, not sure why I told her what I was thinking.

"That's not even a little bit true. I do like you, Seal. You are the one most like me. I trust you implicitly because with you, what you see is what you get. There is no pretending.

"I'm not altogether sure you like me, and I know you don't trust me, but I trust you to keep your word because I would do the same. Once given, my word is ironclad. Know that. Yes, I can twist the truth more than most, but my word is binding.

"Saige has a gentle heart, Laith is scared to death of me for some reason, and Lann still has a hint of boyishness in him that you do not. I trust you with this, Seal. It needs to be you."

"Ari, Saige…" I started to say that he would be better for her, gentler, maybe kinder. She was right; it is his nature.

"No. I need it to be you. You will be doing us all a favor, even if you don't understand that now. You must trust me on this if nothing else," she interrupted.

I had no idea what she was talking about. Saige and Laith had seen her naked and mentioned nothing about sharp teeth or extra limbs. I couldn't understand what she was going on about.

I did the only thing I could do.

"I swear it," I said, feeling the binding settle over us like a veil. She sighed in relief, and her shoulders sagged, making me worry more.

She smiled then, a real smile, meeting my eyes as she untied the gown, dropping it to the floor behind her. Goddess, but she was glorious. Her skin glowed with soft pale light, the nipples of her small breasts already hard.

She put her hand on my chest, tracing the lines of hard muscle through my shirt with the fascination of a girl who has never touched a man, regardless of how many damn classes she took. She rose on her tiptoes to kiss me.

I dipped my head to her and gave her my lips, letting her lead the kiss where she wanted it to go. Her tongue slipped between them and met mine. At first, it was soft and unsure, but she urged it deeper.

I wrapped her in my arms and ran my hands down her back, dipping to the swell of her ass and pulling it to me. She moaned into my mouth, and I gave up letting her take the lead, for she is right; I am what I am. I picked her up and walked her to the bed, laying her down. She was a tiny thing and weighed nothing at all, despite her soft curves.

I studied her eyes for any sign that she didn't want this, and finding none, I untied my pants and pulled them off, then slipped my shirt over my head. She watched me through hooded eyes as I slipped next to her onto the bed.

She put her arms around me, pulling me to her and running her hands down my spine, sending electric sparks along the nerves there. I kissed her again, tasting the sweetness of her mouth. Her tongue met mine, and she did not shy away. I kissed her neck and to the soft swell of her breast, taking her nipple in my mouth. She arched against me, and I thought about that promise and how easy it was going to be to keep, unsure why I had to make such a thing in the first place. I was already halfway there, and if I wasn't careful, I'd finish way too fast.

She was so soft against me, where a man is all muscle and corded flesh; she was strong but yielding at the same time. It felt so good. Amazing. More so than I imagined.

I kissed down her belly and nestled myself between her legs. She was waxed bare, and it took me off guard. The skin there was so soft I nuzzled against her, rubbing her like the damn cat. Her moans got louder, and she clutched at my hair.

Slowly, I drew my tongue over the soft nub of flesh and around the skin under her lips. I held them open and repeated the move until she shivered against me. I never tasted anything so good, like one of her cookies, sweet vanilla, and sugar. The girl is infused with it.

My hands found her breasts, and I cupped them, running my thumbs over her nipples as I slid my tongue over her core. Goddess, but she was so sweet. Amazing.

Maybe it was her magic to be so perfect under my hands. I ran my tongue down her opening and then back up to her nub, and then I focused on it, drawing a sweet, startled breath from her.

She gripped her sheets and cried out, bucking against my tongue. I darted and flicked it over her, alternating light pressure with hard until I felt her give way and come against me. She was wild then; I placed my hand on her to keep her still as I finished taking her orgasm into my mouth.

I thought I would go right then myself. I had to think about Orcs and Goblins to keep from finalizing our deal early. Her legs shook, and she pulled me up to her and away from her sensitive flesh. I covered her mouth with mine, letting her taste herself on my lips.

She kissed me, clutching at my back, opening her legs for me, and locking them around mine. I could feel her readiness, the tip of my cock pressed against her, and in one thrust, I pushed hard and deep inside of her, feeling her rip in two.

And then I knew.

I knew why she had made me promise to finish. Why she said it had to be me, and she was most assuredly right about that. The others would be too tender for this.

I felt her stiffen under me, but she would not cry out with pain that I could see was terrible, as her face was frozen in agony. A single tear escaped from her clenched eyelids, and her body trembled under mine, but not from pleasure. I wondered what she did to make her mother hate her so.

Ari had not had her maidenhead breached. Never. We knew she was a virgin when we petitioned for her, not that we cared about that. Still, the Queen had insisted The Eight stay virgins so that any children born could be assured of their lineage.

Fae women have notoriously tough maidenheads. If allowed to stay intact, they become quite thick. It is extremely painful to both parties when they are broken. It is midwives' practice to use a small tool to breach the thing at birth and then again once the girl begins her cycle so that she is not ripped in half the first time she lies with a man.

Since the beginning of time, this practice has been in place and is the norm, not the exception. Ari's mother had not done that. I felt her flesh rip from her, and hot blood soak me through. My cock twinged with pain from the resistance I met and the force I had used, thinking at the time that faster would be gentler.

Ari had to have known it would be this way. This is why the Queen asked to see her sheets. She would have known Ari was lying. I stilled in her, afraid to move.

"You promised," she said through clenched teeth. Her body was tight around me, and her blood still flowed. "If you stop now, it will just grow back. That is part of my magic; I can heal from most injuries. I don't want to have to feel this again Seal, please, you must well and truly break it. I am sorry, but I am begging you," she growled; her look said it all.

A part of me broke from the pain I saw on her face, but I had promised, and a promise is binding to the Fae. Thanks to that promise, my cock was still hard, despite my shame and fear over causing her so much pain. I began to move again, and a sharp intake of breath was all she would allow herself.

She must have gotten an A in the tolerating torture class. I hated myself just a little, but she had trusted me to see this through, and I would. She brought her arms around me, pulling me to her. Her eyes watched mine; she kissed my lips, keeping her eyes open, letting me see her gratitude.

After a few strokes, I felt the torn flesh finally fall away, and she relaxed into me, her chest arching into mine. I stroked her deeper and deeper, hitting the spot in her that held all the nerves.

I kissed her hard, melding my body with hers. I let her control the angle of her hips so that she was as comfortable as possible, instead of pinning her legs against my ears and going as deep as I could like I wanted to because this first night was about Ari.

I watched her face to find the perfect stroke, and she came hard, clutching my chest to her and crying out. Her flesh contracted tightly against me, and still, I stroked her harder. Nothing had ever felt so delicious.

The binding of the promise I made to her slipped away as I stroked once more and emptied myself into her with a groan. I held her there, pinned under me until the last wave passed, then pulled her to me, kissing her neck.

"Thank you," she said.

"Ari, I."

"No," she interrupted. "I mean it. Thank you, I am grateful. But could you please get me the smallest green bottle from the shelf where the flour is? They are hidden in the back. Not a dark bottle, never touch those, a small green one," she said, her voice breaking just a little.

"Of course." I got up, and she rolled onto her side, gripping her belly as heat like a fever radiated off her.

I could see her pain. Yes, she had had a moment of pleasure too, but now there was only pain. Blood fanned out from her on the sheets and covered my torso and hips. It smeared down my thighs. I couldn't stop staring at it as my hands shook.

Saige would have been devastated, Laith would have likely never touched her again, and Lann, who likes some kind of pain and blood, would have been forever changed by causing this scene. She had chosen well.

I grabbed her robe and slipped it on, not wanting them to see the blood. I walked into the living room and shut the door behind me.

I said nothing as I rushed to the kitchen and grabbed the bottle she wanted. We all knew where she hid them; we are warriors, not stupid men.

"Saige, she needs you," I said, scrubbing my face with my hand and not looking at him.

"What? Why? Why is there blood on your arms? What did you do?" He asked, striding to me, angry.

"She made me promise to finish. I didn't know," I said; I think my voice cracked too, I'm not sure, but the others stood up and came to me, looking at me in accusation. "Our little Faerie keeps secrets."

"What didn't you know?" Lann said, moving past me to open to door to her room.

"I didn't know that her mother knows no mercy; she couldn't even show her the one small kindness all females deserve," I whispered. I pushed past Lann and went to her on the bed. She lay curled on her side, holding herself in silence while tears coursed down her cheeks. I pulled her to me and gave her the bottle.

"Ari, drink it." She didn't open her eyes to check which bottle I offered, just tipped it back. I felt her relax against me as the potion hit her stomach.

"Let me help, Ari." Saige came to her side and placed one hand on her back and one on her belly; he pulled heat to them and sent his healing energy into her. He was not a true Healer, there hadn't been one of those in centuries, but he could do minor healings and offer her some pain relief.

She moaned and went limp in my arms. Lann ran his hands over her hair, his dark face furious. No one said anything.

Laith came with hot towels and sponged her off; I took off her robe and cleaned up as well. Trying to hide the worst of the blood from them and failing. They understood, though. They patted my arms and gave me tender looks. I hadn't done this thing to her, not really, and we were uniform in our desire to take the head of the one who did.

I carried her to my bed. I would burn hers tomorrow and replace it, so we never had to look at it again.

Saige stayed with us, keeping his hands on her until she slept. I pulled the covers over the three of us and dragged Ari to my chest; she sighed and nestled in so perfectly to my body. I lay awake long after she slept, listening to her heart pound in her chest, only when its beats returned to normal and her body temperature drop, did I sleep.

I dreamt of killing the Queen.

Chapter Eighteen

Ari

I awoke under the crush of limbs. Seal lay naked facing me, and Saige held me from behind fully clothed. I had planned on making a special delivery for Ravena today, but as the Queen had declared a day of celebration, I knew the Rowan brothers would likely be with her. The men had wanted to spend the day doing other things anyway.

I watched Seal's face as he slept. He looked older than the others as if worry had changed him more. He was beautiful, his blond curls wrapped around his face. He smelled like pine and earth.

He felt so good inside me last night, even if he will never believe that. Yes, there had been pain, but it wasn't as bad as I thought it would be, and between the medicine and Saige, it was over quickly.

I took a finger and traced it down the lines of his chest. He was hairless, and his olive skin was soft under my touch. I watched him breathe, captivated by him. My breath caught in my throat. I peeked down at the soft part of him that lay between us.

I hadn't got to look last night, and I had wanted to. It lay there, harmless-looking and asleep. I grinned, wanting to wake him up, but knowing he never got to sleep in. When I brought my eyes back up to his face, I found him watching, his golden eyes glued to me as he watched me look him over. He brought his mouth to mine and began to kiss me even though Saige was with us. I sank into the kiss, my body already wanting more.

I didn't know how to feel about Saige being there, but Seal didn't seem to care, and this was our life now. The five of us living together means there will be no privacy. There is no monogamy among the Fae; there never has been. There are commitments, but monogamy is unheard of. There once was a Fae killed over the idea, the same one whose death my mother somehow cocked up.

He pulled his lips from mine and watched again as I ran my finger down his chest and lower. I brushed the tip of him and felt it harden under my touch. I ran my fingers over the shaft lightly, the skin on it the softest thing I had ever felt. I kept touching him, enjoying the feel of his cock rising and twitching. It was a powerful feeling that I caused it to awaken. He gave a soft groan when I explored lower, brushing the base.

I knew how to please a man with my hands; there had been a section on that in our sex class, but I didn't want to do that. I just wanted to feel the silky softness of the thing and to touch him everywhere, all at once. His body was such a contrast between soft and hard; muscles twitched and flexed under his skin, drawing my eyes. I couldn't take him all in. Reaching behind him, I pulled myself to him for a kiss. He turned me, placing himself between my legs.

"Do you need to go more slowly, Ari?" He asked, watching me for signs of discomfort, his face serious. Some old pain showing in his eyes made me want him even more.

"No," I whispered. "I'm fine." I felt the head of him brush me, I was already wet, but still, he kissed my face, my neck, my breasts, my ears, making me grip him harder, tilting my hips to him for more.

I ran my hands down him again, gripping his cock and marveling at its hardness. It was perfectly sized and hot in my hands. He rolled my nipple in his mouth, causing me to lean into him. I used my hand to rub the head of him on my core over and over until I was dripping wet and ready to come. He let me use the tip of his cock to bring myself as he alternated between my breasts, nipples, neck, and lips.

I felt the bed shift just when Seal pushed into me slowly, as I spasmed around him, teasing my orgasm out. Saige lay watching us, a smile curved on his lips. His eyes memorized my face as Seal slid in and then back out of me, drawing out the strokes, until I arched my hips against him, crying out.

I was self-conscious and unsure of what to think about being watched. Seal bent to kiss me, pulling my attention to him. Saige slid close enough to run his hands down Seal's back, resting them on his ass as he moved between my thighs, and my breath caught in my throat at the sight. I gasped into Seal's mouth.

Saige traded his lips for Seal's, kissing me for the first time. He tasted sweet, like mint and vanilla; I sank into his kiss. Seal increased his pace and twisted his hips against mine, bringing a deeper moan from me.

Saige pulled from my mouth and kissed Seal deeply, wrapping his hands around the other man's head, crushing their lips together. It looked like they had done it many times before; their timing was perfect. Seeing them like that almost pushed me over the edge. Goddess, but that kiss was beautiful. Then Saige pulled away to watch; his eyes twinkled at my open-mouthed reaction as he followed our every move, keeping his hand on Seal so he could feel him move.

Seal rolled his hips, holding pressure on a spot deep inside of me, sending shudders down my spine; he slowly slid out then repeated the move until it had me coming off the bed. I looked between us and watched him disappear in me. Seeing that tipped me over once more, and I came in a shudder, rocking hard against him. He covered my mouth with his, teasing me with his tongue and taking my groans into him, thrusting faster.

He leaned up, biting his lower lip, and with a pained noise, came inside of me. I could feel him pulsing like a heartbeat before he sagged against me, sliding to the side at the last second to land next to me. He pulled me into his arms in a satisfied sigh.

Saige watched with a happy grin, and I stopped wondering if he cared that his friend just fucked me in front of him. It was obvious they didn't care.

Saige traced the lines of my face, and I let him, closing my eyes in pleasure. It felt good. I sank into the warmth of bodies around me and let myself enjoy it.

It was much better than the life I came from and certainly much better than the one some of my friends currently enjoyed. My heartbeat pounded hard in my chest, pounding in my ears. Saige leaned to kiss me, "I'll make breakfast; we have a busy day planned for you." He left with a smile and a soft look over his shoulder, shutting the door behind him.

"You feel too good, you tricky little Faerie," Seal said. I'm not sure I like it."

I elbowed him in the ribs, grinning when he grunted. "You seemed to like it just fine a few seconds ago," I laughed, grabbing his sheet and wrapping it around me.

"Mmmmm, yes, I did, but I had dreams of pleasuring you for hours, not minutes." He gave me a serious look as I left, heading to my room.

My mattress and sheets were gone, to where I didn't know but wasn't going to worry about it. I pulled a simple shift over my head, brushed my teeth, and, not caring that I was wrecked, went to get myself a cup of tea.

Lann and Saige sat at the table, grinning like fools at something they were talking about. Apparently, it was me as the conversation stopped when I came in.

"You look the loveliest I have ever seen you look, Ari," Lann said with mischief in his eyes. "It's time for some blade practice for you since you enjoy playing with them. I want to see this B Plus effort you warned me of." His grin was rakish, and his eyes on fire.

"Let the girl eat, Jerk," Saige said, setting down plates of food and Ari's tea.

I joined them at the table and found I did have quite an appetite, even if there were no muffins and only a loaf of day-old bread to go with my eggs, potatoes, and some sort of cooked meat. It was delicious. I pushed my plate away with a groan when I was done. "You will have me fat if you keep feeding me like this," I said, holding my belly.

"You'll work it off when you raise your sword to mine," Lann laughed, rising from the table. He was shirtless, wearing only loose pants tied with a string. His skin the lovely color of dark tea with cream in it.

"I have no blade, Lann," I said. "It's going to be hard to raise a sword I don't have." I eyed him over the rim of my mug.

"Laith, surely you have some rusted old thing the girl can hack about with. She promised to show me her skills, and I want to see them."

"I don't think I actually promised," I said, rising from the table moving to grab my dishes.

"I'll get those, Ari," Laith said, coming back into the room with a gorgeous short sword that looked made for my smaller hand. Its blade was multi-layered steel, and it was polished to such a high shine it looked blue. I had never seen a more lovely blade. The handle was some kind of animal antler that was warm and comfortable to the touch; it was perfect. I couldn't stop staring at it.

Laith grinned. "Seems you're not the only one who likes shiny things, Lann," he chuckled, grabbing plates and taking them to the kitchen.

"Let me change, and I will show you that B plus." I raised my eyes, and my grin took on a feral quality. Excitement sparked through my veins at the thought of using such a fine weapon.

"No. Stay as you are," Lann growled at me. The smell of my brother on you and the sight of your bare legs is going to make this a fairer fight for you. It's distracting." His eyes glimmered in delight when I blushed at his words.

"Very well," I sighed, "I'm going to show you a solid B plus thrashing." I narrowed my eyes and grinned. This was going to be fun.

Chapter Nineteen

Laith

"They are going to kill each other," I said, watching Ari and Lann circle like wild animals. He charged her, and she neatly ducked under his reach, slicing him on his calf.

He retreated, and if anything, his grin got bigger because she had drawn first blood. "Lann is Captain of the Queen's swordsman and has two rods of height on her. I don't think this is a good idea; they look entirely too serious."

"They are fine, Laith; she won't hurt him," Seal said, grinning as she twisted from his blade again, slicing him on the other leg. "Much," he added.

We watched as his eyes narrowed on her, and he moved to swing at her again. The problem was, he is an oversized dragon fighting a hummingbird. He is fast, but she is faster. He is strong, but she is lighter on her feet. His reach is so wide, she could duck under it and cut his ankles to shreds.

It was a joy to watch. No way could she beat him strength on strength, but she knew how to play up her advantages. The glint of pure joy in her eyes had me hoping she cuts him down; his ego is overly large, just like the rest of him, anyway.

"I thought she said she got a B plus in swordsmanship," Saige said, watching every move with glee. Fucking Saige and his fucking watching. "Those look more like A-plus moves to me. She's beating him.

"No." We said together.

"He's letting her win," Seal said, his voice lacking any actual confidence in his statement. Lann's skin was slick with sweat, and his muscles strained as he parried with her stroke for stroke. Everywhere he tried to go, she anticipated. Her concentration epic. The glint in Lann's eyes was terrifying. She continued taking little slices off him while she remained remarkably unscathed.

Incredible.

It was the most beautiful dance I've ever seen. They moved their feet in perfect timing, strike for strike. The sound of blade striking against blade rang through the morning air.

She darted in, under, around, and through his moves. The red in her hair catching the sun and his skin so dark with sweat that it soaked up all light. They were both breathing hard. Finally, he got in a shallow cut to her shoulder and drew her blood. There was a sharp intake of breath from where we were lined up watching. The blade in Ari's hand began to glow a soft chartreuse with her aura, and I held my breath. I had not made the blade for her, but my steel responded anyway.

"Our little Faerie does have secrets," I said in a hush.

"Indeed." Seal leaned toward the fighters, watching with rapt attention as her smile widened. She struck at him again, in earnest now, step after step, pushing him back when he became distracted by her glowing blade.

She stopped when she drew a thin line of blood on his neck, a wound that would be fatal if it were real, how she reached up that high, Goddess only knows.

"Remind me not to make her mad," Seal said with a low chuckle. "Why would the Queen teach them this skill when she also apparently teaches them to take a beating?"

"Maybe that was a joke," I said, hoping it was a joke.

"Knowing the Queen, it wasn't," Saige said. "Who knows why she does what she does."

They stood apart, breathing hard and grinning madly at each other, both their chests heaving. Then Lann did the one thing no one has ever seen him do in the history of Lann, he dropped his sword. He was on her in one stride, taking the blade from her hand and slinging it to the side. He scooped her up by the thighs and pushed her back against the wall.

His hands pushed her shift up, and he slammed into her in one stroke.

"Should we, uh, stop that?" I asked.

"No." The others said together.

"It, uh, looks uncomfortable," I worried.

"She doesn't seem to mind," Saige laughed. Watching. Always fucking watching. Goddess, what an ass.

Ari's arms were wrapped around the dark giant, and he pounded into her, picking her hips up and slamming them down onto him. They made no noise except deep grunts. Her head bowed onto his chest, and the sound of their rapid breathing reached us. All we could see was his ass and her arms and legs wrapped around him. He dwarfed her by ten.

"I mean, she's had a bit of a long night," I said, biting my lip. Unable to look away.

"She's not glass," Seal said, tilting his head to the side, fascinated by the two of them tearing each other apart in this new way: Black on red and red on black. It was beautiful, despite my misgivings. We did the same, trying to see what he was looking at.

"I kind of thought she might work up to him. I mean, he's a bit rough, and we all know he's got a fair bit of size to him."

"Shut up, Laith," They both said at once.

I grimaced as Lann pulled Ari by the hair and slammed his mouth into hers, never slowing the punishing force of his hips. He kept her neck taut as he fucked her, biting her like a stallion does a mare.

"She's quite skilled at swordplay." Saige tilted his head the other way, causing us to follow.

"She'd make a hell of a fighter," Seal adjusted the waistband of his pants, repositioning his stiff cock, making me do the same.

"Don't give her any ideas."

We watched as she took her nails and raked them down his back, drawing more blood. He grunted deeper and curled his body into hers. She came again, throwing her head back, almost banging it off the stone wall. He grabbed her hair and pinned her neck again. She cried out in pleasure.

"I wonder if she knew that he would like a little bloodletting as foreplay and that he might like all the little cuts she made on him. I wonder if they got profiles on the men who applied for them." Seal narrowed his eyes at the scene in front of us.

"Interesting thought, Seal."

We leaned forward as finally, Lann shuddered, bringing her hips onto him one last time. They sagged against each other, breathing hard. He put his forehead on hers, resting it there.

"That's going to be hard to follow," Saige laughed gleefully, rubbing his hands together as he went to start cleaning up the kitchen.

"It's not a competition," I said, grinning, thinking that not everyone wants a barbarian tearing them apart from the inside out. It made me proud to see my steel glowing in her hand, beautiful girl that she is.

They leaned against each other, using the wall for support. Lann did not offer to put her down. Her arms slung loosely over his back, and their heads bent together in a conversation we couldn't hear.

Finally, he put her down, and she swayed on her legs. Picking her back up, he carried her into the house, her face buried against his neck. He walked past me with a wink and a wide, boyish grin, taking her into her bedroom before coming right back out.

"She's just going to, uh, get dressed." He said, grabbing a drink. "Hell of a blade handler, that little Fae."

"We noticed," Saige said, laughing.

I think I growled, "You'll be lucky if she doesn't poison you after that, Lann."

"Shut up about poison," all said at once.

"So, what's our plan for the day?" Seal asks, grabbing an apple from the dish.

"Well, I thought we could take her into town and see about some more clothes for her," Saige said, leaning on the counter.

"Most of the shops are closed, right?"

"Not all, most likely. We could take her to your forge, Laith, and show her your blades. Maybe she could pick a longer one than her knife." He answers.

"I think she already picked her short sword, or at least it picked her. Her aura is beautiful. I don't think I've seen another one like it."

"Everything about her is lovely, but that's one of your best blades, Laith," Seal surprised us by saying. He had been on the fence about applying for Ari, and now he was smitten with her.

"It's hers now," I said with a sigh. Like everything else, my blade was lost to her now. With a small smile, I moved to my rooms to get ready for whatever the day brought. She was already becoming our perfect center. Peace settled over me as I shut the door to my room.

Chapter Twenty

Lann

I tossed Ari on the back of her horse and noticed the slight grimace when she settled upon the mare's back. She turned her head away, but it was too late. I had lost control with her for sure, and I felt a little bad about it.

A little, not a lot.

She didn't seem to mind when she clawed my back like a cat and rode my hips in the most delicious fashion. I had liked her already, and then she nearly bested me in the fight, which made me like her more. My heart sped up when I looked over at her. I didn't like it.

Her smile was wide and beautiful in the warm spring sun. She needed a long hot soak in her tub and one of her green potions, and I'm sure she would be right in no time. I adjusted myself on my horse as well; I did not come away from our encounter unscathed.

The cut on my neck stung and was an angry red, and I wore it with pride. I had not allowed her to win, she had me on my heels, and I can't remember the last time someone had managed that. What a good match she is for me. Our child will be glorious.

I watched her from the corner of my eye as we rode to town; she looked relaxed and happy on Solas. She listened and laughed at whatever conversation was going on around her but said not much of anything.

Laith fretted and worried over her, and I caught her rolling her eyes a little at him. Of the four of us, he is the most delicate. He makes fantastic weapons and knows very well how to use them, he just doesn't have the heart to leave his forge and fight, but then not every man needs to be a fighter.

There need to be some gentlemen in the world to take the edge from the rest of us. Their kind hearts provide balance and light, especially in a world with so few women to do so. I loved him all the more for it.

We met some traffic on the road to town, and I did not like the way others looked at Ari. She had dressed in hunting pants that came to her calves and had tossed a loose dress over it since this was a holiday of sorts. She rode with the ease and confidence few do, and others watched as she passed them by. We kept near enough to her that no one would get ideas about our beautiful little Fae, but not so close, she would think we were hovering.

In town, we rode by the shops and found all but a few of them open. We let our horses go and began to pick up things she might want or need.

She argued about everything we bought for her, saying she didn't need anything more than what she had. That made us buy her more, and we laughed as her eyes rolled even harder. This is a thing she has quite a lot of skill in. She can roll them in different ways to convey different things. I wonder if she had a class in this as well, or if it comes naturally.

"Saige," she complained when he bought her lavender scented soap and some kind of goat's milk lotion for her skin. "You must stop; I don't need any of this stuff." She put her arm through his as we walked the rows of scented things in the square.

"Well, you need the vanilla to go with it, Ari. You can't have the lavender and not the vanilla," he said, grabbing more things and tossing them in the basket Seal carried.

The sight of Seal carrying a basket cracked me up on the inside, but not on the outside. Never on the outside. Seal is the worst of us, in truth, and by far the most dangerous. For him to be carrying her basket just told me how screwed we all were when it came to Airmed, call me Ari. She sighed as we paid for our purchases and headed to the clothing rows.

We all picked out clothes for her because she refused. The more we picked out, the more she started helping since, Goddess knows, we know nothing of what the lady would want.

She picked soft doeskin riding pants and new moleskin boots that were as soft and supple as they could be. She added a few dresses that we liked and some simple shifts to sleep in. We added more of the things when her back was turned.

"Get this one in green; it will make her hair stand out," Laith whispered when Ari turned from us to look at something else.

"I like the yellow one," I whisper yelled back at him. "The fabric is softer and will make the curve of her leg stand out."

"Do you want the curve of her leg to stand out?" Saige asked, looking down his nose at me.

"Yes," I answered.

"In the bakery?" he said.

"No," I answered, scrubbing my hands over my face and looking away when she turned to see what we were looking at with a scowl on her face.

"What are you boys doing?" she asked.

"Nothing." We answered in unison. She rolled her eyes and walked to the next row.

"Get them both," Seal snarled softly, grabbing them from our hands and tossing them in the basket along with some more riding pants and another pair of boots he picked up.

"Good thinking," I said.

Everything that Ari touched and seemed to like, we picked up when she put it down. She scowled at us, placing her tiny fingers on the bridge of her nose in frustration. The shopkeeper was quite happy when we left her after bundling our purchases for the ride home.

We stopped by her bakery, and she let us in; we sat watching as she placed wood in the ovens and checked ingredients for her

104

day tomorrow. The place smelled so strongly of her that we all inhaled the rich, deep scent of Ari and baked goods. This had been her home, for sure, before she had come to ours and took us in hand.

The deepest feeling of peace slithered into my heart as I sat and waited for her to finish. Saige and Laith talked up a storm, but Seal and I just watched as she moved in pure muscle memory around her bakery. When she was done, we locked it up and headed to pick up more stores for the house.

We were picking up flour, milk, eggs, and salt when we ran into Keelin and her men. Their arms were filled with purchases too, and we ducked our heads and mumbled awkward acknowledgments as we waited for the girls to talk.

"So, it goes well by the look of it, Adair," I said, shifting my bundle and grasping his forearm.

"It goes well; indeed, the girls seem happy." He said, looking at Keelin with a smile.

"Yes, they do. It is a good match for both our homes from the look of it." Adair hoisted his heavy bundle onto his hips and nodded his head in agreement. We stood, a little embarrassed and a little proud at how quickly we had come to this point as the girls made quick small talk before hugging and parting ways.

Seal came back and joined us, nodding to Keelin's men and putting a few new packages into his basket. I wondered what the sneaky bastard had gone and bought for Ari.

Asshole.

We stopped by Laith's forge and watched as Ari touched each blade with soft awe at their beauty. In this place that is Laith's, you can see his true genius. His blades are the most beautiful things made in the land, and the appreciation on her face was plain.

"Pick any you like, Ari. Everything here is yours."

"Oh, Laith, you have already given me two beautiful blades; I can't take another one. You've all given me so much, and I have nothing to give back. It's a bit embarrassing, if I am honest."

"That's not true, Ari. You have given us so much in such a short time," he said, grabbing her hand.

"I've given you nothing," she snorted, looking as the sunlight glinted of long swords and crossbows.

"You've given us peace," Seal said, echoing my thoughts.

"You've made us a home," Laith said, brushing his lips to her cheek.

"You've made us all very happy," Saige said. Smiling at her.

"Well, maybe I've made two of you happy," She said, winking at me with the glimmer of mischief in her eyes.

"That's not what it's about, Ari," I said, giving her a lopsided smile I didn't mean to give. Goddess, but I am a hopeless fool.

"Well, I appreciate your kindness, but you have given me tons of gifts, and I have none to give," she said, her face falling, just for a blink, before she picked it back up and looked cheery. I hated that she felt like she had to hide from us.

We called for the horses and piled our bundles onto them, riding home in the dying spring light. The trip was slow as the horses were loaded down, and moving fast would be awkward.

Seal peeled off, doing whatever it is he does when he hunts. Checking for dangers ahead, most likely, or killing some small furry creature for our dinner. He rode back to us with four rabbits across the rump of his stallion. It was his gift, his magic, but I was always jealous of the easy way he moved among the wild. He looked over at me and smiled as if sensing my thoughts. Jerk.

We unloaded in companionable silence; Ari took bags to the kitchen and began to bake. We had caught on that she baked when she felt some kind of strong emotion, but she was quiet in the kitchen as she made bread and pies for dinner.

Saige took our other purchases to her room and put them away because he knew damn well she would not. The new mattress we sent for was on her bed. Seal went outside and returned with soft sheets and a colorful fur blanket he had made for her. I glared at him; he never made one of those for us. All these years. I guess he was a hopeless fool too.

We moved about the house, tidying up and making dinner. Saige took the rabbit and made stew with it, cutting up little potatoes and carrots and making it into the gravy. It was a peaceful scene. I hoped to have a thousand more nights just like this one.

Ari said very little as we made short work of her baked goods and cleaned the table of food. After dinner, she excused herself and went to her room, shutting her door.

"What did we do?" Seal whispered.

"I'm not sure," Saige answered.

"Go find out," Seal ordered in a whisper.

"You go," I said.

"Make Lann go; he's the swordsman," Saige said to Seal.

"She's but a girl," I said, "and a small one at that." I snarled.

"She kicked your ass," Seal smirked, winking at me.

"Oh fine, I'll go," Saige said, pushing back from the table. "If she's asleep in the tub again, I'm going to lose it."

Chapter Twenty-One

Ari

I sat on the bed and stared about my room. Everywhere I looked, some new thing awaited me. The men had bought nearly everything at the market, and I was overwhelmed. I couldn't come to terms with their kindness; it was sudden and unexpected.

I mean, I hadn't expected them to be unkind or rude, but they had taken me in and done everything in their power to make me comfortable.

They had let me take the lead sexually, even Lann, who I had nearly pounced on after our fight. I was humbled and embarrassed by it all. It was too much. I needed just a minute to gather my thoughts. I wasn't used to this much companionship, even among the girls. We stayed to ourselves a lot, understanding that our futures would not be spent together.

Here in this house, though, they were my future. This was my forever, and I was grateful for their kindness, just as I was overwhelmed greatly by it all. It was hitting me that these relationships were going to be my life. Always.

It wasn't a bad thing, it was just a new thing, and it scared me a little. I sat, breathing harder than I probably needed to, listening to pans rattle and pots being cleaned.

My room was cool and quiet. Seal had brought the softest, warmest blanket and quietly laid it across my new mattress when he thought I wasn't looking. I felt tears well in my eyes as I rubbed my hands across the short, soft fur of whatever creature he had stitched it from. They gave me so much of themselves, and I had nothing to give. Well, one thing to give. It made me sad. Angry at my mother and sad.

"Ari, can I come in," Saige asked, softly knocking on my door.

"Of course," I said, wiping my eyes quickly. He opened the door, closing it behind him and leaning against it.

"Are you okay?" he asked, watching my face.

"Yes. I'm fine. It's just a lot," I said, watching my hands rub the soft fur of the blanket.

"I'm sorry, Ari." He looked at me carefully, waiting for me to meet his eyes.

"Don't apologize, Saige. Could you yell just a little bit? Maybe stomp your feet and get mad because I didn't clean up the kitchen." I smiled up at him, a soft smile, but not a real one.

"No. I Can't do that. I understand, Ari, I do. It's a lot, and we are so happy to have you that we can't be normal around," he laughed. "We're acting dumb and stupid. Would it help if you yelled at us?"

"No. There's nothing to yell about. You all fit perfectly together, and I just want to make you happy and not mess up what you already have. I'm overwhelmed," I said, putting my thoughts into words.

"We weren't perfect until you came, Ari. That's the truth. You make us a whole."

"No pressure."

"No pressure," he laughed, tilting his head back. "Let me start your fire; why don't you take a bath? You promise not to fall asleep in the cold water, and I promise not to come in here and drag you out of it."

"Deal," I said, rising to go to my tub while he lit a fire in the hearth. I ran the water hot and let the steam fill the room. My new scents were arranged around the tub, and I dumped some in, sighing as the warm water eased muscles sore from the sword practice and sex.

I heard Saige leave, shutting the door behind him. The soft voices of the men tempted me to sleep, but I had made a deal, so I washed instead. Massaging vanilla shampoo into my scalp and finger combing my loose curls until the tangles were gone. I scrubbed and rinsed until I was clean and smelled good. The bath had done wonders for my mind, and it was calm and settled again.

Tomorrow, I would need to get up early enough to deliver a bottle to Ravena while her men still slept. I drained the water and pulled on a new dressing gown someone had bought for me. I sat on my bed and massaged oils into my skin to keep it soft.

Slipping one of my new shifts over my head when I was done, I curled onto it, luxuriating in the soft feel of fur against my skin. Isa curled at my feet, and I enjoyed the soft warmth of her body.

I listened as two of the men made love in the room next to mine, which belonged to Saige. I couldn't tell who was with him because they were quiet. Their soft grunts of pleasure gave me peace.

I didn't care that they slept together. Four strong, virile men would be too much for one woman to keep satisfied on any level. I appreciated that they weren't shy about being together with me next to them or trying to change habits long in place. I listened as they talked and made love, laughing a little and groaning a lot. I curled under my new blanket and enjoyed the comfort of their friendship. I was asleep in no time, and no one disturbed me.

I awoke many hours before dawn and dressed as fast and quietly as I could. I grabbed a black bottle from my hiding place and tiptoed out the door, shutting it softly behind me. I walked several hundred yards from the house before I called Solas to me. She came, treading softly as if she knew our trip needed to be swift and secretive. I mounted her, and we raced through the night.

I was unsettled. Something seemed amiss from the moment I left my house, but I could not say what it was. We raced through the dark and were not bothered. I heard no footsteps and saw no wolves, but I still felt followed.

I left Solas at the bakery and slipped next door, burying the bottle in the leaves of her dead plant. It made me sad to see it hadn't even been picked up. That was not at all like the Ravena I knew. Her house was dark and silent though, at least that was a mercy.

Back at the bakery, I lit ovens and torches and began my day. My fear eased as the sun rose, and the feeling of being watched faded. I baked cakes, cookies, bread, and cupcakes until the shelves were full.

I made tea on my little stove and traded bread for a plate of eggs, meat, and fruit from the place next to me, waiting for business to start.

Chapter Twenty-Two

Saige

"There is a bottle missing," I said, my heart sinking, and the visceral feeling of worry seeped into my bones. "She told me to never touch the black bottles, and now one is gone."

We stood, arms crossed and staring at the place Ari thought she hid her medicines. Yesterday there had been ten smallish black bottles behind bags of sugar and flour. Today there were nine.

"Poison," Laith said, and this time no one disagreed.

"I did not hear her get up and leave," Seal said. "I can't believe I missed it. It's not like me," he finished.

"My fault," I said. "After yesterday, though, I needed you."

"It's not your fault," he smiled at me warmly. "It's her fault. That little pixie set some kind of magic on us as we slept."

"Maybe," Laith said.

Lann remained silent, his face dark and angry.

"She didn't make tea or any other food, and we all ate last night and didn't die," I said, trying to reason it out.

"I don't think it's meant for us," Laith said, "but it matters not. We are all at risk."

We called for our horses, needing to head to town anyway, and followed her trail. Seal stayed impossibly quiet as he hunted her, following her breakneck path into town. Large clumps of sod were ripped up and thrown along the road as she had raced at full tilt. We didn't need a tracker to tell us that.

"Something was following her," Seal said, after one of his many forays off the road. "I don't know what, as it left no scent, but it matched her speed almost perfectly, never moving to intercept her," he finished, the dark look on his face making us worry.

We picked up speed and reached town at full gallop, sliding to a stop in front of the bakery. From the road, we watched in relief as Ari packaged bread and cakes for customers. One of the Rowan brothers waited in line, and Ravena watched curiously from her window as we reined our horses in, letting them catch their breaths.

Solas must be incredibly fast. The big mare, like her rider, had many secrets. Ari looked up and was startled when she saw us standing there, not missing Lann and Seal's dark scowls.

"We should go; our jobs await. I, for one, have to head to the easternmost part of the country with the archers to look for a melee of Goblins that are causing trouble," I said, trying to deflect some of the tension.

"We need to speak with her," Seal snarled, flashing his eyes my way.

"Not right now we don't. Let it wait, Master Huntsman," I countered, giving Ari a small wave and heading to my barracks. Laith said nothing, just rode away to his smith to leave Lann and Seal scowling. Eventually, they broke apart and went their separate ways.

I spent the day worrying about Ari. My troop rode out to the east's furthest borders and found the Goblins in question, putting them down. Individually, Goblins are weak little creatures, but they become quite dangerous when they form a melee of more than ten or so. This melee was fifty strong and had been accosting travelers and traders. It took us the better part of the day to hunt them down, but only fifty arrows to remove the threat.

My company is the best in the land, and our shots never miss. We were done with the melee and on our way home before late afternoon. The Queen had sent a message warning that we might need to pack for a week or more to handle our next assignment.

I desperately did not want to leave my family, but it was my job, and there is no arguing with the Queen. I would wait for further instructions and hope that they did not come. The ride home left me only time to worry.

Chapter Twenty-Three

Laith

Ari walked through the doors of my smith around dinnertime, carrying a basket over her arm, her red hair loose around her face, and pulled behind her back in a long tail that graced her hips. She wore her new simple riding pants, a loose-fitting cream shirt tucked into them, and her new moleskin boots.

She looked lovely as she walked to me, setting the basket down and taking a seat, saying nothing. I was shirtless and hammering out a particularly difficult piece of steel on my anvil, alternating between the flames of my forge and the hammer. She watched, seeming to understand this process was at the tricky stage, and she did not interrupt.

The thing about metal is that it can be molded and shaped, but it cannot be forced. It is a delicate job, even though it looks brutish and hard. It must be forged and tempered slowly to be worth anything when it is completed. The heat of the fires must be just so, and the quench of the fire on the blade done at the exact perfect moment, or it will become weak or shatter.

It takes a great amount of strength and patience to make one single blade. I make the best blades in the land, and they are never weak. When I could take the silence no more, I tossed the steel to the side and went to her, standing with my hands on my hips, waiting.

"I brought you dinner," she said, taking in the lines of my disgustingly sweaty chest. Her eyes never meeting mine.

"You swore never to make our meals, Ari. Why are you here?" I asked.

"I don't recall swearing any such thing. I just mentioned you shouldn't expect it," she said, rising from her seat and taking her basket to my table where she laid out bread, soup, roasted meat, and some sort of salad with fruit. She pulled out a jar of tea and poured two cups, making a point to drink hers, meeting my eyes. I sat with a sigh and ate. If she was going to poison us all, I imagine that there was nothing we could do about it.

The soup was good, and the roasted meat better. I used her fresh, warm bread to soak up all the juices. I would die, or I wouldn't. She sipped tea and watched. I seldom saw her eat. She's such a tiny thing, no more than six stones and half a rod tall, but I may exaggerate that a bit. I know we all dwarf her to the point of embarrassment.

"Thank you, Ari," I said, watching her carefully.

"You're welcome, Laith. I came hoping you might have a sheath for the short sword I stole from you; I will gladly pay for it," she said, rising to walk along the rows of supplies I carry.

"You will pay for nothing and take what you need," I said, moving to my forge. The steel was ruined anyway, and my day was almost over.

I banked the fire for tomorrow and began to clean up for the evening. I walked to get my shirt, only to find her holding it, staring at me, her emerald eyes curious and sparkling in the evening light.

"I have a sheath for that sword at home, Ari; I will give it to you there." I had worried about her all day. I knew that Lann and Seal would have harsh words with her; I would leave that to them. Not that I'm a coward, but I have seen the size of her fireballs and do not wish to taste their heat.

"I'm not going to hurt you, Laith," she whispered, walking to me, holding my shirt to her chest.

"Ari, you must know how it looks." I crossed my arms over my chest and felt my muscles tense. She traced the lines of my muscles, dropping the shirt and unbuttoning her blouse, pulling it off her shoulders.

"Ari."

"Yes, Laith?" She looked up at me through impossibly long lashes.

"Don't try to ease what is coming. I have nothing to do with it." I watched, fascinated as she dropped her shirt then moved to the tie on her pants.

"There is nothing to ease, my Lord," she said, dropping her eyes and driving me crazy. She pushed her pants off the curve of her hip and stepped out of them.

We were in the back of the forge and couldn't be seen from the door, but anyone could walk in. She took her delicate fingers and ran them over the muscles on my chest.

"You are beautiful, Laith. I wanted to see you here, in this place, and I was right that it is truly your home." She leaned into me, her naked breast skimming my skin, her nipples hardening from that simple touch. Despite my misgivings, I wrapped my arms around her.

"Get dressed, Ari; the others will be here soon to ride home," I said into her hair.

"The others already went home, Laith. You must have drawn the short straw without trying and are the only one left to escort me." She pulled from me, taking my hand and walking to the pallet of blankets I keep to rest on during the long workdays of summer.

I cursed under my breath when her nimble fingers found the ties to my pants and began to undo them.

"Ari," I said, through clenched teeth when she ran her fingers of the shaft of my cock, teasing it to firmness.

"You will never take me, Laith, I know that. You are afraid of me for some silly reason and will never come to me of your own volition." She took me in her mouth, and I gripped her hair, trying to move away from her. Instead, I sank with her on the blankets as she touched me everywhere all at once.

Her small hands were warm on my skin and brought chill bumps everywhere she touched. She teased me with her lips and tongue, and I lay there and let her. She felt delicious, and she was right. I would be the last one to go to her, and she sensed this somehow.

So, she came to the place that is the seat of my power and did exactly what I said she could. She took what she wanted, having some plan in mind, I am sure, for I do not believe anything she does is without a plan.

She pushed me from my side to my back and teased me with her mouth until my hips shook with restraint, then she climbed up the length of my body and straddled me. She placed her lips on mine, and at first, they were tentative and unsure. I hadn't touched her yet, hadn't given her any sign that I wanted her.

I wrapped her hair in my hands and pulled her to me, breathing in the vanilla and sugar scent of her, and deepened the kiss. Goddess, but did she feel good pressed against me. I wanted to be in her, but still, I held back.

Pulling from her lips, I traced the line of her breast with my tongue and scraped her nipple with my teeth as she curled her hips against me with a moan. I went to the other side and ran my tongue over her nipple, alternating soft licks and bites until I could feel her wetness against me. She sat up, pulling away, and watched my eyes. Her breathing was fast, and her eyes hooded.

I could feel the heat in my own eyes, and I watched as she raised, gripping me and guiding my cock into her. The soft give of her flesh surrounded me, causing my breath to catch. She placed her hands on my chest and worked me slowly, too slowly; it was divine and torture at the same time.

She lowered herself, rubbing the core of her against my base until her head tilted back in pleasure. Placing my hands on her hips, I brought them forward and back until I felt her wetness drown me and her muscles convulse around my cock.

Once she had finished taking what she wanted, I gave her what I wanted to give since the first moment she walked in my door. I used my hands and lifted her up my cock, raising her and then bringing her back down, making her take me deeper. Her eyes went wide with the loss of control at how deeply she took me.

I used my length to reach a core of her that the others could not. Lann may be the widest, but I could touch her in places the others couldn't. I used my reach to destroy the shutters she kept in place with me, only me. Not the others.

In my mind, she had kept me at arm's length. I had done the same, and I was still not sure why she came to me today. She rode me, and I guided her until she came again, bowing into me with her heart pounding, gasping for breath.

She may have thought me the most reluctant, but there is a reason for this. I didn't trust her. I didn't trust that she wanted me, and I used my body to straighten out any misunderstandings between us. She would be mine just as she would be theirs; there would be no distance between us. That was the arrangement, but there was something that kept her from wanting me. I did not make it fast, and I made her work for it, but I worked even harder to change her mind. I was not punishing her, just making her rethink whatever impression about me she had.

I took the wall she had built between us, and I tore it down, brick by brick, with my hips and fingers, bringing her over and over again, until her cries were hoarse from too much pleasure. Until she begged me to stop, lying nearly limp on top of me. Only then did I guide her hips, using my strength when hers was gone, letting myself go in a sharp cry, as I filled her with everything I had held back from her for days.

She collapsed against me in a tangled, sweaty mess, her legs shook from pleasure and exhaustion, the mixed fluids from both of us scenting the air. She said nothing as I held her to me; it was too late for her to rethink whatever plan she had when she came to me hours ago.

She lay against me and trembled as I ran my finger along her spine and tangled them in her hair. I feathered her face with kisses. She had misjudged me, maybe we had misjudged each other, but we would be fine now that it was all worked out.

She couldn't even dress; her fingers shook so badly. Perhaps I had been too hard on her. I dressed her, wrapped her in a blanket, and pulled her onto my horse; she cried out when she settled along the animal's bare spine. I pulled her face to my chest and cradled her limp body to me with one arm, kissing her hair, holding her as I took her home.

Chapter Twenty-Four

Ari

Oh, had I misjudged Laith, Goddess knows how badly I misjudged him. I had gone to his forge, remembering the scowls and anger from Lann and Seal and thinking that the tender and delicate Laith would be a good ally for the fight that would surely ensue when I got home.

Only there is nothing tender and delicate about that man, and I got far more than I bargained for when I tried to seduce him. He destroyed me. Not in a bad way, no, not at all, but I couldn't speak when he was done with me, couldn't even button my shirt.

He let me take the lead and pretend like I knew what I was doing when I came to him, but when I thought that I had accomplished my goals, he showed me how wrong I was and exactly what a strong Faeman was capable of.

The others had been gentle; even Lann with his crazed fucking had been gentle compared to this lesson I was taught today. Laith wore me down, bringing me over and over again even as I swore I could take no more, showing me no mercy. He broke me with his body and changed my perceptions of him.

Every. Single. One.

Yet, he cradled me to him as we rode his horse in tandem because Goddess knows, I could not have sat on mine unaided; every movement of the beast caused the delicate flesh between my legs to cry out. I had made a huge mistake.

Laith often says very little around me and watches me with fear; I thought him the weakest of them all and perhaps the most easily swayed to my side. Only he showed me. He knew I had a plan; he knew I was up to something, and even though he said it would be Seal and Lann to have the final word, he punished me for every incorrect thought I had ever had about him.

Let me tell you, there is nothing weak about that man. He rode, kissing my hair and holding me to him, and I knew he is the first one I truly loved. What the actual fuck. I have never had a plan backfire so completely.

Unbelievable.

He rode home slowly, knowing full well the shape I was in, as he had caused it. He tore me apart stone by stone, and my mind was raw from it, not just my body. I had never been in love before, and now it consumed me, causing hot tears to fall from my eyes. I didn't like it.

We rode, quiet as a whisper, into the yard, but the others were waiting. I cried out as I was pulled from the horse by Saige and carried into the house. I said nothing, just lay limp in his arms.

"What the fuck did you do to her, Laith," Lann snarled, blocking Laith from moving forward.

"Nothing she did not come to me for, Lann. Now step aside." They growled at each other and stood firm, chest to chest. Lann backed down and moved first. Saige laid me on the chaise in the living room and ran his hands over me.

"I'm fine, Saige," I croaked, my voice hoarse from hours of attention by the very thorough blacksmith. I closed my eyes, drifting off immediately, listening to them argue.

"What did you do, Laith," Saige said, walking to the cabinet in the kitchen. I heard glass shifting but couldn't open my eyes.

"I gave her all of my attention, brothers, nothing more. She came and offered me dinner, as well as her body, and I showed her my appreciation, that is all," he said.

"Sometimes, your attentions are a bit...intense, Laith," Seal said, breaking his silence. I opened my eyes to see Laith shrug and walk to the kitchen to get a drink.

"Ari, I brought you a green bottle," Saige said, offering me the cool glass.

"A short one or a tall one?" I asked, unable to focus on the thing.

"A short one."

"Thank you," I said, drinking it down and closing my eyes again.

I felt my strength return when the potion hit my stomach, and I could sit up. Laith came to me and sat down, pulling me onto his lap. I whimpered into his neck but sank into his arms.

"I will not apologize, Ari," he said into my hair.

"I would never want you to, Laith. You were...there are no words for that," I chuckled. "It was just more than I was prepared for," I finished, snuggling into the warmth of him.

I felt him smile against me as the others watched in transfixed silence. I had slept with them all, except Saige, but they had never shared a moment of tenderness with me like this one.

"You need to eat, love," he said, picking me up like I weighed nothing and settling me carefully at the table.

I drank the water he placed in front of me and rested my head in my hand. Laith placed a plate of meat and potatoes in front of me, and I forked it into my mouth greedily.

The others came to the table and joined me. Laith placed plates in front of them as well, and we ate in silence until they placed a tray of my muffins on the table for dessert.

"We need to talk, Ari," Seal said between bites of muffin.

"About?" I asked, knowing what was coming.

"Why did you race to town this morning before one of us could go with you, and why is there a black bottle of potion missing? What exactly is in those bottles?"

"Medicines. Medicines for women." I answered, savoring my lemon and sugar muffin.

"Ari," he growled, low and dangerous. "Why did you leave alone and race to town? Why was your scent all over the Rowan's yard?"

"I got up late. I was in a hurry. The wind must have blown my scent."

"ARI!" he shouted, angrily pounding the table in emphasis. "Look at me and stop lying. I can smell it on you. You must have gotten an A in your lying Faerie class. Be honest." I met his eyes and saw only anger.

"I have done nothing, my Lord," I said, straightening my spine and matching his glare.

"You lie." He stood up, smashing his fists on either side, causing me to jump out of my skin and knocking over my drink.

"Seal," Lann growled.

"Do you want to watch them take her head, Lann? What if the Queen demands you do it yourself as Captain of her Swordsman? What then? She is putting us all at risk with her secrets," Seal said, turning and putting his fist into the wall.

"Stand down, Master Huntsman," Saige hissed.

I rose, saying nothing, and walked to the cabinet. Pulling out a black bottle, I glared at Seal and drank it down, pinning his eyes with mine and daring him to say anything before I walked to my room and slammed the door.

Their argument was quick and vicious. Whether they thought I lied was not the question, they likely thought I had just committed suicide. What they did not know is that I am almost immune to my poisons by now, and as long as I don't get excited sexually within the next few hours, I would be fine. Probably.

I ran a bath and sank my tired muscles into it with a sigh as the fight in the kitchen grew louder, and doors were slammed. I wondered who lost the argument over which one had to check on me later. I didn't care. I bathed and threw a simple shift over my head, leaving my room to go to Laith. I wanted to feel his body next to mine; I didn't want to sleep alone.

I knocked on his door, waiting for an answer before opening it and closing it behind me.

"May I lay with you tonight, My Lord?"

"Only if you never call me that again."

I went to him, pulling back the covers and sliding in next to him. He, too, had bathed and smelled of citrus, smoke, and metal. My guess was it is so deeply ingrained in him to ever be cleaned away.

Isa was perched on his bookshelf and hopped down to join us at the foot of his bed. He pulled me to him and let him envelop me in his warmth and strength. I sank into him and let my eyes close.

"You will not die from the poison in the bottle, Ari, promise me," he whispered, his lips soft against my neck.

"Women's medicine. I will be fine, Laith, I swear."

I fell asleep listening to the sound of his breathing.

Sometime during the night, I heard my door open and slam shut, and then Laith's door open, and a deep sigh of relief come when I was discovered breathing and in Laith's arms.

I felt the bed sink as heavy weight was lowered onto it and felt a hand trace my cheek. Laith pulled me closer to him, his arm draped over me possessively.

"I love you, Ari, and I apologize," Seal said before leaving once again, shutting the door behind him. I rolled over in Laith's arms, inhaling the warm scent of him before I drifted back to sleep.

In the morning, I felt him shift from me and rise. I lay longer, enjoying the scent of him and the feeling of love as it coursed through my veins.

I wasn't working today; I had already decided. I was about to drift off again when loud banging at the front door jarred me awake. I heard low voices that raised louder; I recognized my mother's among them. Sighing, I rose from my place of comfort and stumbled out of Laith's door.

In the middle of my living room, my mother stood with two guards at her side. I knew them both, and they were assholes with an unhealthy hatred of me.

"Good morning, daughter." She smiled coldly, noting I had not come out of my room. I walked to Laith and let him pull me to him as I rubbed my eyes.

"Long night?" she asked, glaring at me.

"Long day, Mother, this one is insatiable," I answered with a yawn as I patted Laith's chest, kissing his cheek from my tiptoes before going to the kitchen and pouring tea.

The Guard, Tine Fuar, stared at my naked legs as I went, and the other one, Ciuin Bas, stood there being a fucking prick like normal. I hated her henchmen.

"Ari," Seal started, "Your mother was just saying that the oldest Rowan died last night."

"Rowan?" I asked sleepily, needing my tea to wake up.

"One of Ravena's men," he said quietly.

"Oh," I said, "Is he the big dark one?" I chuckled softly to myself.

"They are all big and dark," Saige said.

"What happened, mother? Thanks for checking on us; as you can see, all is well here." I smiled lazily and walked like a cat to Seal, letting him put his hands on my hips.

The light-haired son of a bitch, Ciuin, glared at me.

"Ravena took two of the brothers to her bed last night, rather willingly, and the oldest Rowan died shortly after they both finished with her," my mother said. Walking slowly to the kitchen, she began opening cabinets. I froze in place, and it did not go unnoticed.

"Why does that pertain to us, mother?" I asked, forcing myself to relax. I followed her and moved to stand in front of one particular cabinet while trying to look bored.

"Because you are rather skilled with potions, and I heard about the incident at the Consummation Ball. You would not let that go,

Airmed; I know you better than that," she said, opening drawers and rifling through everything. I sipped my tea.

"Mother, that situation was handled by my lovers and did not need my attention. What are you asking about it for?" Lann and Seal moved to the kitchen and placed their hands on their swords.

"Ah, is that the way of it? Your tight little cunt must be lined with gold to have my most dangerous men moving to protect you, little girl. Tell me again, which one of them forced his way through your maidenhead?" she snarled.

I heard the light-haired guard hiss out a breath and saw the rise in his breeches, sick fuck that he is.

"It matters not, Queen. Why again are you here if not to check on the welfare of your daughter and her house?" Lann asked, moving to my side.

"I came because Rowan's death has Ari's bloody fingers all over it, even if Ravena and the other Rowan brother both swear there is no foul play. Now move from in front of that door, or I will have you moved." She glared, her eyes filled with hate.

"I don't have the time to make medicines, mother, and certainly am not inclined to make poisons," I lied, not moving. "My lovers and the bakery keep me more than busy," I finished.

"Move, or I will have my guards move you, and if they move you at all, they will move you to my dungeon for interrogation," she hissed in my face.

"Surely, my Lady, there is some misunderstanding," Lann said. "Ari has been with us since the beginning, and due to the dangers in the area goes nowhere unaccompanied," he said, lying smoothly. I could not even scent it coming off him. I moved from my spot.

Aramea opened the cabinet and moved the flour and sugar. Nothing was there. None of the bottles that had been there last night remained.

"Search her rooms," she said, growling at me.

"Mother, why are you doing this. I have done nothing," I said.

"You make me look weak with your attitude and your meddling. I don't even believe you have let these men touch you and have a notion of letting Ciuin check for your maidenhead himself." She snarled at me, and I stiffened in fear. I did not want his hands on me.

"My Lady," Saige argued, we signed a contract. All of us, including you, giving Ari to us. No other man is permitted to touch her based on your written agreement, and that agreement is binding. I assure you, we are taking our job seriously and that Ari has been under our control this entire time. She did not poison the Rowan. Perhaps he is old, and taking pleasure with his brother was too much for his heart. Immortality is a near thing and not a guarantee."

"You say you have control of her and have bedded her, then we shall watch you, Saige, as in the days of old. Once upon a time, all initial beddings were witnessed to assure that royal lineage was accurate. Take her to bed, Saige, while we watch and prove it has been done.

"My Queen, she was used rather thoroughly yesterday and may not be up to the task today," he said, his face paling.

"All the better, for I care not how well used she is," she hissed. I will watch you have my daughter, or she will leave with me, and my Guards will test the veracity of your words."

I felt the tears start. This wasn't about sex or maidenheads or poison; this was about humiliation and control. I knew it, she knew it, we all knew it. She picked the one man I hadn't yet lain with and was going to twist our first time together, even if she didn't know that.

"Come, Ari." Saige walked to me with a sad smile, "It's nothing we haven't done before." He reached for me, paling more at the sight of my tears. I took his hand. He squeezed mine, and we walked to his room, not mine.

That was a kindness I would thank him for later. My room was a place of peace for me; wherever this took place would be ruined forever. The Queen and her men followed, shutting the others out when they closed the door behind them.

I felt their pain, but they said nothing, for there was nothing to say. Perhaps I had caused this outburst with my poison, but I wasn't sure she would not have done this anyway. She does not like being out of control, and this was just another way she could try to control me.

"I will be quick and have them gone, my love, I swear. I am so sorry, this is not us, this is not you and not me, but some strangers forced into this. I promise," Saige whispered to me when their backs were turned so they could settle against the wall.

I loved him then, felt it course through me, and I didn't care if my bitch of a mother watched. I would make her regret it.

"No, Saige." I smiled at him, cupping his face in my hand. That cunt wanted to watch, then I would give her a show.

I loved him. I loved them all. They thought to make us uncomfortable or prove some grand point, I would turn the tables on her. She had never loved anything in her miserable life. I would show her what that looked like and what she missed out on. No one would control me. Not her. Not her henchmen. No one.

Watching Saige carefully, I pulled the shift over my head, and he inhaled sharply, likely thinking I would leave it on and just do the deed. He wasn't the only one who caught their breath as I walked to him with a smile no demon or devil could match.

My eyes only for him. Fuck my mother. I unbuttoned his shirt, placing kisses where the buttons were. I pulled the shirt from his back and dropped it to the floor, my green eyes never leaving his gray ones. I reached down and ran my hands over him, causing him to groan into my mouth.

He was soft, but I felt the first signs that he was stirring when the cloth twitched against my hand. I pulled the string with my left hand, letting my right slide down his entire chest and dip below the waistband.

He lowered his head to me, his silver-white hair forming a curtain between our watchers and us. He deepened his kiss and licked his tongue over mine, tasting me with a soft moan. I slid into him, tracing the muscles of his back and following their lines down to his ass and letting myself feel the hardness of the muscles there.

"Ari," he said, lowering us neatly onto the bed and landing between my legs.

He traced down my skin, using his body to block as much of us as he could, pulling his magic to him and lighting me on fire with every touch of his fingers. I arched, breathing in the delicious scent of mint and vanilla. I focused on him, even as I felt Aramea and her guards stir and adjust uncomfortably.

He was hard against me; I could feel the head of him pressing just there.

"Are you still sore, my love?" He smiled into my mouth.

"A little, yes, but nothing for you to worry about," I answered, licking along the corded lines of his neck; he kissed down my chest, taking my nipple into his mouth and causing me to arch off the bed, everyone else in the room forgotten.

He kissed down the line of my belly and into the waxed skin between my legs, making me wrap my hands into his long hair and pull him closer. He licked around all the soft skin there, pulling his fire to him and warming everything his tongue touched, then blew air across me. I whimpered and curled into him until he flicked his tongue across the hard nub at my center and brought me bucking off the bed.

I cried out, feeling my muscles clench against themselves as I came. He picked that moment to push into me, causing the orgasm to deepen and stretch out as soreness warred with pleasure, and he began to move.

I kissed the taste of myself off his lips and nipped my teeth along his jawline and up to his ear, grabbing his lobe into my teeth and sucking it. He pulled in a breath and watched my face, lengthening his strokes until he was almost out, before pushing back into me.

I watched between us the way I had with Seal. Goddess, but it was sexy seeing him enter me like that. I tilted my hips into him, changing the angle and taking him deeper, causing him to shudder against me and quicken his pace.

I wrapped my legs around his back and held tight as he rolled his hips until the orgasm ripped out of me and left me limp in his arms. He came in me and dropped onto my chest, covering me with his body.

I heard the door open and close as we lay there, breathing hard against each other, and the front door slam shut a moment later. Saige pulled the covers over us and held me close to him.

"I love you, Ari," he whispered.

"I love you too, Saige. I love all of you." I napped in his arms, hearing his door open and close as someone checked on us and left.

Chapter Twenty-Five

Seal

For the second time since I've known Ari, I wanted to kill the Queen. I wanted it so badly I could taste her life on my tongue. I wanted to rip her to shreds.

The look of pain and humiliation on Ari's face and the scent of her tears had me livid beyond reason. I paced as they shut us out of the room, forcing Saige and Ari to be together for their first time under their watchful eye.

I doubted Saige would care, as he liked to watch and be watched, but Ari would be devastated and disgusted over her own mother doing this to her. What kind of sick fuck is she, and how much torture had Ari suffered at her hand?

Then I heard her soft moans through the door and heard her cry out in pleasure, and a very small part of me relaxed. The sound of her with him made me feel better, convinced they had found a way to thumb their nose at the Queen, who stormed out of the house angrier than when she came.

I could smell the sweet scent of Ari's pleasure trailing behind them, and I hated the Queen for taking that moment away from her. Saige came out after and explained what Ari had done. She slept, exhausted from the last few days, on his bed, and I knew I was lost to her.

She protected all of us by not fighting the Queen's wishes, yet took control of a horrid situation and did not allow anyone to ruin what should have been a good memory for her.

Ari is the bravest Fae I have ever known. Saige told us that she said she loves us all. Happiness settled into the deepest part of me at his words, and we moved around the house, cutting wood, wiping up messes, and freshening up the place while our love slept most of the day away.

None of us left the house, choosing instead to regroup and recover from the last week of our lives. Saige cleared gardens in anticipation of the planting season. Lann made a baking table for Ari to place more cakes and pies upon. Laith cut and sewed a sheath that would fit Ari's tiny body perfectly. I made a contraption to amuse the bloody cat. What has happened to us?

Love has happened to us.

Ari rose in the afternoon and stumbled from Saige's room to hers, an unseeing and beautiful mess. Water ran for a long time as she washed and dressed. When she emerged from her rooms, she was fresh-faced and clean, wearing the soft yellow dress I picked for her that showed the curve of her calves. She looked stunning.

"Sorry I slept the day away," she said, pouring tea and preparing the kitchen for a round of baking, something we all knew she did when strong feelings of any kind press down upon her.

We fixed drinks and sat in front of the hearth in the living room while she churned out bread, cakes, pies, and cookies, intending to make us all fat. She tore the feathers off several small hens and set them to baking. She said nothing, but the silence was comfortable as she worked. She laid our table, calling us when the meal was ready.

"Don't get used to it," she growled, glaring at us in the most halfhearted glare I had ever seen.

We each had a hen on our plate and small rounded potatoes covered in some kind of sauce. She is an incredible cook when she chooses to do it. The meat was seasoned with rosemary and coarse salt and melted on our tongues. We gorged on dinner and stuffed ourselves further with pastries.

Ari sat quietly through the meal as we laughed and talked about Goblins and Orcs. No one mentioned the Rowan brother because we no longer cared. We didn't mention poison or the bottles I had hidden in my room but would return to her. They were hers, and I would not throw them away. Regardless of what we told the Queen, we did not control Ari and never would try.

Her spirit is fresh, sharp, and untamed; we would have her no other way. We loved her more for her reckless and fiery soul. She watched us carefully, taking the night in.

We did not push her. So much had changed in her life of late that it must be overwhelming. Saige, Lann, Laith, and I had been together for a long while and had accepted her into our center easily; she had a whirlwind week and might need some time.

She moved to the door and watched the darkness grow through the glass. Her hands pressing on it like she wanted to go but could not. I hoped she didn't feel that way. She was free here.

"Why does your mother hate you so much, Ari," I asked, sensing the shift in her mood.

She sighed, never looking at me. "She wanted a child for all the prestige and power it would bring her, but she did not want a powerful child, and that is what she got. One day I will rival her power and vie for the throne, should I live that long, and she knows it.

"I can't stand her either. Everything she has done is to try to control me. All of this. Yet, it is a game we like to play, acting caring and interested in each other, but there is only hatred at the heart of it. You must keep your enemies close if you want to best them," she said, her voice hard.

"Did you know I had a brother?" she continued. "He was born before me, proving she was fertile and strengthening her influence. She and his father killed him. I was just a little thing and still living in her palace. He was older than I by quite a lot, and they let him live halfway to being considered an adult. They took his head and made me watch." She looked into the night, her face sad, her back still to me. The other men had stopped everything to listen. "He was a good brother, kind to me when no one else was."

"She will never let us win. You must know that. Should I get pregnant and have a boy, he will die. Should I have a girl, she will take her. We will never be allowed to be parents, never be allowed to be happy. Once I have a baby, my usefulness to her will cease, and I, too, will die by her hand.

"She does so hate a challenge, and all I have ever done is challenge her. I can't help myself. I am not afraid because I know how this story ends; I have already seen it play out. There is no use fearing the ending when you know how it will come." She pushed the door open and walked out into the night, not looking back.

We stood in silence, struck speechless. Hearing what she said explained everything. The thing was, deep down, I knew she was right. I watched her until she disappeared, not moving to follow.

Chapter Twenty-Six

Ari

I don't know where I was going; I was just going. I walked until I couldn't walk anymore, then sat down. Solas haunted me on the edge of the woods like a wraith. I could see her out of the corner of my eye. Isa curled onto my lap, and I wondered that the men in my life could give me a minute, but the animals could not.

Interesting.

It was a warm night, soon we could let the hearth fires go out, but for now, they chased the damp away, if not the cold. I sat in the grass in the middle of the field outside our home.

I was exhausted, and I was a fool. I allowed myself to feel happiness and joy for the first time in my life, and now reality had come crashing back in. As long as Aramea lived, I would never know peace. What new horror would she visit upon me? I pledged to make her believe my life was miserable, so she would not be inclined to act on my happiness.

I sat with my arms curled around the cat and watched the moon rise. Dew formed on the grass, and I began to get cold, but still, I sat. I just needed to be alone for a little bit. The warm crush of men and emotions was too much, and I needed to be cold and detached from it all. I was used to that; it gave me comfort.

I saw it coming, a white wolf the size of Lann's horse. It glowed a soft purple by the light of the half-moon. It raced towards me. I moved to pull my knife, but as I did, the animal folded into itself and out stepped a naked woman.

Her long hair was silver with a hint of amethyst, her eyes shone softly violet, a circlet of silver sat on her brow. She brought her hands down, and clothes formed out of the air. Hunter's breeches, like my own, threaded up her legs, and a soft tunic covered her torso as boots wrapped themselves around her calves.

She never missed a step as she walked to me. I jumped to my feet, surprised that she was shorter than even I, not by much, but by a little. I had always expected the Great Goddess to be ten feet tall. I moved to bow.

"Dispense with all that, will you Airmed?"

"My friends call me Ari." I stuttered, unable to speak clearly.

"Am I your friend?" she asked.

"Are you my enemy?"

"Certainly not," she answered. "Let's walk a bit. Your four are getting restless and will be unable to fight looking for you much longer, and please, call me Dani," she said. I fell into step beside her.

"You are in a unique position, Ari," she started. "You see the way of things very clearly, more clearly than most."

"I may have the gift of lying to others, but I cannot lie to myself, Goddess," I said.

"Dani," She cautioned.

"Right."

"I am going to give you a gift, Ari. You will know when you receive it. It is a gift that you may not want but are destined to have. Your power grows daily, and your soul remains kind. You look after others at great risk to yourself and don't even realize that it is optional behavior.

"I have made mistakes. Mistakes that have cost my people. They have made mistakes too, but that is the way of it. As a child, your job is to test the limits of the higher power. It was not my job to cause you suffering, and that is what I have done. To you all." She stopped walking and turned to me. Isa flopped down at my feet, showing the Goddess her belly. Dani picked her up and snuggled her. "She is a good cat."

"She is. She was a friend to me when I had none," I answered.

"You have always had me. I know that you have suffered; all my children have. My son was to rule this place, and he would have been a kind and just king. Instead, your mother killed him, and I took revenge upon you all. For that, I apologize.

"I am beginning to right the wrong, but it will be a long journey. Remember this, Ari, with this gift comes sacrifice. I am sorry that I have to ask this of you when you are so young and have already sacrificed so much, but I promise you this. I will not forget your sacrifice, not ever.

"You and your four will give up what seems like everything, but remember, it will not last forever. That is my promise for accepting the gift you do not want. It will not last forever. With my gift, you will make the world better. You will survive this, and your people will thrive and be happy. That is my promise."

"I don't understand, Dani. It's been kind of a long week or so. Why me? I'm not special," I said.

"That is where you are wrong, my child. You are very special, and you are the only one who can bring about the change that must come. Immortality is a long time; just remember that. Thirty or forty years in the totality of that is nothing," she said, walking again. I followed.

"I am not yet forty," I said, confused.

"I know, child. I know. Just remember how quickly your years have passed and know that I will keep my promise to you." She turned to me once more.

We heard feet approaching, and I could see the outline of the men walking this way. The Goddess and I had traveled more of a distance than I imagined, and I could no longer see our house or the little field behind it. We had walked nearly to the wood line, and I could feel quick their approach.

"They are good men," she said with a smile.

"Yes, they are. Of all the things that could have happened, I am grateful for them."

"As am I. Your mother did a few things right, but only a few. You are one of them. They are another. Goodnight, sweet Ari." Her clothes disappeared, and she was once again the wolf. She ran from me with a howl. Howls answered her in the distance, and she was gone.

"Was that?" Saige came at a sprint.

"Yes," I said, shaking my head.

"What did she want?" he asked. The other three stopped next to him, following the retreating wolf with their eyes.

"I think she wanted to tell me that our lives are going to get a shit ton worse before they get better." I sighed. "Other than that, I'm not sure. She promised we would survive and that it would get better, so that's something." I shrugged, walking away from them back toward the house while they stood transfixed and staring after the largest Dire wolf of all. The Goddess's howls echoed through the night; I took my cat and headed to bed.

Chapter Twenty-Seven

Lann

We stared after Ari as she walked back to the house like it was every day that the Goddess approached you. We stared after the Great Goddess as she ran the opposite way in wolf form. Our Goddess was known to walk among her people, but that had changed over the centuries. I had never seen the Goddess in person, not ever, and yet she came and sought out Ari.

We watched the wolf run straight to her and were stunned when it became a woman in the next stride. I wondered at the nature of their talk and hoped Ari would share. Instead, she walked, defeated, into the house and shut the door behind her.

Then she made an apple pie and two trays of lemon cookies. While the pie cooled, we all took baths so that she could have some peace and a respite from our hovering. She was done when we emerged, and the door to her bedroom open. Seal found her asleep in her damned tub an hour later, ice-cold and blue.

We thought we had stopped her from doing this. I lit her hearth fire, and Seal tucked her under his blankets of fur after fighting her frozen body into a light shift. She never stirred. We eased into bed next to her, shivering at the touch of her ice-cold skin on ours.

Laith came to the door but turned away. He does not agree that we should all sleep together, I think he would take Ari for himself if he could, but that is not the way of it. We all knew. We were all raised the same. He touched the ring on his finger then walked to his room, closing the door.

"Keep your big paws to yourself, Lann and let the poor lass sleep," Saige said from the door.

"I had no intention of even touching her at all, but the girl is blue from cold. Seal even put clothes on her, imagine that," I said, shifting my weight so that Ari's round bottom snugged into me perfectly.

"Just going to sleep, Saige; you are welcome to come too. I think she has been overwhelmed enough for a bit. Why would she lay in a bath of ice if she was feeling comfortable with us?" He said, kissing her hand and the ring she had yet to take off.

"She has been through a lot. We discount that because she seems to handle it effortlessly. She is half our age and has no real-world experience. She is comfortable, just a little shaken tonight," Saige said, slipping in behind Seal. Good thing we got Ari an extra-large mattress. We warmed up the air under the blankets, and soon Ari stopped shivering and settled into a comfortable sleep.

I pulled her to me as tightly as I could, wanting nothing more than to slip inside her body, but I did not. I didn't think I could sleep and was surprised when I was out in a matter of minutes. The sweet scent of vanilla and sugar filling my nose and the feel of her soft hair against my chest.

In the morning, she was gone. We did not wake up until long after sunrise, which is not normal. Even Seal slept late. She hadn't been gone long. The cat lay on the table in her spot of sun, and the bread and tea were still warm. Ari had waited a bit before going, not wanting to wake us up.

I hated that she traveled the distance to town alone. This area was wild. Creatures roamed about that even Seal would struggle to manage. We drank her tea and ate her bread before we dashed out the door to work, late already.

We became even later when we stumbled across the bodies of two Orcs. One had been leveled by what I would guess were really large fireballs; the other had been stabbed through the eye with a pristine blade that no doubt had a chartreuse glow when held by Ari's hand. Hoofprints and the prints from tiny feet circled both bodies. We stood staring, unsure of what to say.

"I smell her blood," Seal said. "Not a lot, but enough. It smells like cookies."

"How did she kill not one but two Orcs?" I asked.

"She used her B plus swordsmanship skills on this one," Laith said, poking his finger in the dead thing's eyeball.

"She used your favorite sword," I said.

"Her sword now. I just hope she cleaned the blade; Orc blood is hard to get out of steel." He said, flipping the dead Orc only to have the head slide off its shoulders. The blade work from the cut so fine that we did not even notice she took the thing's head.

"Has to be more than a B Plus," I said, kicking at the head a little.

"Our little Faerie keeps secrets," Seal snarled, moving to mount his horse and track Ari.

"The Goddess wants her for something; we know she is not weak. She said she loves us. We must trust that."

"She killed Rowan and two Orcs," Laith said.

"No great loss," I said. "We did not want a weak wife, and we do not have a weak wife. Let us enjoy the fire until she poisons us too." Saige grinned, mounting his horse to follow Seal into town.

"He has a point." I jumped on my stallion and galloped past them both, leaving Laith to deal with the dead Orcs.

Chapter Twenty-Eight

Ari

Ravena and I were sitting on stools in the bakery talking when Lann, Seal, and Saige flew down the road, sliding to a stop in front of the bakery. I gave them a little wave.

I assumed they found the Orcs.

I had waited on them to get up. I even made them breakfast, but the strain of the last few days was affecting them too, and they slept past the point I could wait, so I left.

I had woken up smashed under Lann, Seal, and Saige and had to struggle to get out from the pile in which we all slept. Much different than seven other girls, I assure you. The three of them probably weighed more than the eight of us combined.

Laith had slept by himself, and I wondered about that. He seemed the least willing to share and was often possessive when his hands were on me, not to mention how he makes love. His intensity would disallow sharing.

I stood and walked to the door; I had even dressed for them today, wearing the flowing green gown they had picked out for me at the market. Their scowls got deeper, and I wondered if the small stain of blood I tried to wipe off still showed. It wasn't mine anyway, but it had marred the prettiness of the soft green color.

"They are rather protective," Ravena said, waving at them from her stool. This is the first time we had been alone together since she went to the Rowans. Now with the biggest one gone, she had more freedom and seemed much happier.

"Not in a bad way; I was attacked by Orcs this morning and left two of them dead. I imagine they are checking for wounds."

"Just two this time?" she asked, sipping her tea and watching the men stare at me open-mouthed.

"The third one got away, slimy bastard," I said, smiling at my men and watching their scowls dip lower when I turned from them in a swish of skirts to go back to my stool. They could come in or not; I was finishing my muffin either way.

"Are they good to you?" she asked, her blue eyes striking against her pale blue skin and black hair. Ravena's beauty is uncommon, and I'd always found her ethereal in her grace.

"They are. They are also a bit complex, and I haven't quite figured them out yet," I said, taking a bite of my muffin.

Out of the corner of my eyes, I saw my three ride away. They were late for work anyway, and their boss was a royal bitch, so they were better to get going. "Are things better now that?" I stopped, waiting.

"Yes, things are better, thank you. The oldest Rowan was a cruel man; the others are not so bad. He was cruel to them and not just me. It is a mercy to us that he is gone.

"The Queen says she will replace him once she can find someone suitable, but the other three are in no hurry to see that happen. It's like we can all finally breathe." She slumped in her stool and placed her hand on her belly.

"Are you alright? Did he permanently hurt you? I can get Saige to look at you or make you a medicine," I offered.

"You have done enough, sister. I have healed from the worst of it. We all knew rape was a possibility or even a likelihood. They prepared us for it. I was willing to give in to him; he just took more than I offered. I will be fine, Ari. Your men?"

"I would kill them, and they know it. They have found my medicines and seen my B plus swordsmanship skills," I laughed. "They are very kind, and for that, I am grateful," I said, placing my hand over hers and praying to the Goddess that Ravena found kindness too.

"Do they know who gave you the B plus? That elderly Fae is the still best in the land, your Captain included. A B plus from him says a lot." She laughed, throwing her delicate neck back, her bruises almost completely gone.

"No, they do not, and I will never tell," I chuckled.

The door to my bakery slammed open, and a very large, very angry Laith filled the entire frame.

"Ah, Laith, would you like some tea or perhaps a muffin?" I said, ignoring his posture.

"You killed two Orcs," he stated, looking me over. "In a bloody dress." He stalked to me, arms crossed and waiting.

"I got the blood out of the dress, Laith." I smiled sweetly at him. He placed his fingers on the bridge of his nose to keep his brains from oozing out and closed his eyes. My guess was he counted to ten to keep from saying much more. I understood the gesture.

"The third one got away, my Lord," Ravena said, a twinkle in her eye that I had not seen since her matching. Laith's eyes snapped to mine.

"Third one?" he snarled at me.

"Take a basket of muffins, my love, and a jar of tea. Are you not late for work?" I gave him a knowing grin as his face became darker. I packed four muffins, a loaf of bread, and an assortment of cookies for him while he stood there with actual steam coming out of his ears.

Walking to him, I placed a chaste kiss upon his lips from my tiptoes and patted his arm before walking away. In one step, he pulled me to him and held me against him, staring into my face. I just smiled and waited. He kissed me, urgent and demanding, before leaving with more relaxed shoulders and a softer slamming of my door.

"He's very cute. Deadly, but cute," Ravena said, grabbing another muffin.

"He's probably the least deadly of them, likely why the other three didn't come in. They might need a minute."

"Indeed. Knowing you as I do, it's hard not to feel sorry for them." My friend sipped her tea with a smirk on her face.

The remaining three Rowans came not long after, buying bread and cake for later. They watched Ravena laugh and talk with me, and their shoulders eased too. They had all suffered cruelty, she said. From the looks on their faces, I thought they would be okay.

Ravena left with them, and they walked to the market, two of them holding her hands and the other trailing not far behind. I grinned at that.

My day was busy, and I was out of baked goods by mid-afternoon, so I cleaned up and closed for the day. I went by the market myself and picked up a few things for the house before calling Solas and riding home. The men had cleaned a section of the gardens away, and I wanted to plant onions and potatoes. The sun was warm and bright, and it would feel nice to be outside. The ride home was uneventful and contained no Orcs. Their bodies were gone; the blood had soaked into the ground.

Mostly.

I pulled out a hunk of some sort of beast and set it to slow cook with herbs and spices before changing clothes and going to sink my hands in the Goddess's earth. I pulled weeds and planted seeds in the late afternoon sun, enjoying the warmth upon my face. My soul settled, and a deep peace washed over me.

My life was good. I loved it so much. I had freedom, kindness, and large men who liked to please me, I thought with a slow grin. The Goddess said we would face sacrifice, but I wasn't worried because it would be fine as long as we had each other. I enjoyed the late day sun and waited for them to come home.

Chapter Twenty-Nine

Saige

"Where is the little sprite now?" I asked, seeing the darkness of her bakery, knowing she was gone.

"Killing more Orcs," Laith growled, rubbing his free hand over his face. "What are we going to do with her?"

"I have some ideas about that," Lann said, a feral grin on his face.

"Your ideas are a bit violent, Lann," Laith said.

"And yours are not?" Lann argued, "She couldn't even ride her horse home after your day with her. She was done with me in minutes," he laughed.

Laith growled low and dangerous. Our little Ari had changed him somehow. Had changed us all.

"How does she do it?" Seal whispered. "Two Orcs. They are not an easy kill."

"One Orc got away, or so Ravena says," Laith snarled. "Maybe she dipped my blade in her poisons."

"They are women's medicines," I said. The other three looked at me, throwing their hands up.

"Like I believe that," Laith said.

Shrugging my shoulders, I reined my horse towards home and wondered if perhaps we might come across the bodies of Giants or Ogres. It wouldn't be a surprise at this point.

"She is little, but she is fast," Lann said; you should fight her and see. Orcs are lumbering things. They probably presented little challenge.

"Really? That's what you're going with?" Laith said, urging his horse after mine.

"I mean…yeah," Lann laughed.

Seal was quiet, as he often is. Going off the road, always searching for something. He came back to us when we came to the junctions where the Orcs had lain. There were no fresh bodies; I took that as a good sign.

"There were six Orcs," he said. "Why would she claim only three?"

"She's embarrassed that she didn't kill more?" Lann asked.

"Why are so many things stalking her. It is every day and not normal, not even for this wild country," Seal worried. "How many Orcs have a single one of us come across in years?"

We got quiet because what he said was true.

"She said that she will one day rival the Queen for the throne. Do you think she is serious?" I asked.

"I think she is barely finished growing and is already almost as strong as the Queen. I think she hides much from us," Seal said.

He had always been on the fence about applying for her. He does not trust easily.

"I'm not so sure I want to go down that road," Laith said.

"Too late, brother, where she goes, we go. We are in this together, all of us. You knew it. We all knew it when we signed that contract," I said seriously.

They would no sooner give her up than I would. Even Seal and especially Laith. She had done something to him in his tiny brain, and he was sorting it through. We all knew it. You could smell the burning from between his ears.

We rode the rest of the way in silence. When we were within shouting distance, the delicious smell of food came to us on the breeze. Ari had been busy. We pulled the horses to the gate of our garden and let them go.

Fresh rows had been dug in the earth, and spring flowers bloomed in pots hung from the walls. The warm smell of vanilla, sugar, and cakes mingled with roasted meat and potatoes. We walked into our house and found the table laden with hot food and steaming bread. The house was spotless, and she had the hearth fires lit in anticipation of a chilly night.

This is what it meant to come home. We stood there, feeling it wash over us. No way any of us would change this. We had waited too long to find the feeling. Ari lay asleep on the chaise, her delicate arms thrown over her head and her soft white shift riding up to her thighs. Her head was turned into the cushion. Her hair lay about her in a beautiful tangled mess, still damp from a bath.

Her plate was not in the sink, and I knew without asking that she hadn't eaten. At least she didn't lay in her tub of freezing water. We were trying to break her away from the horrible teachings she had survived, but it was hard going.

She trusted us, I think. She was happy here, but having never known comfort is a difficult thing to overcome. We sat at the table, piling food on our plates without changing from our dirty clothes. We enjoyed her meal as she slept on; no one had the heart to wake her.

Killing Orcs is hard work.

We cleaned the kitchen after demolishing the cake she left for us. This one was orange flavored with vanilla icing, and we ate until we were sick.

I gathered her into my arms after my bath and carried her into my rooms. Lann followed, and I let him. Laith scowled, and Seal just smiled as we went. She snuggled into my neck and placed a kiss against me. I would never give her up.

If she wanted to be Queen and save us all from Aramea, I would lend my bow to the fight. We belonged to her, and that was final. I lay her on my bed, and her eyes popped open. They roamed over my chest and then to Lann.

"So, this is the way of it?" she said, her voice husky and eyelids half closed.

"Yes," Lann said, stripping his shirt off and tossing it on the floor, closing the door behind us.

Ari drew her shift over her head and tossed it to the side, holding her hands out for us, her breasts rounded and nipples taut and pink. The sight of the curve of her pale hips and the crease between her thighs had me hard instantly. Her sleepy eyes and delicate arms opened to me. I almost came at that moment, the sight of her naked and on my bed, reaching for me. Goddess, I needed to think about Orcs, but then Orcs made me think of Ari, and I was right back to almost coming. I didn't like it.

Lann snuggled between her legs, and I watched as he licked over her bare skin, sending her back into the pillows. I stroked myself a minute longer, enjoying the sight of them together.

She reached for me again, and I slipped in next to her. She placed her hand on my cock and gripped it hard, sending a shudder through me. Lann slipped two fingers in her, and she moaned; I covered her mouth with mine, sliding my tongue over hers. Never had anything tasted better.

I kissed her like it was the last time. Lann flipped her on her knees and began licking her from underneath, her thighs trapping him to the bed. He gripped her hips, not allowing her to escape him. I slid in front of her and brought her mouth to my cock. She cried out against me as Lann teased her, not allowing her to come.

She sank her lips around me and took me to the base. I reached around and grabbed her nipple, twisting it just enough to make her back arch and push her deeper onto Lann's face. She cried out again and lost her rhythm as she came hard, clutching at everything. I moved away from her, sliding in to take his place. He raised an eyebrow at me, and I gave him a pointed look. We both knew that he was bigger than I and had no business taking Ari from behind. Not yet, anyway. He smiled when he got my point. He knew that would take some working up to.

I slid between Ari's thighs and flicked my tongue over her center, bringing a soft whimper. She was so wet. It dripped from her in steady drops, and I licked at them and ran my tongue over the hard nub. I heard Lann groan as her mouth found his cock, and she took him to the root. Her lips were the softest thing I had ever felt in my life, Lann, no doubt, was experiencing the same thing. Hard not to let her finish you when her mouth feels like that. Maybe someday, but not today.

I looked up her body and watched as she sucked his cock in a steady rhythm. I lashed her again with my tongue, making her lose her pace and shudder against him. Not ready to finish her, I slid out and entered her from behind, coating myself in her slickness.

I moved in her, watching as she worked him with her mouth. Lann's eyes met mine, so black they smoldered. I pulled out, smiling at her soft cry of displeasure, and adjusted her body over

Lann. He pushed into her from below, taking her wider than I ever could. He pulled her chest down to his and took her mouth as he pushed in and pulled out of her, bringing her closer.

His black skin against her white was stunning; it took my breath. The red of her hair contrasted with everything about him, and I could only stare at how beautiful they looked together, like obsidian on fire. He kissed down the line of her neck and kept her in position for me. I moved behind her, tracing her spine with my hand. She bowed her back, and I pushed her harder onto him, making her take him to the base. She barked in surprise at her loss of control. It was a cute noise. So, I did it again.

Lann's hips bucked to meet my push, and he tilted them just so. I adjusted and, using the slickness of her, eased into her from behind as Lann stilled his hips, letting me take my time and not hurt her. He pulled her to him to give me a better angle, and I could see her bite her lip. I waited until I was settled in, and her body relaxed around mine before I pulled almost out and then slowly pushed back in. This time, Lann moved with me, and we filled her.

"I don't. I don't think I can," she said, her voice shaking and her breath coming fast.

"Shh," Lann said, covering her mouth with his and reaching up to tuck an errant curl behind her ear. "We will take care of you, my love." I could feel his cock filling her as we moved together, making her almost too tight. I increased my speed as she was able to take more of me, and she began to moan again.

She felt so good that it made my heart ache. I had taken a man this way but never a woman and was amazed at the difference. It was like nothing I ever felt. She was amazing, brave, giving, and mine. The thought caused my heart to skip about twenty beats and made my head swim.

Lann took her hips and her control and pushed into her. I pulled her up to me and went still inside of her, enjoying the tightness of her on my cock and the feel of him moving against me inside of her.

I ran my hands down her breasts and flicked a finger over the nub of flesh between her legs, and bit down on her neck, causing her to shudder and sink deeper onto me as Lann rocked her onto him. She laid her head back on my shoulder, and I held her still as Lann went into her over and over again; it was like holding the entire world in my hands.

I felt her loosen and ran my hands over her, faster and faster, until she screamed her orgasm, her muscles clamping down around us both. I pushed her onto Lann, and he took her fast then, unable to help himself, as she came again with a shortened scream and followed by silence, her body clamping down tightly, the wetness running onto both of us and easing my way even more.

Lann finished violently, his dark eyes closed and his face slack with pleasure. I could feel him pulsing inside of her, and it sent me over the edge. I bucked into her one last time, giving her all I had.

I pulled her down between us, holding her to me. I kissed the back of her neck as she shook and tried to catch her breath. The sweet smell of her pleasure soaked my senses. Lann faced her and wrapped us both in his arms.

He kissed her forehead and my arm before going to get a towel to wipe us off. He carefully cleaned her first, then handed her a glass of water before handing it to me, then taking some himself. He pulled us to him again and wrapped us in his arms, and together we slept.

Sometime during the night, I felt him move and make love to her again. I had never known him to be so gentle as he was at that moment. He took his time, enjoying everything she gave him, and he gave her a side of himself I didn't know he had. Not in all our years together. She was quiet in his arms, and I listened to the sound of her rapid breathing in the dark until she came one more time and was still. I just lay against them, trying not to get in the way, but so satisfied that I couldn't even open an eye to watch.

Chapter Thirty

Ari

I awoke under the crush of men. Again. Lann and Saige had taken me to bed, and oh my Goddess, did they show me a thing or two. It's one thing to have a class about this stuff and entirely another to experience it. I sighed and snuggled against them for just a moment longer, enjoying the feel of them. I was sore, but not in an unpleasant way. They had known what they were doing.

Breathing in the scent of mint, vanilla, citrus, and oak, I sank into the feelings that ran through my veins before getting up and throwing my shift over my head. I had never felt love before and wasn't sure if that was even a real thing, but I did enjoy them, and they made me happy.

The sex was better than I had hoped it would be. I had always believed it was something to be tolerated, even though our class taught us otherwise. I just thought that was a thing men said to make you willing. My heart sped up when I looked at them, and there was a warmth in me that hadn't been there before. I wasn't sure what that was all about.

Someone was up and tea already made, and I could hear the swing of an ax. The sun was just rising, and already the day was warming. I went into my room and ran the water into my tub as hot as it would go, sinking into it in pure joy. I scrubbed myself clean with my new soaps and oiled my skin to softness, then braided my hair down the side so that it lay over my shoulder. I dressed in loose pants and a light chemise before going back out.

Laith stood in the kitchen with his shirt off and sweat drying on his skin. The sun came through the window, striking off his auburn hair, ringing his head in flames. I smiled at him, and his scowl deepened. Cocking my head sideways at him in question, I went to get some tea.

"Good morning, Laith," I said, coming around to bake some bread. He tossed his towel down and stalked back outside, picking up his ax and starting again on the wood. He didn't speak to me. I put two loaves of bread in the ovens and a made tray of muffins before taking my tea out into the garden.

Laith swung the thing like the wood did something to offend him. I sat in a spot of sun with Isa on my lap and watched as he chopped wood, scowling and angry. Fluffy white clouds moved overhead, casting shade on him in intermittent shadows. The others were not yet up.

I pulled my knees up to my chest, hugging them to me. "Why are you angry, Laith," I asked, fingering the hem of my pants.

"I'm not angry," he said, pausing to lean on his ax and glare at me.

170

"You look angry." I looked up and met his eyes. His face was flushed and his jaw tight. I could hear his teeth grinding from where I sat.

He stared at me, then went back to cutting wood. I went in to take the bread out to cool then came back to wait him out.

"Laith."

He swung the ax and let it go with a grunt, slinging it high over the wall with a frustrated scream.

I went to him and placed my hand on his arm. "Laith, I don't understand. Why. Are. You. Angry?" I asked through clenched teeth.

"Because I do not like that they shared you," he growled in my face in feral fury. "It's crude. I don't like it. I don't want to share you at all. With any of them," he finished deflated, he sat down on a bench.

"Laith." I started.

"Don't, Ari. I know. Okay? I know that is not the way things go. I don't understand why I feel this way. I can't help it; I just do. I love them." His voice shook with emotion, and he refused to look at me. "I have loved them for years, but this is different. You are different." He growled, rising to storm out of the garden and leave me in tears.

"Ari." Saige touched my shoulder. "He struggles sometimes," he said, running the back of his hand down my braid. "He doesn't mean anything."

"Oh, really? It seemed like he meant a lot. You all said you wanted a center, but here I am, tearing you apart." I sniffled and wiped my nose with the back of my hand.

"It's not like that, Ari. Laith is the oldest of us. As you know, in the grand scheme of things, age doesn't matter much, but in this instance, it does." He sighed, sitting next to me. I looked up as Seal flung the door open, running a hand over his face as he looked us over before going after Laith.

"Laith remembers when Talamh na Sithe was stronger. The rest of us don't. Laith used to be able to take the shape of several animals. He preferred the company of them to his own kind most of the time and spent his downtime away from others." He stopped, looking off into the distance, trying to decide where to go with this.

"Over the last few decades, he has lost the power to do that and has been stuck in his Fae form. From time to time, he gets very frustrated. You aren't tearing us apart, Ari. Faerie is. Laith loved his Dire wolf form, and he stayed in it perhaps for too long a time. Dire wolves mate for life, and they do not share. He understands he is not a Dire wolf in truth, but those emotions sometimes flow through him and make him more complicated.

"Perhaps he always had those feelings, and that is why he loved that form, I don't know. He will move past this. He will. Please don't take his jealousy as any kind of criticism of you. If anything, it speaks to what he feels for you. We have shared each other for more decades than I can count and been friends since I can remember, and he has never once protested any of that. You make us all feel something different, Ari," he said, pulling me to his lap. I turned and wiped my face on his sleeve. "It's new, fun, scary, exhilarating, and terrifying, but not one of us would change it."

"I'm not sure I believe you, Saige."

He kissed the top of my head, standing up and setting me on my feet. "Believe me. We want to take you someplace special today. What you are wearing is perfect. I'll pack us a basket." He left me sitting in the garden feeling chilled despite the sun. I rose, moving quietly to my room and shut the door.

Chapter Thirty-One

Laith

Seal walked up to me and punched me so hard that I saw stars. Then the fight was on. I punched him in the gut, taking him to his knees. He swept my legs out from under me and reversed our positions until he was straddling me, and then he punched me again, drawing blood from my lip. I bucked him off and jumped to my feet, drawing my short sword.

Seal drew his blade, and a dark smile crossed his lips. I am not a swordsman but had I taken the same class Ari did, I might be capable of a B minus. Seal preferred the short sword and was quite good with it. I did not back down from the fight. I wanted to bleed.

He feinted left, then whirled and slashed me on my right side. I brought my blade up, twisting sideways and avoiding the next slice, landing my own across his arm. He jabbed right, and I dodged left, our swords meeting in the center, each holding them in place. Sweat ran down my arms and chest, making my cuts sting. Seal would never hurt me, nor I him. He knew what I needed at the moment, and he gave it to me. Much better than when I tried to take my aggression out on a girl weighing six stones.

I am an ass.

Sensing my distraction, Seal twirled his sword and sent mine flying before placing the tip of his sword at my throat.

"Brother, you went too far," he growled, glaring at me.

"I know," I sighed. "Sometimes, I have trouble controlling myself. You of all people should understand that," I said, walking to get my sword.

"I do understand it," Seal yelled, and I know he did understand; he out of all of them would. Not Lann or Saige, who were light on the inside compared to our darkness.

"I will fight you or fuck you if you need help reining it in," he said, his voice softening. "You must find other ways of dealing with aggression than attacking Ari. Take one of us. Woo Ari to you, but do not- do not tear down that woman. I will not allow it. She did not ask for us; we asked for her. Our position with her is precarious still, do not threaten what we could have with your wolfish ways." Seal wiped his sword on his shirt and sheathed it behind him.

"It's getting harder," I said. I feel the lack of power pressing down on me. Aramea has done this. She has done this to us all. She is a horrible Queen. What was Saige thinking about applying for her daughter? It keeps her too close." I walked to an outcropping of stones and sat down.

"Ari is nothing like her mother; you must see that," Seal said, moving to sit near me.

"She is powerful and deadly. She can lie well, and she is not afraid of anything. She could be like Aramea," I said. I wanted to love Ari; I wanted to trust her. I desperately wanted to steal her away for myself, but I did not want to be betrayed by her.

"She is not cruel. She is not unkind. She will be nothing like her mother unless life twists her in that direction. Do not be the thing that twists her, brother. If she says she is powerful enough to someday be Queen, we should encourage her. Aramea is a blight upon the land. Perhaps with her gone, our strength will return," he said, placing his hand on my knee and squeezing it. "Don't discount anything, Laith. The Goddess of our People is telling her things will change. Let us hope they do." Seal rose and reached for my hand to pull me up.

"She also said there will be a great sacrifice," I said.

"She also said it would end well," he countered.

"I'm not sure that was exactly what she said."

"We don't know what she said word for word because we didn't hear it." He waved his hand at me, urging me to take it.

"Exactly," I said, slapping my hand into his and allowing him to pull me up. "Let's go home."

"Just remember that it is our home, Laith and that she is now a part of it." He gripped my hand hard in warning, staring at me with his intense golden-brown eyes.

"I will try, Seal. I will. Thank you for being there."

"We are always here for you, brother. The Queen has already pulled one of The Eight from her home and given her to another, let's not allow them to make that mistake with us."

"What? Who?" I asked, shocked. The Eight had only been in their homes for a few fortnights at the longest.

"Teagan. The men would not bond with her. They had been left to themselves too long to feel real desire for her," he answered with a short laugh.

"We don't have that problem, Seal; if anything, we have a bit too much desire." I laughed, seeing the ridiculousness of my behavior.

I had a beautiful woman in my home. Something I had never had before. She had come to me, and I had made her weak and felt her pleasure roll through me until she was weak from it. She had made me feel things I had not felt with anyone else. Being inside her was like being on the highest plane of happiness. I should be happy and not let the darkest parts of my mind have their way. I would do better.

"Yes, but we should still be careful. Despite our contract and our desire to keep her, I do not trust the Queen. Let us watch where we step." We walked back to our house, coming to the edge of the wall. I hugged him to me, and we went inside without another word.

A basket sat on the counter, prepared for our trip. The door to Ari's room was closed, and I went to it, knocking softly. I heard her sigh, and it was not one of pleasure. She sounded annoyed.

"May I come in?" I asked, pressing my hands flat to her door. There was a long pause before she answered with a yes. I opened the door and shut it behind me.

"I apologize," I said before she could say anything. "I don't blame you; I blame myself. I don't know why, but I feel very possessive of you. This is a new thing for me. It's my problem, not yours, and I will deal with it." She had changed into a dark green dress and sat on the chair by her window, looking out. She hadn't looked at me when I walked in, just stared out into the garden. The damn cat perched on her bookcase gave me the evil eye.

"I didn't want to be here, Laith. I wanted a life I could control at least one aspect of," she said, stabbing me in the heart with her words. "I've had no real choice. Ever. Understand that. I don't think you wanted me here either, and I know that Seal did not."

"Seal loves you," I said quickly.

"And I love him. Now. But that was not always the intention. For any of us," she said, still not looking at me. "I don't want to leave here, Laith. You were the first one I had feelings for, but I care for you all.

"I understand that things are new and complicated, but I ask that you respect me enough not to get me taken from here because that will lead to nowhere good. You know it, and I know it. I am the Queen's livestock, and there is nothing to be done about that other than try to survive her. If you don't respect me for having your brothers together, refrain from speaking about it. This is our life now. We can have five in a bed, and no one would question its appropriateness." She looked at me then, and I saw how hurt and angry she was.

I also saw a side of her I had yet to see, one she must refrain from showing others. If the Queen saw this face, it would mean Ari's death. I had no doubt. Her fierce defiance and determination shined in her eyes. She would do what she could to keep it from falling apart, which is what a center is. The center is what holds the edges of a thing together. Without one, they fray, and it all crumbles. I would still be jealous, but she would accept it and work with it, and I would work on keeping it from damaging us as a whole.

She looked so regal sitting there that I saw something else. She would be Queen. Saige and Seal were right. She would be Queen, and we had a hand in what sort of Queen she would become. She had not wanted to be here, and her life had already been shaped by being forced into every aspect of it.

The only choice she had was which one of us would take the burden of being her first into their heart, and she had chosen well for that task, but outside of this home, she was nothing and had nothing. We did not treat her this way, but her mother did.

To us, she was everything. All we could do is provide her a safe and loving home until she was grown enough to go to war. Then we would go to war with her. It was already preordained, and it showed on every line of her beautiful face. I went to her and bent my knee, bowing my head.

"My Queen, I am yours," I said, lowering my eyes.

"And I am yours." She looked at me finally, her green eyes so bright that they shimmered; the look of determination I saw there seared my soul. She placed her hand on my shoulder. "Do not forget that."

I wanted to take her and kiss her, to lay her on a proper bed, but she was still angry, and the others were waiting to take her to the lake for a day of relaxation. I rose and left her, going to my rooms to get ready, my thoughts heavy but determined to do right by her. To do right by them all.

Chapter Thirty-Two

Seal

I prowled the outside of the group as we rode to the lake. It worried me that so many odd creatures had been on Ari's trail since coming to our home. I saw nothing out of place but kept my eyes open anyway.

Despite what Laith was feeling now, we all knew that the only way to keep females safe in a land as wild as this one is to have a higher male to female ratio. It has always been this way. What better way to protect your family than by surrounding it with strong men who would care for any child born like it was theirs?

We are one unit, and any child would be ours, regardless of actual parentage. When one man goes to war and leaves his wife at home, he can fight freely, knowing his brothers will care for her. There is less worry and more comfort.

Once upon a time, it was nothing for a female to have six husbands. The genetics keepers paired that down to four, saying that was the ideal number for genetic diversity. Whatever that means.

Many homes have no females and never will. I do not want to live in one of those homes. Last night, walking into the place I built with my brothers for my wife and finding her asleep like that? There is no better feeling. None. We make her safe, but it takes the group of us to do that, especially this one.

A fiercely independent woman like Ari would crush one man and then dash off to be murdered by a melee of goblins. Laith will calm down and settle in. Funny that the tiny Fae who had lived only three decades adjusted much better than he. She was taking things in stride, including Saige and Lann. The thought of them together made me chuckle. I would love to see her at that moment myself. I screwed up by hesitating, and those two assholes never hesitate.

She rode her big white mare, looking like what she is. A Queen. I saw it the first moment that she stared down her mother and threw herself on my couch in rebellion. She will be a good Queen. Maybe she can fix whatever her mother did to cock up Talamh na Sithe.

She wore an emerald dress instead of the pants she wore this morning. This one had silver inlay and long flowing sleeves. I didn't remember buying it for her, but she has her own gold and could have bought it herself.

She rode her horse bareback with both legs off to one side to accommodate the dress. A small pack on her mare contained swimming clothes, I assumed. We had told her to bring them.

She did not chatter. She listened intently to the conversations around her but kept her eyes moving. Much the way mine do. I wondered how she learned to be so observant. She acted like a Huntsman. Perhaps creatures had stalked her before, and she knows she needs to pay attention.

Once we got to the lake, we could all relax. The place was warded against intrusion by any of the wilder Fae that roam. Her short sword was slung across her back, and I caught the glint of steel on her thigh when she mounted her horse.

Maybe she was still cross with Laith. Who could say? She rode mostly in silence, happy to listen to Saige and Lann verbally spar like the brats they are. I wove in and out of sight, checking for signs of danger. We reached the mouth of the valley leading to the lake, and I kicked my horse ahead to make sure there were no traps or ambushes.

There are other ways in and out of this place, but this opening was the most traveled, and all knew it. I sensed nothing off and smelled nothing of danger. No murderous hordes were lurking, so I awaited their arrival more relaxed, feeling the wards of protection snap over me.

This place was lovely. A large, warm lake that was clear blue to the depths shimmered in the distance. A pink sandy beach surrounded it, and there were tables to dine on and benches on which to relax. Three hot springs pooled under flowing falls of water before feeding the lake that were marvelous to soak in. The day would be warm enough to swim, and Ari could play at the lake's shore all day if she wished.

The others joined me, and I moved in beside Ari.

"You've never seen this place?" I asked, noting the stunned look on her face as she looked around.

"No, my Lord, I have not. It's magnificent," she whispered, reverting to her more formal manner as she often does when she is thinking too hard." She slid off the back of her horse and reached down, touching the soft tips of the lavender flowers that bloom here. The scent of the plants filled the air. It mixed with the lake's smell and the scent of distant pine; it calmed my soul.

Solas walked beside her, keeping the tip of her nose even with Ari's shoulder, mirroring the girl's steps. With her mouth open in shock, she took in everything.

Large purple mountains framed the valley, and their white snow-covered peaks were visible above thin layers of clouds. Ari walked, her hands flared out over the tips of the lavender. We could do nothing but stop and watch her beauty. She was breathtaking; the green of her gown and the red of her hair blended into the paradise surrounding her, making it perfect. The soft mid-morning sun made her pale skin glow, and her eyes brimmed with tears, for reasons I did not understand.

She bent her knee into the lavender, bowing her head. I could not hear what she said to our Goddess, but that is between them anyway. Then she rose, pulling a stalk of lavender, inhaling deeply.

Our Queen was stunning. She took our collective breath. Then she turned to Solas and pulled her pack off the mare, whispering something into her ear. The mare turned and trotted off with a swish of her tail. We moved to follow.

"Lann, do you think she speaks with animals the way you can?" I asked, not taking my eyes off Ari as she walked slowly, almost reverently, to the lake's edge.

"I don't know. It's possible, certainly. She never mentioned it before," he replied, watching as she pulled out a blanket and spread it on the sand.

She hadn't known what kind of place we were bringing her, and she looked down at her gown and the pink sand clinging to it. She pulled the laces in the back, sending the thing to the ground before stepping out of it. Beside me, Lann sucked in a breath.

"Is there anything more beautiful?" he asked.

"Not that I have seen. Even this place does not compare to our tiny Fae." I turned my horse loose and watched as Ari laid her dress over a bench. Her simple white shift blew about her legs, silhouetting their shape.

"We should have mentioned the sand," he said.

"Then we would have not seen this particular view," I chuckled.

"Indeed." We walked towards her as she pulled her shift over her head, dropping it. Naked and unaware of her stunning beauty, she made her way to the water. Saige and Laith, momentarily paralyzed by the sight of her, joined us as we followed her.

I laid out our basket and a few other things we had brought with us before stripping out of everything and going to one of the hot springs to soak. The other men dropped what they had brought as well and began to undress.

Ari could not take her eyes off the mountains and the beauty of the place. She stood at the edge of the lake, late morning sun kissing her skin, and I knew there was no hope for me. She tested the lake's temperature before wading out. I closed my eyes and enjoyed the hot water and the flow of the waterfall, feeling nothing but peace.

Then I heard Saige yell and jumped to my feet, already moving to the lake's edge. Ari was gone. I did not see her. Saige ran to the edge and surged deeper in.

"She disappeared under the water," he said, frantically searching for her.

I swam out, yelling her name. I could hear the others splashing as they searched.

She appeared then, a hundred feet away. She rose out of the water, taking a breath, and then dove under again. I stilled.

"She's swimming," I said. "She swims like a seal." Around me, the others froze. Few Fae can swim at all. Out of our group, I am likely the only one who can swim, and even I do not swim under the surface of the water. There are dangers there one would be wise to avoid.

Ari not only did not care about the dangers but had done this enough to be an excellent swimmer. We watched, stunned, as she breached the surface of the lake again and lazily floated on her back, occasionally stroking her arms to bring her back to us.

"What manner of creature is she?" Laith asked.

"I have no idea," Saige answered.

"She is our creature," I answered,

Swimming out to meet her. I gripped her from behind, pulling her to me. Her back melded to my front with perfection.

"Which one of my men has caught me?" she asked with a laugh, turning in my arms to face me. "Ah, Seal, I would expect that you could swim," she said, her eyes bright with laughter.

"And I did not expect that you could, little pixie. You terrified the others. They thought the lake monster had taken you." I smiled back, bending to her and taking her lips with mine. She let me claim her mouth, I teased her tongue, and she wrapped her arms around my neck, drawing me to her. My cock hardened in the water, and I pressed it against her thigh. She broke the kiss and dropped under the surface of the water. A trail of bubbles showing the way she went. I had never seen anything two-legged swim this way. Laughing, I followed, stalking her above the surface as she swam below.

When she surfaced for a breath, I grabbed her again. I held her more tightly this time so that she could not slip away. She faced me, bringing her legs around my hips. I felt the dagger I gave her dig into my hip, making it hard to hold a conversation with her. She hadn't taken her blade off to swim; she is a true warrior.

We were close enough to the opposite shore from where we started that the others looked small, and I could touch my toes.

"You never cease to surprise me," I said. "Where did you learn to swim?"

"Keena. It is part of her magic. Her people come from the sea," she said, nibbling down my collar bone.

"That doesn't explain how you learned so well, Little Fae," I asked, nuzzling down her neck and breathing in the scent of her. Her red hair floating around us tangled in my arms.

"I have learned many things," she said, tilting her hips into me.

"Yes, you have." I kissed her harder, cupping her ass with my hands and pulling her to me. She moaned, and I took the noise into me with a kiss.

Slipping my hand under her thigh, I palmed her sex, feeling it hot despite the water. I wanted to taste her, but there was nothing except sand and a blanket that involved three other men. She rubbed her core against the head of me and bit lightly up my neck. I eased my fingers into her and found her not only hot but wet.

Water is not the easiest medium in which to make love, but Ari, like everything else, defied that. Using my thumb, I traced lazy circles around her core and felt her shudder against me, pulling me tighter and trying to angle my cock into her. She buried her face in my neck, and I slowed my thumb so she wouldn't come.

"I'm not going to let you come, Ari," I said, teasing her. I bit down her shoulder and positioned myself under her.

"Why not?" she asked, her green eyes meeting mine, and I could see the need heavy in them. There was no way I could tease her much more; she was almost there already.

"It's just morning," I grinned, we have all day."

She groaned against me, dropping her head onto my chest.

I shifted her again and, in one stroke, buried myself in her as far as I could. She shuddered, and I held her just there until her body adjusted to having me in it. She pulled me to her with her calves and took my mouth, kissing me hard. Her mouth took mine, and the tingle started in my spine and spread down.

Her breath came in short gasps, and I knew that neither one of us would make it long, the Gods be damned. The feel of her surrounding me was too much. Maybe someday, when it was our one hundredth time together and not our third, I would be able to do this right and take my time.

Today my body betrayed me, and I thrust into her hard and fast, angling her hips so that the sweet and sensitive part of her was crushed against me and taut with friction. Her muscles clenched around me, making her impossibly tight, and she groaned her release into my chest. Hot fluid made her slick, and I was done;

despite my best effort to make this last, I emptied into her with a grunt, bending my face to her head.

Little shocks of pleasure trailed down my spine and made my cock twitch in her causing her to moan, and her little body shudder against mine.

I held her while I remembered how to breathe, my heart pounding in my ears. My legs threatened to stop holding me up, and I had to force them to do their job. She took a deep breath, too, in and out, then reached up and pulled my lips to hers.

"You are amazing, Seal; I love you." She looked at me with such ferocity that I believed her. Whether it was love or lust, I didn't care. I was hers regardless.

"I love you too, Ari." I curled around her and held her there for a long time. Then she slipped under the surface of the water and was gone.

Chapter Thirty-Three

Ari

Gods, I love to swim. It is the most freeing thing I have ever felt. It's how I imagine true freedom or flying must feel. I like swimming almost as much as I like sex, I thought to myself as I swam away from Seal, my limbs barely working. Perhaps I floundered more than swam. Goddess, but that was amazing; I smiled to myself. It must be near my time because I was flush with need and overcome with desire nearly every moment these last few days. My sex class hadn't covered this.

It didn't matter that Seal had just made me come; I was not sated, I could feel the ache between my legs already building. That's why I had worn the damn dress and rode Solas sideways; I did not want to come on my poor horse, and riding astride would have caused that.

I couldn't stop thinking about them. I wanted them all. Now. Immediately. One or four. I had seen cats in heat, and that is what I felt like. I tried to keep my mouth shut for fear I would only be able to mewl and growl while I stuck my ass in their faces. It was horrible. I was glad I had renewed my potion because this feeling is where babies came from. If I didn't need to ride a horse home,

I would go and force myself on Laith right this minute. He would strip the need out of me and leave me punished and exhausted.

They had broken me- done something to me. I didn't like it, but I kind of did. I swam in lazy circles; I could swim all day and never tire. The girls that wanted to learn to swim would sneak away on the days without classes and swim in the dirty nasty water outside of town; we didn't care.

I watched Seal go back to his hot spring, his muscles rippling as he walked naked to his pool. His beautiful body moved like a wild animal, all grace and sinew. I loved that he didn't hover and worry. He took my need and gave me his but did not demand more. He was okay with letting me take care of myself, and I loved him for it.

I floated on my back, looking at the bright blue sky, occasionally doing a backstroke that would take me back to shore to the others. I wanted to feel that hot spring myself and maybe take one of the others, by force, if necessary, to ease this horrible need. Laith had joined Seal, but Saige and Lann rested naked on my blanket, letting the sun kiss their skin. They were both propped on their elbows, talking and laughing while they watched me swim.

I felt a tug on my hair and let out a yip. All the men turned their faces to me. I was still a hundred yards from the beach. I felt another pull on my hair; I swam faster and pulled my knife. I could not touch and did not know what was pulling at me.

Placing my dagger in my teeth, I dove under and swam as fast as I could, which is faster than I can swim on the surface. I popped up and took a deep breath, I was halfway to the shore, and at least my toes touched here. Before I could submerge myself again, I was surrounded by heads popping out of the water around me. I palmed my dagger, waiting. I could hear the men shout and splash my way. I held up my hand to stop them from making that mistake.

I knew these creatures. They looked very much like my friend Keena. Their skin was a pale blue, and steel gray hair hung long and straight, floating in the water around them. Five sets of piercing blue eyes watched me. Only one had her head above the water; the others breathed in and out, their eyes breaking the surface. Little bubbles trailed from their noses. I sheathed my dagger.

"Well met, Maighdeann Roin," I said, bowing my head to them. They stood then; five tall, slender women circled me. Their breasts covered with only their hair. I heard a sharp intake of breath from the shore where my men gathered; I raised my hand again to calm them. These are peaceful Fae, at least Keena said they were.

"Are you a Selkie? You are not of our blood, but you call to us," one asked.

"I am not a Selkie. I am Fae." I answered.

"We are all Fae," she said, cocking her head at me.

"I am Daoine Sidhe," I corrected the minute difference between us. Though many would have called her race lesser fae, we were all Fae. She was actually more fae than I.

"You swim and make love like Maighdeann Roin," she laughed at me then, reaching for my hair.

I groaned on the inside, knowing they had probably watched Seal, and I make love in the water. She played with my hair, running her fingers through it and shaking out the curls from the front like an embrace before she began to braid it again without thinking. "I am Conley. I wanted to see the creature who has captured my lake today. You are welcome here; take all that you wish.

"I thank you, Conley. Your lake has no rival to its beauty," I said, ducking my head to her as she was Queen here. "My name is Airmed, but you may call me Ari."

I know you, regardless of your name. You are Prophesy. You are Legend. You are Spaed. You are welcome here, always. This place will protect you, do not forget that." With a smile, she slipped below the surface and was gone, the others following in silence. No bubble trails pointed their way.

I walked back to the men, a huge smile on my face. Seal's face was closed, Lann's stormy, Saige's curious, and Laith's murderous. Oh my. Lions and tigers and bears.

"What did they want with you?" Laith asked. I walked to my blanket and lay down, catching my breath from the fast swim.

"Just to introduce themselves and see who was mucking about their lake," I answered, throwing my arms over my head and letting the sun warm me.

"Selkies? Wanted to introduce themselves?" he asked.

"Those were Maighdeann Roin, not selkies, Laith. They are very peaceful."

"The wards?" Saige asked.

"This is their lake, Love; the wards will not hold them." I laughed, sitting up; it did not go unnoticed that I was now ringed by four much less peaceful types.

"Relax. They just like the way I swim," I said, leaving out the rest of the conversation. They don't need to know everything, even if they think they do.

"Now show me this hot spring," I said, grabbing a muffin and taking a sip of the ale they left by the blanket. I stood, undoing my braid, and walked naked to one of the pools, my hair wet and straight fell to cover my backside.

Chapter Thirty-Four

Saige

I was starting to see Seal's point. Fucking Mermaids? Are you kidding me? The girl gets hounded by every creature known to Faerie. I'm just waiting for a blessing of unicorns to show up and carry the lass off. Gods be damned.

We watched in surprise as Ari walked uncovered to the hot spring. She had never willingly shown herself to us at the same time. Only the night Seal broke her maidenhead did she lay naked before all of us, and that was not something I wanted to remember.

Maybe Seal's lovemaking and swimming with the damned mermaids made her less shy. I liked it. I followed behind, unable to help myself, and I don't even like the hot springs. Or water, but my cock liked her backside very much, so I followed it anyway.

"I brought my bow, Ari; let me see what score you got in your archery class later," I said, dogging her heels like every other depraved creature in the land.

"Oh, Saige," she laughed. "I am a terrible archer, but I will show you my lack of skills after I soak a bit in the hot water.

"Lann brought his sword; I'm sure he'd be happy to use it on you," I waggled my eyebrows at her when she turned to see my meaning.

"Lann used his sword on me quite well last night, love, as did you, if memory serves," she said, a wicked light in her eyes. "That is the reason I am interested in the healing powers of this hot spring." She shifted her ass and winked at me. Little sprite. I was going to fuck her there again at the earliest opportunity. I chuckled low, knowing she sensed my thoughts.

"Memory serves you well, wicked girl. All your fault, I assure you."

"My fault?" She barked a laugh. "You pinned me between you two like bookends in the library." I raised my hand and ran it down her spine, and she arched her back, letting out a very catlike noise. I laughed out loud and pushed her into the hot spring. She squealed, splashing me as I jumped in beside her.

"Bastard," she said, pushing her hair out of her eyes and going under the surface to get it back into place. When she rose out of the water, her nipples tight, droplets making little trails down her perfect skin. I knew we were all in trouble.

She settled on the rock bench near the falling water with a sigh. She arched her head into the waterfall, letting it flow around her like magic. Laith joined us, slipping into the water so quietly that I almost missed his entry.

Seal was grabbing a snack on the blanket and keeping a watchful eye on the lake. Lann joined him, and the two talked softly, his hand smoothing the rough skin of our most dangerous warrior.

Lann is a powerful lover, and so is Seal. I hoped they would fuck right there so I could watch. I kept one eye on them and one on Ari. She had never seen any of us together. It happened less and less since she came to us, and I wondered what she would think if they took each other in front of her.

I leaned back against the smooth rocks, letting the heat soothe me. Ari had been a handful last night, and my thighs ached from holding us both over Lann, though I would never tell her that. I think she believes we do that sort of thing all the time, but she is wrong.

Laith moved toward her with predatory grace, and a glance back at Lann and Seal told me I wasn't getting what I wanted on that front, so I pulled my attention to this one, even while I pretended to ignore him and kept my eyes half closed. He stood in front of her and watched as the water split around her shoulders and teased her pink nipples to hardness. Watching her with Laith would be amazing too. His intensity and focus are unmatched. She kept her eyes closed, even when he reached for her and traced the line of water between her breasts.

"Laith," she growled, making my cock stand. How she knew it was him and not me, I do not know. He straddled her then, placing his knees on either side of her thighs, and pulled her from the fall of water, settling her on the smooth rocks surrounding the pool before claiming her mouth. His kiss was slow but insistent. It made my breath catch in my throat.

She opened her eyes then, meeting his green eyes with hers. They were evenly matched, looks wise, only his hair was more auburn than red. The look between them was heated, and I could feel the heaviness in the air.

I stopped pretending I wasn't watching.

I placed my hand on my cock, unable to stop myself. I stroked it as I watched Laith's slow and careful attention destroy her. Not one of us can do what he does, his focus is extreme, and he has a sense of when you are at your most exposed and vulnerable. That is when he begins to build you back up, leaving something stronger than what he found behind.

Maybe it is his magic or his ability to forge that allows him to do this. We all lose our focus in the pleasure of the moment, but with Laith, at this moment, there was no one else in the world but her, not even himself. That is simply the way he loves.

She grabbed his hair and arched her hips into him with a little cry that caught the attention of the others, and they looked our way; Lann smiled and shook his curls. Poor girl will never sit on a horse this evening, I heard him say and then slap Seal on the back.

Laith and Ari heard nothing, each so deep into the other that no one else existed. I could smell her arousal in the air, and it fueled my own. He brought her hard, taking his time when she begged him for more, making her wait until she was shaking with need.

I stroked myself until I came at the same time she did, spilling into the hot water around me. Laith is a master of seduction, and my cock still didn't soften. He slipped two fingers into her, and she cried out again, clutching him closer. When she sagged against the stone, he turned her. Laying her belly on the sun-warmed stones, he slipped into her, giving her time to adjust around him. He is the longest of us, and there is no slamming that thing home. He eased inside of her, and when she arched off the stones, he pushed her back down, pinning her with his giant hand.

I watched as he buried himself in her, forcing her to take all of him; she tried to come off the stones again. He pulled her arms roughly behind her back, holding them with one hand, while he used the other to caress her skin until she relaxed around him and her flesh allowed him to move.

She turned her face to the side, resting her soft skin against the stone. Using his hips, he pushed her against the wall of the pool, holding her there for a space of several heartbeats before easing back out and then pinning her again.

He used his cock like another would use a blade, countering any move she made and meeting it with his own. It was a thing of beauty. She made a guttural noise deep in her throat, and he dug in, pulling her arms tighter and using them to bring her to him.

Sweat ran down his wide back, and he stared intently at her face and half parted lips. He tilted his hips and hit the spot deep in her, and she began to pant and writhe against him, begging for him to finish her, but he did not. He kept his pace slow and thrust deep, taking her higher and higher, but not allowing her to go over the edge.

Her face flushed, and she tried to pull her hands away from him. Still, he held tight, pushing her hard into the stone until she cried out, saying his name over and over, asking him, pleading with him. Still, Laith is a hard-hearted bastard, and he will strip you down to nothing before building you back up, and that is what he did to her.

He turned her over, pulling her legs around him and using the ledge while he stayed on the bench in the water, flicking his finger over her core. He almost finished her but pulled away so she could not.

He moved his hips faster, her naked back rubbing raw on the stones, and I knew I'd be healing that later. I couldn't look away as he pounded into her. Her eyes were open now, staring into his with so much intensity. Even when she screamed and arched against him, she did not look away.

She stopped begging him and watched as he entered her. Their breathing came hard, and I knew Laith was straining not to come, so he changed his tactic to delay yet again. He switched places with her, sitting on the edge of the pool, and guided her onto his lap backward.

He crushed her back to his chest and spread her thighs, so I could see him fucking her. Her head was thrown back on his chest, and there was no more noise to be had from her throat. One big hand wrapped in her hair, keeping her tight to him. Looking at me over her shoulder, he quirked his eyebrow.

Before he could change his mind, I kissed him hard, crushing Ari between us. I let my tongue explore his mouth and felt him shudder against her. Laith does love being kissed, and I know my little pixie loves watching it.

I could feel her head tilt up as she watched the violent clash of our tongues from below. Her shudder followed his. Someday, I will have Laith take me so she can watch. Or better yet, take me as I take her. Yes, that will be one hell of a day right there.

With that thought in my mind, I pulled away from them and stood on the bench in front of Ari, guiding my cock to her lips. She took me to the base without preamble, making my eyes close in pleasure. Her tongue rolled around the underside of me, and when I managed to open my eyes, hers were glued to my face.

Wrapping my hands into her hair, I pushed into her mouth as far as I could, her eyes widened, but she did not pull away. The feel of her mouth drove me wild, and she could see it. She wrapped her arms around me, digging her fingers into my ass cheeks as I gave in and fucked her mouth. The feel of Laith pumping into her from below and me from above had me on edge again quickly.

Laith gave a low moan as Ari arched into him, and I knew he would break soon. Never taking my eyes off her, I alternated fast thrusts with slow as she took me deep into her mouth with no complaint.

I felt it coming from the base of my spine and forced my eyes to stay on hers. Surprise flared across her features at the force of which I emptied myself into the back of her throat. She would have pulled away, but I gripped her hair as I came, not letting her release me.

She closed her eyes in a soft moan and swallowed what I gave as Laith changed the angle of his hips, heightening her pleasure. She licked the last drops off of me in delicious kisses and long licks. She met my eyes again with a satisfied smile. I had never experienced anything like that in my life. Hands down amazing, and I could've easily curled up and taken a nap in the sun.

Instead, I dropped between her open legs and traced her core with my tongue, placing my hands on her thighs when they tried to take my head off by tightening around my neck. She cried out and arched against Laith; he wrapped his arms around her, placing them on my head, urging me on.

There is a point in sex when you go so high and wait so long to orgasm that the act itself becomes difficult to achieve, and Ari was there now. He had held her off too long; her body was rigid from it. I licked her, sucking her firm tissue until her legs shook against my hands. I ran my tongue over Laith's balls, sucking them gently before gliding it up onto Ari, and I felt him falter his pace.

I did it again, licking Ari's pleasure from him before clamping my mouth over her; I held her core tight to me until she shattered and went over. It was glorious and so worth the wait. She pulsed against me, letting out a guttural scream as she finally found her release.

I tasted the wetness as it flowed from her. Laith slowed his strokes once, twice, then came with a groan, pushing deep inside her. She sagged into my arms, and even though he was still inside her, I pulled her to me, cradling her limp body like an infant. She was out. Instantly out, her soft breaths ruffled the few hairs on my chest, fucked to sleep by the true master.

"Laith, sometimes you are too much," I laughed over Ari's head.

"It's the only way I know," he grinned with a shrug of his shoulder, slipping down into the water to sit next to me. He pulled her feet onto his lap and massaged them. I pushed some healing power into Ari's back so that it would not be sore. Laith's chest was streaked here and there with blood, so I knew her back was raw. She slept through it all.

Lann came when I was finished and plucked her from my arms, taking her to the blanket and laying her down. He placed another cover over her and let her sleep in the warm sun.

"What was our life like before she came to us?" He asked when he came back to the pool and settled in with the rest of us.

"I don't remember," I said.

"Dull," Seal said.

"Empty," Laith said, shocking me. He had fought against trying to get her.

"Well, it's not empty anymore," I said. Laying my head back against the rocks.

"No, it isn't," Laith agreed.

Chapter Thirty-Five

Lann

I laid the lass down on the blanket, her body boneless in my hands, just like she had been last night. She enjoys pleasure so much that she gives herself to it completely that it often leaves her wiped out. I like it. Her breaths were soft on my arms. Her light skin against my dark is lovely, and I have to stop myself from taking her in her sleep. At this moment. Right now. What is the matter with me?

The sweet smell of her sex and my brother's pleasure filled my nose, and I practically dumped the lass and ran, knowing she was done for now and that I am not a monster.

Her scent had been stronger lately, more intoxicating, and I wondered if that meant we could be fathers soon. Her eyes have been heavier, and she has wanted us more, though she has not said as much.

She hints about not wanting Faelings, which is difficult for me to understand despite her valid points. I would love to hold a tiny piece of myself and Ari in my hands. No one would take that piece from me without going through my blade first. I would assure her that if she allowed me, but children are something she does not talk about.

I wonder about her deliveries to the other girls and the green bottles of medicines that she takes regularly. It is her body; we spoke of it before she moved in, and we will try to give her a child, but we will not count days and cycles for her to have one. We will enjoy our time and take what comes.

We sat in the hot spring and talked about life before and after Ari. Not one of us would change a thing. Our lives had settled into so much peace and happiness that, for once, we were satisfied. It didn't matter that Ari killed Orcs and seduced Mermaids; she was Ari. We were hers now. Her will be done.

Even Laith seemed to have settled in. He let Saige join them while they made love, and that is a huge step for him. It did not matter with whom she was with, she was with us all, and we loved her more for it. We talked as she napped, saying things we would not want her to hear about how we felt. Even Seal opened up and admitted his happiness, and he is the darkest of us.

She changed us.

She makes us whole instead of parts of a whole. We are united in all things now and not just many.

We left the pool when we were wrinkled, pale, and done professing our love for the tiny red-haired pixie. We dressed, pulling food from the basket. Ari stirred then, stretching and yawning, the blanket pulling down and revealing her small rounded breasts and deliciously pink nipples. We stopped breathing and stared at her for a moment.

After a few more minutes, she opened her eyes and stretched again before popping up and looking around. Her hair was a wild mess from the water, and it floated around her in stunning waves of red. We were right in our thinking that she would delight us with her soft curves and warm flesh. We just had not known the depth and scope of how she would consume us with her fire.

It is all powerful.

She stood naked, still, and not caring as she rifled through the blankets looking for her shift before coming to join us at a table. I poured her a glass of lemonade and cut meat and cheese for her plate. I added some bread she had baked earlier and enjoyed watching as she ate. She rarely did, not that we saw. Her waist was so tiny I could splay my hand across her entire back, yet her hips flared out nicely, and she seemed to be unbreakable despite her size. At least, so it seemed to me.

After our lunch, Saige pulled out his bow and set his shirt as a target. He pulled the string, his muscles rippling with the draw and sliding with the release. It was beautiful to watch. With a bow, Saige is an artist; he never misses, much like myself with a blade. Well, unless I am fighting Ari, and then I miss a good bit if memory serves. It is part of our magic and what makes us the Queen's best warriors.

Ari held the bow and struggled to draw the string. I laughed when her arrow went flying, released too soon, and landed haphazardly nowhere near the target. She tried again and again, and I believed we found the one thing Ari failed in school. Archery.

We stood watching as she struggled to draw the bow to a full draw. Finally, taking pity, Saige moved behind her and placed his arms over hers, covering her hands with his and nocking her arrow. Bringing his cheek down to hers, he helped her draw the bow and brought the string even with the corner of his lip before telling her to release it. The arrow went flying and hit the center of the target.

With a yip, she turned to him, hugging him to her. Turning in his arms, they did the same thing again and again until she pushed him away and drew the bow one last time, hitting the nearest corner of his shirt without help. She glowed with excitement as she shook out her arms.

"Thank you, Saige; I never understood the concept of the bow until now. Perhaps I can join your ranks as a junior archer." She smiled at him with a wink. He groaned, thinking she would likely try to do just that. She kissed the tip of his nose and handed the bow back before walking away.

Seal and I were trading blows with our swords in easy familiarity, shirts off, and muscles straining in the sun, our faces focused. So focused that we missed Ari taking up her blade and stepping into us with a wicked grin.

"Ari," I said, lowering the tip of my sword when I finally noticed her. She countered into me, twisting my blade away with her own, letting it fly. I have never been disarmed. Not ever. I am the best in the land and was just disarmed by my mate. The mate that is half my size. I grinned and moved to pick up my blade.

She stepped into Seal's reach in my absence, her blade raised and ready. The glint in her eyes daring him to fight her. She cocked a smile at him while his eyes gleamed in anticipation.

"Come now, Huntsman, will you not show me your skills with a blade?" she asked, one eyebrow quirked up in challenge.

"I thought I showed you those skills just a bit ago, love," he said, keeping his blade raised, but his posture relaxed. Sun highlighted the contrast between his skin and the tattoos etched on his spine. Goddess, he is lovely.

"Always thinking with your cock, do I not satisfy you, Seal?" she asked as her face scanned his form, looking for a weakness. Seal was shorter than I, and she would have difficulty evading his reach as she had with me. I settled back to watch, knowing this would be entertaining.

"Oh, you satisfy me very well, little Fae."

She twirled in, ducked under his reach, twisted around, and landed a thin cut to his torso before he could even parry her strike. Seal's eyes narrowed at the sight of his blood, and the grin on

Ari's face got wider. He advanced on her, and she met him strike for strike, their blades glinting in the early afternoon sun. The sound of them clashing was like low bells ringing.

Twisting again, she placed her blade in her left hand; taking him off guard with the crossover, she pushed him back. Seal's olive skin and blond hair flew about him as he tried to get one step ahead of her and failed every time.

Ari's feet barely hit the ground, and her eyes never left his face. The muscles in her arms rippled and flexed, showing definition I had somehow missed before. As much as he tried, he could not land a strike on her.

When she fought me, we seemed almost evenly matched, even though that should not be possible, for I have no equal in the land, but she had Seal on his heels the entire time. Switching her blade hand often and making her short sword sing. I would give anything to see her fight with two.

Her hair flew wild and red around her as she danced, not breaking a sweat. Whatever instructor had given her a B Plus had cheated her out of an A. She was truly a master swordsman and could easily be a warrior with her blade skills.

Suspicion as to her teacher was formed in the back of my mind. I thought that old codger dead and gone, but watching Ari now, I had other thoughts for she fought just like him.

After Ari landed yet another small slice to Seal's torso, she pulled her blade to her lips in salute, bowing to let him know their sparring was done. Seal just let out a low and vicious growl before bowing back, acknowledging her win with a shake of his head.

She laughed high and pleasant before sheathing her sword, whipping her shift over her head, and diving naked into the lake for one last swim.

"What the hell is she?" Seal growled as he watched her disappear under the calm surface of the lake, only to reappear far away, crest out of the water, and disappear again.

"She is Daoine Sidhe," Laith said, "There is a core of her power that the failing land has not touched."

"We are all Daoine Sidhe," I laughed, "What makes her shine where others do not."

"That, I do not know," he answered. We moved to pack up while she played. The spring sun would be setting, and we did not want to ride home much past dark.

"Why would the Queen teach her to fight with a sword if she worries she might lose her throne?" Saige asked. This is a question we have asked ourselves many times.

"Perhaps the Queen did not know their exact curriculum? I can't say; it does seem odd. Many in the land would love to see a new ruler; there are just none bold enough to challenge her. Perhaps the class was placed without the Queen's knowledge for that reason," I said, crossing my arms and watching Ari swim.

"Ari is bold enough," Laith said, watching her with narrowed eyes.

"That she is." Saige moved to fill the final basket and shake out Ari's dress.

With our baskets packed and blankets folded, we sat waiting while she swam, none of us wishing to shorten her day. The five mermaids joined her, and together they splashed and swam in some kind of game.

At one point, they all disappeared under the water, and Laith jumped to his feet, fearing they had taken her to whatever place they lived. Then six heads popped up further out, and the chase began anew. The sound of their laughter floated to us, and we couldn't help but smile.

When they tired of their play, they floated in a haphazard circle and talked. We could not hear their words, just made out their laughter and the low hum of conversation. Only Ari could make friends with mermaids and hold their attention this long. They took turns petting her and playing with her hair. It was a sight to see.

Finally, they parted, and Ari slipped under the water like a seal, swimming our way. We whistled for the horses, and all five came, even Solas though Ari did not call her. I stood with a towel, waiting for my girl to pop up. I dried her off from top to bottom and bottom to top.

I loved how she cared nothing about standing in front of us all naked. Her pale skin had pinked up in the sun, and tiny chill bumps raised on her flesh. Water dripped down and caught the definition of her muscles, running along them in little streams, and I have never seen anything more lovely. She truly is our girl. She helped me get the water out of her hair before moving to dress again. I ran my hand down the back of her head and let it trail on her spine as she walked away from me with a swish of her lush hips. Goddess, but I am a lucky man.

She rode Solas astride on the way home, the skirts of her dress riding up to her thighs. She leaned over the mare's neck and closed her eyes, wrapping her slender arms around it and rubbing her lightly.

"Thank you for such a wonderful day," she said, addressing all of us.

"It was our pleasure, Ari," Saige said.

"Yes, it was," she sat up, winking. "Mine too."

As the sun began to disappear and the Dire wolves stir, we kicked our horses faster, cantering the rest of the way. Once there, we separated, moving to our rooms to clean up and change for the night.

I sat with Saige and Laith in the garden, sipping ale, while Ari baked cookies in the kitchen, singing softly to herself.

Seal prowled the boundaries of the garden, unsettled for some reason. His instincts are flawless, but we wondered about his unease. After such a pleasant day, it was hard for us to imagine why he felt this way.

We were jarred from our easy conversation by a knock at the door. Seal blew past Ari and beat her there, even though she was much closer. He opened the door with a growl. It was late, well past the time when visitors would be expected. I paced by Ari to stand next to my brother. Knowing Seal as I do, I trusted that there was good reason to worry.

"Hale, Captains, I have orders from the Queen." One of her heralds stood at the door in full livery and at attention. My heart sank, and I felt Ari still unnaturally behind me.

"Orders?" I said, stepping up to the man and extending my hand. He placed three letters bearing the Queen's seal into it before bowing his head, turning crisply on his heel, and walking to the horse he tied to our gate.

Seal closed the door behind the man and leaned against it, pinching the bridge of his nose. In my hands were letters addressed to myself, Saige and Seal, bearing our formal names. I took mine and handed the others off. The air in the room was heavy and suddenly cool, despite the warmth of the day. I slide my finger under the wax seal and read the letter, first to myself and then out loud.

"By order of the Queen, you are called to duty on the southernmost border of Talamh na Sithe. Plan to arrive at the palace for more detailed instructions on the morrow at dawn." I read them again, hoping I had misread them.

"We knew it was coming," Saige said. "There have been Trolls and Goblins disrupting the travel ways for weeks." He sat heavily on the chaise, and Ari moved to stand next to him, placing her small hand on his arm.

"How long will you be gone?" she asked, her voice barely above a whisper.

"At least Laith will be here," I said, not answering her.

"How long?" she repeated, louder this time.

"There's no way to know weeks? Months?" Seal said. "Why now? Why all three?" He paced the room, barely containing his fury. "Why do they need a tracker on the border? Huntsmen are not infantry. I don't like it. Ari will be vulnerable."

"I will be with her, Seal," Laith said, almost angry.

"The Queen will have you in your forge working day and night to supply the lines, Laith. It will take more than one busy Faeman to protect her," he growled back.

"I'll be fine. Don't worry about me." Ari walked to Seal, leaning up to kiss on his lips, hoping to diffuse him. He grabbed her arms, pulling her up to his eyes.

"You will not leave without him. No early morning trips to town alone. Do you understand? No deliveries unless he is with you." He looked into her face intently."

"Seal, I," she started.

"Swear It, Ari!" He shook her once gently, begging her with his eyes.

"I swear," she croaked, and I felt the promise settle over us all.

Seal hugged her to him hard before setting her down and stalking to his room, slamming the door.

"The timing is a bit suspicious," I said, pulling Ari to me and crushing her to my chest. "Just a few days ago, the Queen threatened us all, and now we are being pulled apart. I don't like it." Goddess, but I did not want to leave this place. I would almost rather be tried for treason than leave Ari alone, but the Queen's punishments are notoriously severe, and to go against orders would likely cost me my life.

"Neither do I," I said, but the borders have been unstable for a while; we knew it was coming. Hopefully, it will be a quick deployment, kill a few trolls, chase a troop of ogres, and we'll be back in no time.

"Hopefully." Saige pulled Ari from my arms into his lap, playing with her hair absently. "Ari, I know you can lie, but please promise that you will keep your word." He buried his face in her hair, scenting her deeply. For all her bravery, her eyes were round with concern.

"I will keep Laith safe, I swear it. I will not allow him to travel alone," she said, her face solemn. She met my eyes and held them. I could see her worry, despite her attempt at humor. Her brows furrowed and caused fine lines between them. She said she loved us, and maybe she did; she held my eyes, not letting them go. I walked to her and wrapped my arms around them both. Laith walked to us, ruffled Ari's hair, and left us alone with her.

Chapter Thirty-Six

Seal

I paced the floor of my room, my control slipping and rage bubbling to the surface. I knew the Queen was up to something. It couldn't be a coincidence. Huntsmen don't go to the front lines; we go after specific targets and neutralize them. We track, we hunt, we kill. We fill the Queen's meat house and feed many families in Talamh na Sithe who cannot provide meat for themselves, but we do not fight on the front line. We are assassins, we work mostly alone, and we take down our prey regardless of species. There is nothing we can't track. That is our magic. For the Huntsmen as a whole to be ordered to the border is unheard of.

Archers, yes. Swordsman, yes. Huntsman, no. To my knowledge, it has never happened. Yes, we can fight and fight well, but our skills are better served hunting one on one. Anything. No creature born does not fear the Huntsman, but we do not fight in rows or back to back with swords.

I will find a way to slip away from the front lines and circle back. They would not expect the Huntsmen to stand around, waiting for a foe to strike, and they will not have the ability to know our location in the grand scheme of things. I will find a way.

I threw clothes into a bag and packed what little I might need so that I could travel fast and light. I would get more information in the morning. Another of my Huntsmen is mated to Keena, one of The Eight; I would ask his thoughts on the matter. He could be trusted, and likely does not want to leave his mate either.

Feeling calmer now that I had a plan, I returned to the living room to find Ari alone in the kitchen, biting her lip as she iced cookies, her red brows scrunched together in thought.

"Seal." She dropped her knife and came to me, pulling me to her.

"It'll be okay, Ari; Laith will keep you safe."

"I'm not worried about myself; I'm worried about you. If there wasn't a threat, you wouldn't be going," she said, not letting me go.

"Ah, Ari, I'll be fine."

"I love you, Seal. I want you to come home to me." She met my eyes, the pulse in her neck pounding against her skin. Maybe she did love us. I don't know how she could since she had no say in being here, but maybe she did care. I gave the first real smile of the night.

"I will come home to you, Ari. I will always come home to you." She hugged me harder, burying her face in my chest.

Leaning down, I placed my lips on her hair and breathed in the scent of vanilla and sugar that is uniquely hers.

She relaxed in my arms, the tense muscles of her back eased, and she sighed before pulling away and going back to her cookies. I followed, grabbing them up as soon as she iced them and shoving them in my mouth.

"Save some for your brothers," she said, smacking my fingers but smiling when I took my seventh cookie.

"They should pack faster; to the victor goes the spoils." I smiled over at her again.

Saige and Lann eventually joined us, and we stood around the table, shoveling cookies in their faces as fast as Ari could make them, which is pretty damn fast. When we could eat no more, we sat in the living room talking while she made several more trays, packing them in tins to keep them fresh. She handed each of us a tin of cookies and a warm loaf of bread for our trip.

"Where's Laith?" Saige asked, glancing at his closed door.

"Asleep. I checked on him. He's still dressed." She laughed a little.

"You wore him out."

"He wore himself out." She chuckled low and satisfied at the fact that she could at least pay the greedy bastard back for his attentions.

I was jealous that Laith would have my girl all to himself, for Goddess knew how long. Let the stingy fucker sleep.

I put wood on the fire while Ari cleaned up the kitchen, then helped Lann chop enough wood to last several weeks since Laith would undoubtedly be in his forge most of the day and into the evening.

Saige checked the meat house and brought in enough items to keep Ari and Laith comfortable for a while. None of us wanted to leave our family behind. Our unease hung heavy on the air, and we worked silently as the hours passed.

Finally, without any discussion, we piled in Ari's bed. There was no sex; we just wanted to feel each other one more time. The fear of leaving her and the worry of the unknown left us wanting physical contact. We are not immortal. Not really. Incredibly hard to kill, but not impossible. Where once these deployments brought excitement and thrills, now they brought reluctance. Ari was our home, and we wanted nothing more than to be with her. She settled in the middle of her mattress, and we surrounded her with arms, legs, and love. I don't think any of us slept, but we dozed comfortably until it was time to leave.

Chapter Thirty-Seven

Ari

We rose in the morning, my heart so heavy I could barely breathe. The men went into their rooms to dress, leaving me alone for the first time in days. I didn't like it.

I dressed quickly in pants and a loose white shirt, braiding my hair over my shoulder so it wouldn't be so wild. I planned to see them off before working in the bakery until I didn't feel so distressed.

Laith had risen early, and when I came from my rooms, he had a meal laid on the table for us. We ate in silence before calling our horses and riding into town.

"Don't forget your promise, Ari," Seal said, dragging me from my thoughts.

"I won't," I answered him through the darkness between us.

"It will be more dangerous for us if we are fearful for you, love," Saige added. "If we know you will do everything to stay safe, then we can focus on our jobs."

"I said I would, and I mean it. I will stay with Laith and take no risks." I felt them sigh in relief around me.

They knew I could lie, which is unheard of among our kind, but they trusted me, and I knew that any distractions could be fatal for them. I would not risk them for some foolishness.

At the palace gates, we stopped. Many men were gathered and saying farewell to their families. Keena stood with her men not far from us, her silver-gray hair unmistakable in the lightening sky. She hugged two of them, holding them for as long as she could before watching them leave. I recognized them from the ball and knew one to be an Archer and one a Huntsman.

I eyed the rest of the crowd and was surprised to find so many of The Eight here and so many of their mates leaving that it put me more on edge. I didn't think this was part of the Queen's plan, not the way Seal did, but it made me nervous that so many of us would be vulnerable in the absence of our strongest warriors.

I couldn't believe the Queen would muck up her broodmare program by getting any of us killed, but the unease was there like black mist in the back of my mind.

Seal caught my eyes and held them; I felt the surprise show on my face and knew he understood. I finally got it. Something was off about this. I slid off Solas and went to him.

"Laith will keep you safe, but know this. I don't plan on lingering along some border waiting for trouble. The Huntsmen should not be there at all. I will get with the others, and we will come up with a plan. Something is not right here, and I know that you see it now." He gripped my hands in his tightly.

"I don't like it," I said, my heart racing faster than it should.

"Neither do I."

Lann and Saige said their goodbyes to Laith, bending their heads in serious conversation before walking to me. Each of them held me as long as they could. I leaned up, kissing them deeply before they turned, and walked away.

When I could see them no more, I got on Solas and walked with Laith to the bakery. He knew my heart was heavy and said nothing on the short ride there. He squeezed my hand, giving me a smile before riding on to his forge.

I turned Solas loose and went inside to light ovens. I baked all day even though half of the population was missing, fighting some unknown enemy on a border I have never seen. Many of the girls stopped in, and we spoke in hushed tones, all of us worried.

Not every girl loved their mates, but we were all mated, and they shared the same unease I did at their sudden absence. All of them had at least one mate gone; most had two. I was the only one to have three mates deployed.

They stayed in the warmth and safety of my bakery for most of the day, even Ravena, who was the only other girl to have only one mate at home, because the Queen had yet to replace the one I poisoned. We planned to spend as much time together as we could. With the men occupied with work or fighting, we felt safer together.

It was early evening when my mother came. Ravena and I sat at a table, talking together when she walked in. Ravena's back straightened, but I just sat watching the Queen look around the store.

"Are you well, daughter?" she asked, her eyes lingering on Ravena just a second too long.

"As well as can be expected, mother."

"My two favorite murderesses together, what are you plotting now?" she asked.

"Nothing, my Queen, I assure you, Rowan died with a soft cock and a smile on his face. It is no fault of mine that he was unhealthy and weak," Ravena said, rising and giving the Queen a deep curtsy.

"Mmmm. Perhaps. Neither of you appears to be bred yet." Aramea walked to the counter and placed bread, cakes, and cookies in a basket.

"I am not bred yet, mother, but not from lack of trying. There have been no children born; I doubt that will change. Surely all Fae have not given up sex, and still, no children come," I answered, rising to pull a strawberry tart from the back counter. My mother loves strawberry tarts; it is a small concession to see if I can get more information from her.

"We are all trying, my Queen. I want nothing more than to fill my house with children," Ravena said, shocking me. I did not think she could lie and know for a fact that she did not want children. Maybe things had changed. My heart thrilled at the thought that my favorite sister might have found happiness with her men.

"Ari, is there not a potion that will help with conception?" The Queen asked, turning my way.

"We take a potion, mother; I have mixed red raspberry and clover with motherwort and shared it freely. It has only been a few months. The genetics class said that it can take a year under the best circumstances. I promise we are trying. The matches were good, and The Eight are largely happy," I lied. "If children are possible, they will come." I handed the strawberry tart to my mother and kept my face placid.

"Well, my match for you was a success; if nothing else, their attentions have evened your temper." She watched my face; I lowered my eyes so they would not show my true thoughts.

"Are the men safe, mother?" I asked, turning from her and school my features to blandness before facing her again.

"There have been reports of Clans of Trolls that have been killing travelers along the border. They seem to be working together. Some women have been taken, and men found dead. There was a melee of Goblins causing trouble as well, and there is some talk that they are working for some end we do not know."

"That is unheard of," I said, my eyes snapping to hers.

"Yes, it is. There has been a lot of unrest among the lesser Fae, and even the wild creatures are acting out of character. The men are fine, but the borders must be safe, and the lesser Fae brought to heel." She took a bite of my tart and closed her eyes in pleasure. "Your tarts have gotten even better," she said, smiling at me.

"There's tea if you would like some."

"Thank you, no, I must go. I need to speak with Laith about an order for the front lines. I will send him to you when we are done."

"Very well." I bowed my head slightly, watching her as she left.

"It doesn't make sense," Ravena said as soon as we were alone.

"No, it doesn't, Ravena." Lesser Fae do not work together, and Trolls and Goblins would not associate regardless of a common goal.

"Agreed."

Lochlann came to fetch Ravena, and I sent them on their way with a basket of bread and cookies. I had kept her all day, and she looked tired as they walked across the yard to their home, Lochlann's hand resting lightly on her back. She smiled up at him and laughed at some comment he made, and I was happy to see her in a better place than she was.

I cleaned up the bakery, banking fires and bringing in wood for tomorrow. Laith came just after dark, walking through the doors and calling frantically for me.

"Ari?"

"I'm here, Laith." I came from the back with a bag of flour and from my storeroom. I was tired, and my back hurt from the long day, but I felt lighter just seeing him.

His eyes were wild, and his hair a mess. His smell was wrong, somehow. I couldn't put my finger on it, but something wasn't right with him. I watched him carefully, looking for a clue as to what was off.

"I'm sorry for being late; your mother stopped by," he said, calming down and taking the bag of flour from me. He placed it under the counter and went to the storeroom for sugar, and I followed for eggs.

"She said as much when she stopped by."

"She came here?"

"Yes, she came for bread and tarts. She mentioned needing to talk to you about an order."

"Ari," he said, pausing. His brow furrowed, and his breath caught. "She came looking to bed me." It came out as a growl and was barely recognizable as speech.

"She what?" I asked, slowly turning to face him, my eyes on fire.

He took a deep breath in and let it out slowly. "she asked me to take her to bed; she said her consort was on the front line."

"Oh," I said, seething on the inside. That bitch came into my store, ate my tarts, then planned on taking my mate to her bed. I was incensed. I could feel my hair rise on the breeze of my power, and I planned her death for the thousandth time. She knew no boundaries and had no care for me at all, despite what her brilliant acting skills pretended.

"I would not, Ari. I don't think anything…I told her no," Laith said, coming to me to take my hand but pulling back as the feel of my power coursed through him.

I met his eyes and saw the truth in them. There was nothing to keep him from taking any woman that was willing, only I had to stay faithful so that lineage of any child born to me would be known; the men were free to do as they pleased. It was all spelled out clearly in the contract.

"Ari," he said again, his tone forceful. He did not sound at all like himself. "I did not…I'm confused." He stopped, unable to continue and unable to lie.

"It's fine, Laith. It shouldn't surprise me. It just took me off guard. You are free to do as you wish. You know this."

"Please. I told her no." He choked on the word.

"I believe you," I said, turning to him and letting my power go.

I didn't know what she had done to him, but she had done something. Maybe even something he didn't completely understand. His scent was so corrupted, and that could only mean that she had magicked him. The air around us stilled, and I took his hand. "Let's go home," I whispered, turning from him so he couldn't see the tears I tried to keep from falling.

We called for the horses and rode through town and out into the wild at a good clip, both of us wanting to be home as soon as possible.

Once there, we went about starting hearth fires; it didn't take long as there were only two to light. Laith filled the wood stove that kept the water hot, and I went to draw a quick bath. I didn't soak or rest, just rinsed off the day's sweat and washed my hair.

When I came out of my room, I found Laith in the kitchen, frozen and unsure; he stared at his shaking hands with frightening intensity.

"Are you hungry?" he asked, not meeting my eyes.

"No, thank you," I said. "The girls and I ate all day."

"I smell your lie," he growled, causing the hairs on my arm to stand.

I cautiously moved behind him and poured myself a cup of water. I felt him tense, and I could hear his teeth grind. Saige had said he used to shift into the form of a Dire wolf and that sometimes, when his behavior was wild, his animal was right below the surface, unable to break free.

As our power faded, Laith had lost the ability to change forms, and it caused him to fight internal battles with his other self. I was tired anyway and not interested in any more conversation or personal battles. Laith struggled with something I didn't understand, and I just wanted to be alone in my bed. My mother's worst betrayal yet stung. I didn't blame Laith. How could I? But I missed the others. The house wasn't the same with all of us not in it.

I felt him move to stand behind me, a growl so deep in his throat that it vibrated through my chest, striking a chord of ancient fear I didn't know was there.

One minute I was standing with my back to him, and the next, I was scooped up in his arms. I struggled against him in vain, my strength no match for his. I could fight him with magic, but that's not what he needed and could possibly make him worse.

He walked to my room, stopping to scent the air there, tipping his nose up, likely catching the scent of the others. He growled again, crashing the door closed and breaking it, before taking me to his rooms. He lay me on the bed and ripped my shift in half cleanly, crushing me to the mattress with one hand.

"Laith, please," I said, trying to move away from him. His eyes were feral and not completely his.

"You are mine," he said, growling low.

"Yes. I am. I swear it. Calm down, Laith, everything is fine," I whispered to him, trying to stay calm. His beast was fighting him, and I would not trigger it to fight harder.

Something had upset him. Maybe whatever happened with the Queen caused him to react this way. He would not lie about sleeping with her, but that doesn't mean he realized what happened. Her magic is that strong.

Laith may not know that he was raped, but his wolf does. Saige said Dire wolves mate for life and do not share. For some reason, Laith's animal felt the need to reassert his dominance over me. I swallowed hard, trembling beneath him as he growled at my throat; I bared my neck to him, turning my face to the side, letting him know he was alpha.

He leaned off me and ripped his shirt off, throwing it. He ran his hands up my chest twisting my nipples and clutching at my breasts before burying his fingers in my hair.

Green eyes had yellowed in the light of the hearth fire, and if he could still shift forms, I knew he would have done so. He didn't even look like himself. His features had thinned, and his muscular body gotten sharper. Never taking his eyes off me or his hand out of my hair, he pulled the string on his pants and pulled them off.

I watched as his cock sprang free and twitched against his abdomen, a drop of wetness already waiting. He pushed my knees further apart. Laith, normally patient and slow, sheathed himself inside me in one hard push. He was too large to push into me like that when I wasn't ready, and I couldn't help but cry out, despite knowing better.

He crushed my lips, covering me with his body. He took my mouth hard before nipping my bottom lip and down the line of my neck, making soft whines as he went. I wrapped my arms around him and kissed him back when his mouth met mine again, trying to slow my pounding heart, trying to tell him with my body that he was okay. He needed something, and I would try to give it.

He moved inside me, bending to take first one nipple and then the other in his mouth, licking and rolling each one over and over, biting them gently. His pace was not slow and very much unLaithlike. He pounded into me hard and fast, hurting me a little with his size. He pinned my hips with his so I could not evade his thrusts, one hand wrapped around my back, pulled me tight to him, and the other bracing us off the bed.

Despite my initial discomfort, I felt my body give to his, and I arched my back as the pain turned to something sweeter. I stopped trying to move away and sank into the sensation of his body possessing mine. That's what he was after, and I wouldn't fight him. If he needed submission, I would give it.

He moaned into my mouth; his head bent to mine as he continued his punishing pace. He twisted his hips to hit my core, and I came hard, my body clenching around his and holding it tight. He cried out, pushing deep into me one more time and emptying himself. He held me, breathing hard, as the last spasms faded.

He dropped on top of me, positioning himself so that I could breathe but would still be pinned by him. His leg came possessively over my hip and his arm across my chest. He planted his nose in my hair, scenting me, and when his breathing calmed, he slept peacefully.

I lay for a long time, thinking. I was not angry. I wasn't. Not at him, anyway. I loved him. If anything, I was angry at my mother. She had done something to trigger his animal. I wasn't sure I wanted to know what that was, though. I had a sinking feeling that she had taken what was not hers to take. That she had raped him with magic. It broke my heart for the gentle man covering me now.

I hate that bitch. She will die for this alone.

My word on that; in this, I do not lie.

Everything she did was premeditated. She might have even known that he would lose control and that there would be no buffer between us. Talamh na Sithe is a small place; there is no way she did not know what powers he had.

I found it odd that she would wait until we were alone to pull his string and release this particular arrow, but I would not blame him. Never.

Regardless of what her plan was, I would not allow her to win. I curled into him finally and slept.

I felt him awaken and sit up, startled. I heard him scent the air and his sharp intake of breath. His eyes took in our ripped clothing and disheveled appearance.

"Ari, I hurt you," he said, his hands roaming my body for injuries.

"I'm fine, Laith, lay down." I pulled him to me and hugged him tightly, not ready to get up yet.

"I made you bleed; what did I do?" He rolled from me, scrubbing his face with his hand.

"Nothing I didn't enjoy, love. I like the rougher side of you," I said, pulling him back down and rubbing my cheek against his chest.

"You lie," he said.

"No, I would not lie about this. Now hush, and let's lay a bit." My body hurt all over, and as much as I had enjoyed him last night, I was hurting today. He pulled me to him, and I felt his chest heave as he sank his face into my hair.

"Ari, I am so sorry."

"There is nothing to apologize for, Laith." I could feel his tears and worried for him, he had almost feared me when I first came, and I had to go to him. His reluctance was so obvious.

Whatever my mother had done, she would pay for in spades, I promised myself. With a deep sigh, I settled against him, and we slept again until dawn.

Chapter Thirty-Eight

Laith

I think I raped Ari.

I laid with her, pretending to be asleep as her chest rose and fell softly against mine. The Queen had come. I don't want to think about that, but she had come and set the part of me that spent too many years in the form of a wolf off. I don't remember what happened. None of it, my memory is gone, but Ari's lips were bruised, and her neck had bite marks all the way down. I smelled her blood on my sheets, and I know.

She lay in my arms, peaceful, and I didn't smell fear or revulsion in the air. Maybe I was just rough, I can't say because I don't remember, and I hate myself for that. I stirred, and it woke her. She assured me that nothing was wrong and smiled calmly into my eyes, but I smell the pain on her and know I caused it.

She pulled me to her and fell back to sleep. I had wanted nothing more than to have her all to myself, and then I hurt her on our first night alone together. Had the others been here, it never would have happened. I laid there and listened to the soft sound of her breathing before slipping out of bed and into my bathroom. I picked up the remnants of Ari's torn shift and my shirt, tossing them into the low fire.

In my bathroom, I bathed the small smears of blood off of my abdomen and parts lower. The wolf would not hurt Ari intentionally. She is his mate, but he does not understand there is more than one way to hurt a female, and wolves are much rougher than even the Fae can be during mating. He would not understand the word no and take it as a challenge to his dominance. I laid my head in my hands and sobbed into them. Goddess, what had I done?

I went back into the bedroom and dressed, wishing I could run off to my forge and think about this, but I couldn't leave her alone. Instead, I went into the kitchen and put on eggs and tea for her. There were no dirty dishes in the sink, just a cup of water spilled across the counter. Judging by the sounds my stomach was making, we did not eat last night.

She slipped out of my room, wearing one of my clean shirts not long after breakfast was ready. She would not meet my eyes. She walked to me gingerly, but there was no healer to help with her pain this time. Seal had hidden her potions in his room. I would get her one so that her pain would be eased.

"Did I rape you, Ari?" I asked, choking on the words.

"Laith," she started.

"Did. I. Rape. You?" I asked again, enunciating each word.

"No," she whispered, meeting my eyes finally. "You did not rape me." I sagged in relief at her words, closing my eyes tight.

She patted my arm and took a plate off the counter, sliding it to her instead of sitting down at the table. We ate side by side in silence, but it was not strained. Thoughtful perhaps, but not strained.

After breakfast, I took her into Seal's room and showed her where he kept her medicines; he had meant to anyway but had probably forgotten in his haste to leave. She drank two, a small green one and a large green one, then she pulled seven other large green ones out, tucking them in the hem of her skirt before going to get dressed for the day. I was glad to see that she left the black ones alone.

At least I had not angered her enough to poison me to death. I listened, unable to miss her groan as she sank into her tub. Whether she lied or not, whether I raped her or not, I had hurt her. I banked the hearth fires as the day would be warm, cleaned up our mess, and waited for her to be ready to go.

We rode into town at a brisk pace as we were both late. I was glad to see her sit her horse comfortably. She kept up friendly chatter during the ride, talking about the other girls and how they had spent the day in the bakery together. She shared their worry over the other men being gone and generally avoided any serious topic.

She acted as if nothing had happened last night, and maybe she did not view it that way it seemed to me. Her lips and neck were almost healed. She always said her potions were for healing, and maybe they were. There was no denying the pace at which the bruises marring her perfect neck disappeared.

When we got to the bakery, I was shocked to see the rest of The Eight already seated inside, laughing, talking, and drinking tea. Ari side passed Solas to me, pulled me into a quick embrace, then kissed me gently before jumping off the mare and running inside. I sat and stared after her as she hugged each girl in turn, wondering if it was wise or foolish to have the girls together in one place. Heart heavy, I went to my forge.

I was deep in my work and deeper in my thoughts when I heard the first screams. I dropped the piece I was working on and raced into the street, everywhere people were running. A line of Trolls swarmed the market, crushing men and picking up women, some were thrown away, and some were simply whisked away at speeds so fast no Faeman could follow.

My heart stilled.

My sword was inside, and I wasted precious seconds going after it. I cut my way through the Troll nearest me and raced to the bakery and towards the densest area of screaming.

My hands shook as I ran, dodging Trolls and bodies. The scene was horrific. It had happened so quickly. They were not a creature known for their speed, yet they had destroyed this section of town in minutes.

Ari's bakery was a five-minute sprint from the forge, but I made it in three. The destruction was worse the closer I got. Fae can't die, not easily, but many here were dead, ripped into pieces, and left to die slowly. If we had a healer and a place to treat them, they might live, but those services no longer existed here.

I slid to a stop outside Ari's bakery and saw the place smashed apart. There were no walls left, not a door, and not a window. It was gutted. I eased my way through the destruction with my sword raised and nearly tripped over the body of a gray-haired girl, only she moaned when touched her. I bent to turn her over.

"Laith?" she whispered, her voice barely audible.

"What happened, Keena?" I asked, pushing the girl's hair out of her eyes; her face was bloody and her arms at awkward angles, but she would live.

"Trolls. They took some of the other girls." Her eyes slowly opened and fixed me with a stare.

"Ari?" I whispered.

"She fought them. She fought them with her short sword and magic; she held them off while the other girls ran. One grabbed me and tossed me aside. I don't know why. I saw Ari run, and they chased her. They took Teagan and Arlie with them." She started sobbing. I picked her up, placing her in the storeroom on

Ari's resting pallet. She would be safe until someone came for her. I ran back into the street, my eyes racing to find some sign.

The Trolls were gone. I whistled for my horse, only to be stopped by Ravena's hand on my arm. "Laith, they went towards to crossroads, please find them." Her face was battered, and blood ran down her arms.

"Keena is in the storeroom. She is injured," I said, jumping on my stallion, unable to promise her anything. I raced towards the crossroads, pushing the stallion as fast as he would go, and he answered, giving me every bit of speed he had.

I pulled him to a stop, jumping off to check the tracks. I am no tracker, but it was obvious that several large creatures tore through here and headed towards the northern border. My heart sank. It was a ruse. It was all a ruse; the warriors at the Southern borders could not help us, not in time.

I heard screams and the sounds of swords clashing and sprinted forward. In a clearing off the path, Ari stood, short sword in hand and one dead troll at her feet; her arms trembled from exhaustion, but the look on her face was fierce. Her sword glowed bright chartreuse, and her chest heaved as she waited.

Three more trolls ringed her, pushing her back to the edge of a high cliff. Solas screamed at her side, rearing and striking. A long line of blood ran down her side, her mouth flecked with bloody foam. A troll struck the horse aside, and she flew lifeless through the air, landing in a heap, a huff of breath escaping her lungs.

Ari screamed again, not a scream of fear or pain, but of rage, and charged the troll who had taken down her mare. She twisted under his arms, slicing through his torso like butter, and his innards slid out. The others advanced on her in tandem, and I knew that she was lost.

I ducked in behind the largest one, raking my sword across his hamstring, felling him. Ari's eyes snapped to me in surprise, and she gathered her strength once more, fighting back the other troll to try to get to me.

I turned away from the felled Troll, but not in time to avoid his blade. He slashed wildly as he fell, catching me across the middle. I dropped my sword, catching my bowels in my hands before they fell to the ground. I dropped to my knees.

Ari froze, a panicked scream dying on her lips. Her eyes pinned to mine.

The last troll standing took advantage of this and swiped at her with his arm. It was the size of a large tree trunk and upset her balance when he connected with her. She peddled backward; her eyes locked onto mine.

Her heel caught the edge of a rock, and she wheeled her arms to catch her balance. The troll reached for her again, but momentum took her over the edge. Her screams echoed off the wall of the cliff as she fell until they stopped and were no more. I fell forward; my vision narrowed and went dark.

Chapter Thirty-Nine

Saige

Something was wrong. The quiet of the Southernmost border belied the unease of the troops waiting there. The Huntsmen had tracked since we got here and found nothing. Not Goblins, not Trolls, only old trails, and dried bones. Nothing was current.

We had been here for almost two days and found nothing, no signs of unrest, and no aggressive Troll activity. Seal had already decided to slip home tonight and was itching to leave once the sun set.

He and the others had tracked for a solid day without rest and found no threat. A few passersby had been questioned, and they said that there had been activity but that it was months ago. Nothing recent and no new threats.

The Queen's intelligence was either grievously unreliable or a complete lie. The men were all restless to leave and continue our search elsewhere. Worry lined many of their faces, and I knew there was trouble ahead. I could not fight an enemy I could not see, but I could feel it trying to take me into its grip.

I heard the shrill sound of a horse screaming and the pounding of hooves before I saw her.

Solas ran through the center of our lines, her eyes wild, lips flecked in white foam and blood. Her sides were blood soaked, and she searched wildly until she found my stallion among the many others and ran straight to him.

I was off the horse in a second to still the wild mare in front of me. Bloody handprints, the size of a larger child, marred her sides, and flesh hung off of her in pieces where she had been cut with a blade. My heart stopped, and my breath caught in my chest.

Seeing the mare from where he was, Seal raced to my side with Lann hot on his heels, their stallions wild to get to her. The mare stood shaking, trying to catch her breath, and we knew. We all knew. Something terrible had happened. Solas never left Ari's side and stayed so close when not needed to be a ghost in our lives.

"Lann, what does she say? Can you try?" I asked, turning to him. He stared at the horse, taking in her injuries and the total sum of blood on her white hair. I had already done the math; if the horse had lost all the blood that covered her sides, she would be dead.

"I can try." He placed his hands on the mare's nose, and she stilled, her eyes showing less white and more of their usual black. His face twisted and contorted as he talked to her in the way he can. His breath came quick as her tale unfolded, and he sagged against her as tears fell down his face. The horse looked at us expectantly and pawed the ground.

"Ari is gone. Trolls came and sacked the town. In Solas's mind, Laith is dead and Ari over a cliff. Her pictures are frantic and fractured; that is the best I can make of it," he said, his voice cracking as he spoke. I mounted my horse.

"Cory, tell the Hornsmen to sound the alert; we ride now," I ordered. "Lann, ask Solas to follow if she can, but not to hurt herself in doing so; we may need her memories." I didn't wait for an answer; I just kicked my stallion into a gallop and raced back to the capital.

I heard the horns sound and the sound of hoofbeats behind me, but I did not slow. Solas settled into a gallop beside me, and although she was no longer wild, she had run many hours to find us, and the trip home might kill her. I wished I could tell her to leave and rest, but I couldn't, and I wouldn't stop long enough to ask Lann to do it.

Side by side, we raced through the darkening night. It had taken us a quarter day to reach our destination, but we made it back to town in half that time, never stopping to rest our mounts. We crashed through streams and rivers, never slowing.

As we neared the capital, we saw fires burning. We were far enough away to know that they were not a good sign. For us to see them from this distance meant the town was either on fire or funeral pyres burned. We kicked our horses faster, flattening on their necks to speed their travel.

I pulled to the side at the crossroads so the rest of the men could pass. The only cliff I could think of in this area was north of here. Lann and Seal stopped with me, but Solas kept going straight, never stopping. We followed her.

A few hundred paces from the crossroads, Laith lay nearly pinned to the ground with a troll's sword that was the size of a man. His skin was a waxy gray, and his green eyes closed. Bowels looped around the sword, and blood congealed around him in thick puddles.

We had no light, no way to search the area with our eyes, but our noses had no trouble smelling.

Lann took a torch from his saddlebags and lit it against the dark. We made out the shape of three dead Trolls. One sliced across the middle almost cleanly in half, one with the large artery in the thigh severed on both sides and another hamstrung and run through the heart with Laith's sword. The cuts on the others were too delicate to be made with his blade.

Ari had killed two Trolls. Two. The smell of her blood was thick in the air. I went to Laith, pulled the sword from his gut, and then laid my hands on him.

"Laith, we are here, wake up and tell us what happened," I pleaded. He was not dead, his life was ebbing, but with healing, he would survive.

"Ari," he croaked.

I pushed more healing power into him. I could not fix an injury of this magnitude completely, but I could work on the smaller areas of it and give his body time to heal itself. I placed his innards back in his abdomen and willed the wound closed. I stopped what bleeding I could but could do no more. We needed to get him home. Maybe Ari's healing potion would help, but time would help more than anything.

"Ari," he said again, his voice barely above a whisper.

"We'll find her, brother," I said, watching as tears ran down his face. I left him there to go to Lann as Seal was tracking Ari in the way only he can.

"What happened, Saige? By whose design did our town get razed and our mate taken while we sat on the border picking our noses?"

"I don't know, Lann, but we are going to find out." I watched as Solas went to the edge of the cliff and peered over, whinnying, looking for Ari. She paced back and forth, her legs barely holding her up.

Lann went to her, placing his hands on her nose once more, and begged the mare to still. Ari will kill us all if she comes back and finds her horse dead. The mare settled, lying on her side at the edge of the cliff. She placed her head on her front legs, occasionally raising it to scream into the night, but at least she was off her feet.

Seal returned from his tracking, holding three bright red feathers. They were as long as Lann's arm and from some type of creature that I had never seen.

"She did not land at the bottom of the cliff. She went over the cliff here." He went to the spot where the rock was overturned and dirt scuffed, "but she did not land down there," he said. "The fall is not survivable. Her body is not there, her scent is not there, no impression of her is there, she did not land there. I do not feel her. I cannot track her." His eyes were feral in the light of Lann's torch, and I knew what he was thinking.

Where was Ari?

"Something snatched her from the air?" Lann asked.

"There is no creature in Talamh na Sithe with the strength to fly a small woman. There is no bird large enough," Seal growled, moving to Laith.

"Not a bird then. Did the Trolls catch her?" I asked.

"Maybe, but I tracked the only living Troll from this clearing to the north, and her scent was not with him. I will track him tomorrow and take his head, let's get Laith home and do what we can for him," he said, moving to Laith's side and pulling the larger man over his shoulder. Laith groaned in pain.

"Can you sit a horse, Laith?" he asked.

"I will try."

Together we situated him on the back of Seal's stallion, not taking time to call Laith's own. He slumped over the animal's back and lay across his neck. The rest of us walked, leading the animal slowly. Solas stayed at the cliff, whinnying into the darkness.

It was slow going, but we made it home with Laith still living. Carrying him inside, we deposited him on the chaise.

"Lann, go to my room and get one of Ari's little green bottles, actually, get two," Seal said, inhaling the scents of the house deeply and pausing by Ari's broken door jam. He said nothing.

The house was spotless, dishes in the sink, no messes left behind, but there was a feeling of unease in the air. We could all feel it. Seal opened the door to Laith's room and took one step in before backing out and slamming the door hard.

"Not the tall green ones?" Lann asked from Seal's room.

"No. Those are to keep The Eight from conceiving children, the small green bottles, Lann," Seal said, pacing the room and ignoring our collective sharp intakes of breath.

"What? Why?" I asked.

"You have to ask that question, Saige? Now?" he answered, never slowing his steps. He prowled like a caged animal.

I guess I didn't. Why would Ari want to have a baby? She even told us that she did not. She didn't want to see her sons killed and her daughters taken. She had not lied about that. We had made love with her, never dreaming a child could not come from it, and even though my heart sank, I understood. This place was not safe.

"How did you know?" Lann asked, bringing two of the smaller bottles.

"How did you not?" he growled back. "Thistle, ginger root, and stoneseed. How can you not know? You asked for an herbalist to be your mate; perhaps you should have investigated herbs a bit more."

"Gentlemen," I said, reaching for the bottles in Lann's hands, shutting them up. Now was not the time to argue. I placed the bottle to Laith's lips and poured the first one down. He took in choking gulps. I waited a short time and gave him the second; he took that one much more cleanly.

I put my hands on his again and pushed as much healing power as I had into him. It wasn't much, but it would do. Ari was a skilled herbalist, regardless of her goals, and between the two of us, Laith would live. We watched as his color improved and his breathing became easier. I rose to make tea.

The house felt empty without Ari in it. I worried for my brother, but I worried more for her. I would not accept that she was gone.

Laith stirred on the couch and pulled himself into a more comfortable position.

"What happened, Laith," Seal asked, his voice low and carrying the edge of danger.

"Trolls..." Laith started only to be stopped.

"Not with the Trolls. Not yet. What happened here?" Seal asked, stilling his endless pacing.

"What do you mean, Seal?" I asked.

"I'm asking Laith."

Laith laid his head back, and tears fell from his eyes.

"I raped Ari," he said.

"No," I said, taking a step to him. Lann's blade was in his hand, glowing bright orange and at Laith's throat before any could stop him.

"Take my head, Lann, please. I can't stand another minute of this," Laith begged, staring Lann in the eyes.

"Tell us," Seal hissed, taking a deep breath and letting it out slowly.

"I don't know, honestly, but I am remembering," he said, and I saw the grip on Lann's sword twitch toward Laith's neck. "The Queen came to me in the forge yesterday. She." He stopped, swallowing and sitting up a little straighter. "She said that she had been taking medicines to make her conceive and that she wanted a weak man to father her child. She said that the mistake she made with Ari was taking a man with strong magic.

"I refused her. I asked her to leave. She came with a basket from the bakery, and I knew she had just left the place where my mate was. I refused her. She used magic. She did something to me. I got hard, and she tried to make me take her. I don't know what happened. The last thing I remember is her mouth on me and me trying to get away. The animal. The wolf took my mind. I don't remember if the Queen took my body or not.

"I don't remember going to get Ari from the bakery, but I know that I did. I don't remember coming home. I don't remember breaking her door down or tearing up the house to get to her. I don't remember ripping the clothes from her or making her bleed. I don't remember biting her and marking her with my teeth. I don't remember doing any of those things, but that is what I did.

"I awoke with her in my bed battered, bloody, and bruised, and I do not know what I did to her. So, take my head, for this is something I can't live with." His shoulders shook, and the sound of his sobs filled the house. Lann's sword relaxed, and Seal stalked to the couch.

"Laith, did you ask her?" I said, sitting next to him.

"How can I believe a girl who had a class on everything, including torture, and who can lie? She said I did not rape her, yet she walked with such caution this morning that I know she was in pain. She drank one of her potions just to be able to ride her horse and show her face in town. In fact, she drank two. The short green one and the tall."

"Laith, stop," Seal said. "Did she run you through with a sword?"

"Well, no."

"Swords are hanging all over the place, and there are several in your room. Did she fight you with one?" I asked.

"I don't. I don't think so."

"If you raped her, you would be dead," Lann said, sitting on the chair opposite Laith.

"Did she use magic against you?" Seal continued.

"Not that I know of," Laith said, looking around.

"She could hold you off with magic, we know this, she is very strong, and yet the house still stands and remains in one piece," Seal finished. "Whatever you did, you did not rape Ari. She told us from the beginning that if we ever forced her, she would kill us. I doubt that sentiment has changed."

Laith relaxed a little taking a breath. "But the wolf."

"Sometimes we will accept the acts of a man, not because we love the act itself, but because we love the man who does them. Is that good or bad? I can't say, but I know this, Ari loves you. If she sensed some great void in you, she would try to fill it. If she knew of your wolf's need, she would handle it and try to help. She is not fragile. We know this. She has not been broken. Ever. The wolf would never hurt his mate. Never. Whatever happened to trigger him must have been bad enough, but he would not hurt Ari. You would not hurt Ari. And Ari would not hurt Ari; she would not allow it. You must trust her on this. If she said she was willing, then take her at her word. You are not the first to shed her blood, and she does not hold it against us."

"I can't stop seeing her eyes when she went over the cliff," he sobbed into his hands again. "I had her to myself for two fucking days. Two. And that is how I treated her, and now she's gone. I will never forgive myself. Gods, I am a fool. I thought I would be enough. I doubted that all four of us were needed to keep her safe. I thought…I don't know what I thought, but I have never been more wrong. It was my job to protect her, and I hurt her before the Trolls ever had the chance to."

"Laith, did she feed you a black bottle this morning, or did she kiss you and send you on your way?" Seal said, one final time, his voice gentler than I have ever heard.

"She kissed me."

"Then, there is nothing to forgive. Now tell us of the Trolls because I intend to get our mate back with or without your help, but I would appreciate any help you can give." Seal went to the kitchen and poured a cup of tea. Lann put his sword away, and I sat with my head in my hands.

We hadn't slept since before we left, and sleep wasn't coming tonight either. Of that, I was certain.

"The town was overrun," he started, scrubbing his hand down his face and back through his hair. "I could hear the screaming and ran as fast as I could. The girls, all eight of them, had been in the bakery when I dropped Ari there that morning. Not long after, I heard it start, first one, then a few, and then just mass chaos and screams. Keena was hurt. She said that Ari had defended them and done what she could but that Arlie and Teagan were taken. She said that the Trolls ran after Ari, so I followed.

"I found her just north of the crossroads with a dead troll at her feet and three more attacking her. She killed another for striking Solas and was trying to get to me. I killed the third, but not before he cut me. Ari froze when she saw that.

"She was struck and lost her balance, going over the edge. I watched her fall and heard her screams. They just," he paused, drawing in a ragged breath, "Stopped. They just stopped."

"She wasn't at the bottom. I checked. There is no sign she ever landed. The grass there is delicate and unbroken. Her scent is not there, and there is no blood. She did not land there, Laith," Seal said, watching him.

"I saw her fall. I heard her screams."

"What of the red feathers?" I asked.

"I don't know," Seal answered. I have never seen a bird with these feathers.

"I will speak with Solas; maybe she saw something."

"Let her rest," I said. Let's get cleaned up, then we will all go check on the horse, and then we'll go into town to see if there is anything that can be learned there."

Chapter Forty

Lann

Gods, do I want to kill Laith. Why? Why did we trust him with her? One of us should have stayed behind, somehow, regardless of the consequences. The whole deployment felt wrong from the beginning. It's not a coincidence that the capital gets attacked and the girls taken while we are gone. The only question is: who is behind it?

We called our horses and rode into town, even Laith and I want to kill him all over again. Whether or not he raped Ari is beside the point. He hurt her, and there is no doubt she was afraid. I smelled her fear even if the others did not. Our peaceful home was thick with it. We leave for two days, and the girl knows fear again. I. Don't. Like. It.

That Seal is the voice of reason in this situation shocks me. It should be him and not me carrying these murderous intentions. I no longer believe Ari would kill any of us. No matter what we did. I've seen how she looks at us. Gods, but we are monsters. There is no monster worse than man. The Goddess should strike us all down.

Solas slept at the crossroads, and we did not have the heart to wake her. Maybe after she rested, I could get a better sense of what happened, but waking her now would just make her memory worse, so we passed her by and let her be.

The town was a mess. Magic had blown Ari's bakery apart, but that was not even the worst of it. Crews cleaned up shattered timbers and broken carts while the acrid smell of burning flesh filled the air. Our warriors milled about, helping where they could, but most of it was for nothing. Wails shattered the air, and the smell of death lingered.

Aramea stood to the side, her gown pristine and her face unlined. It set me off.

"Where is our wife?" I asked, bringing my sword to her pale neck.

"My Blade."

"I am not your Blade. Where is she? Why would you send us on a wild goose chase? This has your bloody fingers all over it."

"Careful, Lann. This sudden urge to fight your Queen does not suggest your life will be long. "I do not know where my daughter is, but worry not, I will find her. I will also caution you to Remember. Your. Place." Her sick magic tried to consume me, but I blocked it off.

Either I could fight her magic now, or I was so angry that it rolled off me despite her. She brought her arm to my sword blade, lowering it.

"If I can prove that you caused this, I will take your head," I said, stalking to my brothers and not caring that she could have me killed on a moment's notice or that her punishments themselves are worse than death.

I saw Ravena with her men, helping to clean up, and went to her.

"Any news?" she asked when she saw me. I shook my head. "Arlie was found by one of the Huntsman. He tracked the troll carrying her and caught him before they could reach the border, but Teagan is still missing."

"I don't understand why they would go after women," I said. There isn't much a troll can do with a Fae female.

"I'm sure there is quite a lot a troll can do with a Fae female," Ravena said, a shiver going through her. "I just don't think it is survivable." She met my eyes, her blue ones filled with such sadness that my heart sank.

"We'll do our best to find them," I said before walking to my brothers.

"What do we do? Where is Seal?"

"He's tracking. He can't stop," Saige said, tossing another body onto the pyre.

We did what we could, working into the night. We let Seal work his magic and hoped he would find some lead for us to follow. When the dead were burned, and most of the ruble in piles, we gathered the men and waited.

Not long before dawn, Seal arrived with Quinn.

"We tracked Teagan to the border," Quinn said; we need a team to go after her and the Queen's permission to cross over into the troll's territory.

"We have been attacked. We do not need permission to cross," I said. "Ready the men. Ari?"

"There is no sign of her. I should be able to track her anywhere, and it's like she's gone," Seal answered.

"Dead?" Laith whispered.

"I. No. I don't believe so. I think even if she were dead, I could track her, but I can't be sure."

"Then, where?" I asked.

"Maybe she went through the planes?" Quinn whispered, not meeting our eyes.

"Another realm?" Seal asked, his eyes snapping to those of his fellow Huntsman.

"If you don't believe she's dead, then that is the only other possibility. She is simply gone. Not here. Neither one of us could get a sense of her, and our magic would not fail, you know this, Seal." The other Huntsman lowered his eyes at the look on Seal's face.

He let out a roar so loud that everything around us stopped. He stalked off again, not saying a word.

"Thanks, Quinn, thanks for trying. Is Keena going to be okay?" Saige asked, watching as Seal evaporated into the crowd.

"Yes, thank you, Ari saved her life. If there is anything I can do, know that I will do it." He clasped our wrists and left us.

"What do we do now?" I asked.

"The feathers?"

"Some odd coincidence. Perhaps there's a nest nearby, or the Dire wolves dragged something through there," said Laith.

With nothing more to do, we mounted our horses and headed home. I had never been so miserable in my life as when I walked through the door, and she wasn't there. No cookies baked, and no fires burned. It was awful. We bathed and changed, and by some unspoken plan, all slept in Ari's bed. I had never felt so alone in my entire life.

Chapter Forty-One

Ari

I came to on the ground, surprised I survived. I didn't even hurt, not really. I was just stiff from lying. I jumped up and ran, screaming Laith's name. The last memory I had is of him being disemboweled by the troll. As the sun was up now, he was likely dead. My heart stopped at the thought. He would be very hard to kill, but the troll had sliced him through. His pleading eyes were the last thing I remember before that long fall. I turned in a slow circle.

There was no cliff. I saw my sword to my right and went to get it, placing it in its sheath.

Something was wrong.

The air was warm, bordering on hot. The grass was lush and green, not at all like spring grasses should be. The air smelled alive. I took a few steps; maybe my injuries had been so severe that it took a season to heal from them. No.

Seal would have found me before a season passed. That is his magic. He warned me of that. I slipped through the trees, looking for any clue. Any sign as to where I was. Perhaps the Trolls had taken me, and I was in their lands. My gut twisted with fear.

Unusual birds flitted around me as I stalked, and the plants were somehow wrong. This was not Talamh na Sithe. Talamh na Sithe was mostly gray and dying; only parts remained as untouched and clean as this.

I pulled my sword and crept forward towards the sound of running water, knowing that if you follow it, you will most likely reach a town. At least, that is what my hunting class taught me. Maybe I could catch a clue as to where I was if I found a town.

I paused at the stream, washing Troll blood off of my arms as best I could before moving upstream for a drink. My clothes were soaked with dried blood, and there would be no helping them.

A large deer popped out of the grasses in front of me, his antlers thick and wide as he came forward, his head lowered. He was brown with small white spots, and I had never seen anything quite like him. He had no fear, keeping an eye on me as we shared a drink. When he was done, he bounded off again.

Rising, I started following the stream downhill, always keeping it in my sight. In some areas, the terrain was wild, and in others, it was fairly open. All of it teemed with life and sound, like nothing I had experienced before. I looked for the cliff I had fallen from, hoping I could find a way home.

I had no clue where I was. We had taken history classes, and I knew that we had once lived in another realm, but I was assured that place had been closed to us long ago. Now I wondered if that was simply more lies to keep us compliant with our circumstances. If people didn't know there were options, they would make their only choice work.

I don't know how long I walked or how long before that I had been unconscious, but my stomach began to growl after the sun had changed its position many times. For me to be hungry meant that many hours and possibly entire days had passed. Had Laith survived? I didn't think he could have.

I stopped when the sun sank low, gathering sticks and using magic to start a small fire. When the last of the sun sat on the horizon, I moved deeper into the brush and waited patiently.

I was not a good hunter, but I was not a terrible one either. My classes ensured I would not die of starvation by teaching me to get by on very little and hunting and dressing small game where I could. I mean, what household wouldn't want a female who could put meat on their table while they were out doing more important things for the Queen?

My patience paid off when a fat little rabbit hopped into my hiding spot in the brush, likely heading for his burrow. I took the knife Seal had given me and threw it, pinning the thing and killing it instantly.

Arlie had gotten an A in hunting and would have speared it much better than I. I had seen the Trolls carry her away. I prayed to the Goddess for her safety or a quick death.

I dressed the rabbit and roasted it over my small fire, picking the meat off until I was full. I would eat when I could since I knew not when my next meal might come.

I cleaned my mess, washed in the little stream, and made myself as comfortable as possible. Only then, by the warmth of the fire and surrounded by darkness, did I let myself cry. I cried for Teagan and Arlie. I cried for Laith and the many others who died during the attack. I didn't know where I was, but I would do my damnedest to get back to them.

I awoke when the warmth of the sun touched my cheek in a gentle hello. In the distance, I heard the barking of some type of animal. It was not the yipping of a Dire wolf as they do not roam when the sun is up, nor was it the barking of a fox or other small furred animal I had heard before. Rising as quietly as I could, I pulled my sword from its sheath and crept through the brush to the edge of the stream.

A large furry creature, the color of wheat, stared me down. Its head would come to my hip or higher, were it close enough. Its muzzle dripped with shaggy fur, and its ears flopped over. It barked again, looking over its shoulder, and I eased away from it. I had never seen anything like it before, and it had to be some strange cousin of a fox or wolf. Talamh na Sithe has many magical creatures; perhaps this strange place did too.

I kept my sword aimed at the beast and readied my magic, but it did not charge. It just stood wagging its tail and yipping its head off. Just then, three people came into sight around the bend in the river, and I crouched low, keeping my sword between them and me.

They called the creature using words I did not understand, and it came to them. They startled when they saw me. There were two males and one female, all three larger than myself by a half a rod or more. The female had red hair like mine, which is a rare thing in Talamh na Sithe. One male had pitch-black hair, and the other had blonde hair like Seal's.

I could not see their eyes from this distance, but I could see the startled looks on their faces. I leveled my sword at them, knowing it was too late to flee.

The female walked to me, holding her hands out and up in front of her, thinking she would use magic against me. I made a quick protective shield, and it appeared with almost no thought at all.

This place must be filled with magic to allow mine to flow so freely. I readied a ball of flame to shoot at her and held it aloft in my hand. She stopped, staring.

My hair lifted and swirled unbidden as power rushed through my feet, taking my breath. She spoke to me in a language I did not understand. Her voice sounded like those from home, but the words were not the same. I backed up slowly, looking for a way to escape, but she held her hands higher in the manner of surrender, and the others did too.

I stood, watching them for a long moment. The woods were quiet now; nothing moved or made a sound. It was like the place waited to see the outcome of the encounter.

The female backed away from me and came even with the males. They turned from me, waving their arms like I should follow. Then I thought about what I looked like to them, a short woman with crazy fire red hair covered in blood and holding a sword and a very large fireball.

I had wanted to find a town and get some answers; well, this was my chance. I dropped the magic and followed them like a wraith, slipping from shadow to shadow as they walked slowly from the woods. I sheathed my sword but kept my little knife handy.

At the edge of the woods, they stopped, glancing back. They spoke again in their language. I asked them if they understood mine, and they just looked at me and then one another before shaking their heads. They bid me to wait at the edge of the woods, using their hands and pantomiming sitting.

I took a step back, and they shook their heads. I shrugged my shoulders and rested on one knee, palming my knife. They bounded away from me, looking back as they ran. If they brought soldiers back with them, that would be trouble.

I took a moment and glanced around. The woods had thinned to almost nothing, and I could hear the water to my left and the soft sounds of civilization up ahead. Dropping to my belly, I crawled forward. The hill crested and dropped down to reveal many houses crowded together. Children ran by the dozens, chasing and playing. Their laughter reached me, sending shivers down my spine. I had never seen so many children in one place. Never had this many children been born in our history at one time.

I stood transfixed. Metal carts moved across smooth dark roads without the benefit of horses, their wheels gleaming in the sun and their bodies painted brightly. It was a place of great magic for certain. I stood in awe of the place, and if there had been any doubt that I was no longer in Talamh na Sithe, it was gone now.

I watched as a withered old woman, led by the red-haired girl, walked slowly up the hill to where I stood. The woman had hair so gray it was white, and her skin lay in wrinkles upon her face. Her back was rounded, and she used a wooden staff to assist her steps, the girl on one arm and the staff in the other. She must be ancient. As old as the world.

My mother was two millennia old and did not look like this female. Perhaps she was a Goddess. I dropped to my knee and sheathed my knife. It would not save me against a Goddess this ancient.

I kept my eyes down even once they were even with me. The two spoke feverishly back and forth in the language I did not understand but still sounded so much like the voices from home before the ancient creature turned to me.

"We mean you no harm," she said to me in my language, though the cadence was different, the words were clear.

"And I mean you no harm. May I ask, which Goddess are you?" I asked, not raising my eyes.

She laughed then, throwing her head back and causing me to look up at her. Green eyes met mine, and she gave me the kindest smile I have ever seen.

"Lass, You have our roles reversed; I am just an old woman. Come, and let's talk about how a High Blood Daoine Sidhe came to be in Clifden. I promise you are safe." She turned from me and headed back down the hill with the help of her staff. I waited for a bit, but seeing no other choice, I followed.

At the edge of town, I paused, staring after several small girls as they ran by us, freezing at the sight of me. Goddess, but they were beautiful. All different colors and complexions. I had not seen a child since I was one myself. I couldn't help but stare. Their rounded eyes and soft faces were the most glorious things I have ever seen. I saw them notice my clothes and run away, keeping a wary eye on me as they left.

The old woman waited patiently until I decided to move on. She moved through the town with deft agility while I tripped on rocks, toys, and oddities because I couldn't watch where I went as I was too taken with the surroundings.

She led the way up a set of stone steps in front of a brightly colored house; I hesitated, afraid to be in an enclosed space with strangers. She had promised, though, I had felt it settle over us, and I knew she would keep her word.

Inside, the house was cool, despite the heat of the day. I shut the door and put my back against it, just in case I needed to leave in a hurry. Ignoring me, the three young ones spoke for a bit with the ancient Goddess and then left, watching me through wary eyes.

The gray-haired woman moved around the kitchen, pouring two cups of tea before sitting at the large table and waiting.

"Come on in, lass, I won't hurt you," she said in my language. I moved silently through the house, taking in my surroundings as I went.

Lights glowed from lamps but held no fire. Music came from a small black box on a table by a loudly colored couch. Pictures that were not paintings hung on the wall; their details so sharp that the image looked alive. This place was magical. I could feel it thrum through me in hot waves.

Never had I felt the like before. I readied my magic, and it came in a rush, then I went to sit across from the gray-haired woman.

"My name is Paulina," she said, passing me the tray with tea and cream on it.

"I am Airmed," I said, smelling the tea before taking a light sip. It did not taste like poison. "Where am I?" I asked.

"Airmed? The Tuatha de Danann?" she asked, her grin widening. "I am honored, Lady."

"I am no one, great Goddess. Thank you for the tea," I said, sipping it. It was wonderful, strong, and heady. I would've closed my eyes in pleasure but did not want to take that risk.

"You?" she laughed, throwing her head back. "You are definitely not 'no one.' You are a legend. How did you come to be here?" she asked, eyeing me over her cup.

"Where am I?" I asked again, trying not to be impolite, but my eyes narrowed anyway.

"You are in Clifden, Ireland. You are a very long way from home, I imagine."

"Ireland?"

"You would call the place Eire," she said.

I stilled at her words.

I was in the homeland, in the mortal realm. Somehow, I had crossed the planes.

"I need to get home; how can I do that?" I asked, rising to my feet.

"I don't know," she answered, but I have friends who might. Regardless, it will not be a quick thing.

I groaned, rubbing my hands down my face, and sat back down.

"How is it that a High Blood Daoine Sidhe managed to come into this world anyway?" she asked, her face curious. "There are no true Fae here."

"I don't know," I sighed, draining my cup. "There was an attack by Trolls. I fell off a cliff and woke up here. I can't say what happened. We are not taught to travel the planes. My mother doesn't allow it. My mate," I choked on the words. "One of my mates was killed, and I was falling to my death; that is all I know."

"Mmmmm. What year is it there?" she asked, looking at me from the corner of her eyes.

"Year?" What do you mean? How do you measure a year?" I asked, confused.

"Do you know of the Milesians?" she asked, skirting my question.

"Yes, of course," I answered.

"How many winters have passed since they came?" she asked, her smile real.

"I don't know? Many? We don't measure."

"I see. Okay. I was just curious, anyway. I have never had a Goddess in my kitchen."

"I assure you, kind lady, I am no Goddess," I said, chuckling.

"Oh, but you are. Your entire race are Gods."

"My entire race is dying. I am the last to be born, and only a few remain," I whisper. "That is why I need to go home," I said, swiping at tears that hover on the brink of falling.

"We will work on that. Now, my granddaughter is out getting you some clothes that might fit; why don't you clean up, and we'll go visit a friend to see about getting you home."

"My Lady," I started.

"Don't 'my lady' me; you are covered in blood. You can't wander around town like that. Come." She rose from the table and walked down a short hallway.

I had never seen a house like this, it was small and its rooms tiny. She led the way to a room with a tub and a chair, unlike I had ever seen before. She turned the water on, pulling a few levers, and water sprang from the wall in a powerful waterfall. I stepped back, eyeing the wall of water, my hand hovering above my sword.

"Go on. Get in."

"You have waterfalls in your house?"

"It's called a shower. Use the soap and shampoo to clean up. Here is a washcloth," she said before leaving and shutting the door behind her.

I looked silly with my hand hovering above my sword, standing in a small room with water shooting from the wall.

Sighing, I stripped naked and climbed into the water, unable to stop the moan that came from my lips. Hard water pounded against my back, and never had anything felt so glorious. The water was hot, almost too hot, and I wondered what type of fire they must have to keep it so. I looked through the bottles that lined the walls, picking them up and smelling them since I could not read the words.

I found some potion that made bubbles and began to scrub the Troll blood from my arms until the water ran clean. I used the same soap to wash my hair, but it caused my hair to tangle. I went through the bottles again until I found one with a silky liquid in it, and I dumped that on my hair too for good measure.

And then I just stood there.

"Clothes, my Lady," a voice said; I heard fabric drop and the door shut again.

"I am no one's Lady," I grumbled as the door shut.

I stood until I felt the water cool. The knobs on the tub were not dissimilar to the ones on mine, so I played with them until the water stopped flowing.

When I got home, someone was making me a magic waterfall. I didn't know I had to have one until now, but now I had to have one.

I used a towel and dried off, finding soft, thick pants and a black shirt resting on the odd chair in the room. I struggled with the closing mechanism as they did not tie but finally got them to stay on after trial and error. I dressed, amazed that the clothes almost fit. The pants were a bit too long, but then I am short, so there's that. I shoved my feet in my boots and eased out into the hallway.

"In here, Airmed," the old woman chimed.

"You may call me Ari," I answered, following her voice to the kitchen. The three young mortals, for I guess that is what they were, had joined her at the table.

"Ari, it is then. Feel better?" she asked.

"Yes. The magic waterfall is amazing; thank you for your kindness. I am in your debt. Are there any cliffs about so I can try and go home? I cannot repay you and do not wish to intrude longer."

"Ach, it's no intrusion," she said. "You are welcome here."

"My mates will be worried; I must go," I said again, looking towards the door.

"Mates? Plural?" she asked.

"Yes, naturally."

"I'll make you a deal," she said. My eyes narrowed on her, and I put my hand above my sword once again. I did not know these creatures. I did not want to make a deal with them.

"We will take you to try to find your way home, and in exchange, you will answer a few questions about your life," she said.

I saw the younger girl bristle.

"Questions? That is all?"

"Our hospitality and any help you might need to find your way home in exchange for simple conversation." The girl rolled her eyes, and I smiled. Eyerolls are universal. Maybe she understood my language well enough, just could not speak it.

"I will make you a counteroffer," I said. "I will give you information in return for your help and hospitality, but you will ask me to perform no magic that is outside of my abilities, you will ask nothing of me that would cause me harm, and I decide what may cause me harm. You will not impede my departure in any way, and no harm will come to me at your hand or any other hand in this home. In exchange for that, I will protect you with my sword, if needed, as long as I am here. I will answer your questions to the best of my ability, but their asking cannot delay my departure. You will also answer mine in return," I said, leaning against the wall casually, even though my blood was boiling with the need to go home.

"Deal," she said, smiling, and I felt it settle around us.

The three young ones at the table snapped their faces up and looked between us. The old woman just smiled. They spoke back and forth in their language.

"What are you telling them?" I asked.

"They feel your magic. We have mixed Fae heritage from many, many generations ago. It lets them perceive things others cannot. I explained to them that they were feeling the bindings of a deal with a very strong Fae. She smiled at me, and I knew that she set the deal up on purpose so that her young ones could feel it. I was okay with that. The young must learn.

"Let us go find your way home," she said, rising. The three young mortals followed, and I trailed behind them all.

Outside, the heat of the day had grown enough to almost be uncomfortable. Children ran by us again, kicking a black and white ball. I couldn't help but stop and stare. What kind of place was this that so many children ran free? Boys and girls alike.

The boys looked healthy and unworried as if the sword did not hover just above their necks. I could see the beauty of this wild world, if only through the eyes of its children. I must have stared for so long that I caught the attention of one of them, and he walked right up to me, smiling. He was a tiny thing and barely toddled before he fell at my feet. I scooped him up.

He reached for my hair, and I let him. He smelled like dirt, fresh air, and love. He said one word in his language.

"He says you are pretty," the old woman said, suddenly beside us.

"Pretty?" I repeated the word.

"Yes, that's right."

"You are more than pretty, little Faeling," I said, enjoying the squirmy feel of him in my arms. Maybe I was a fool, and maybe I did want one of these squishy things. He felt right in my arms.

And then I remembered my mother.

Slowly, I put the boy down.

I made him a ball of green light and handed it to him to play with. Laughing, he took it and ran. He was right to do so.

"They do not allow our boys to live," I said, watching him leave. I saw her shock and felt her stiffen.

"Only girls. Only the girls can live, and it is no life. We are bartered and contracted for," I said, unsure why I let that secret slip.

"Then why do you want to go back?" she asked.

"Love," I said.

She repeated it in her language, and I repeated it back to her.

"Love makes us do things we otherwise wouldn't," she said. She was right.

"Is there a book I can read that will teach me your tongue?" I asked.

"I will get you one that will work well enough, you speak a much purer version of it than we do, but since you understand my ramblings, it should do the trick."

"Thank you," I said, following her to the road, marveling at the hard surface. Children rode two-wheeled machines back and forth, and there was not a horse to be seen.

"Come," she said, opening the door to a great steel beast. It was colored blue and had no head nor tail. It sat on four wheels. I pulled my sword without thinking.

"It's just a carriage," she said, laughing.

"Where is the horse?" I asked, not sheathing my sword and unwilling to get into a magic carriage.

"It has a motor; it's not magic. I promise it is safe. Well, safe enough with Remi driving." She got into the back of the thing, patting the space beside her. The others had all piled in and waited patiently for me. I sheathed my sword and followed.

"Shut your door, Dear," she said. I pulled the thing to, and we took off smoothly, no lurching. The girl put her hands on a wheel, and we moved silently down the road. Music came from little boxes in the door, and I just couldn't deal with it. I didn't even know what was happening.

"It's called a car."

"Car," I repeated in her language.

"Yes. It runs on gasoline and has a motor."

"Where are your horses?"

"Their spoiled asses lounge around and do not do much of anything," she answered.

"I must see them later. That is the only way to judge a person."

"Well, then you will judge us poorly; we don't even have a horse."

"Oh my." That was all I could say to that.

We rode in the magic carriage to a house, not ten roads over. We could have walked.

I tried to get out of the thing, but the door would not work. The girl named Remi laughed, walking around to release me. I followed them up the steps to a little house that was neat as a pin. Loud yips and barks came through the door, and I whisked the others behind me and drew my sword.

"They're dogs, Ari. Not threats," Paulina said, opening the door. Two large creatures rushed out of the door, wagging their tails and licking my face.

I wasn't much taller than they were, and their heads were larger than mine. I don't know what a dog is, but I don't like it. They are very wet creatures who lick a lot. I sheathed my sword and placed a barrier between them and me. It snapped into place, and the dogs whined on the other side of it. The others just looked at me.

"Why do you have wild animals living in your houses?" I asked.

"Do you not have any pets?" Paulina asked.

"I have a cat named Isa," I answered.

"Ah, you're a cat person then."

"I don't know what you mean; we have no dogs," I answered.

"More's the pity," she chuckled.

I followed them inside as the dogs ran through the house, bumping into furniture as they went. The place was cute, smaller than Paulina's, but just as neat. There was a large box on the ground over which pictures moved. Men dressed in very short pants kicked a black and white ball over a green field of grass.

"What sorcery is that?" I stood transfixed and staring. The men were all very muscular, and their colors varied from light to dark.

"It's a television," Remi answered, saying the words slowly. I understood them and repeated them back. Paulina then explained what a television was, and I was enthralled. They had so many things we did not. How could I step from one world to another in the same time frame and find that nothing was the same?

I sat down on the couch and was immediately beset by dogs. I sank back, letting them maul me. It would be a clean death.

"Egan and Echo, get down." A tall, elegant woman who could have easily been Fae rounded the corner. Her hair was a dark blond, like Seal's but without his white highlights, and her eyes were green, like Laith's. It made me homesick. She did not glow like the Fae, though, despite the resemblance. The dogs moved and sat at her heel.

"You look overwhelmed," she said in my language. "My name is Devin."

"You may call me Ari, and yes, I am a bit overwhelmed," I answered.

"Tell me about Talamh na Sithe, and maybe I can help with some of your questions."

"Have you been there?" I sat up, brightening.

"No, but my grandmother went. It was accidental, much like what happened to you."

"Did she come home?" I asked, sinking back into the couch.

"Eventually. Yes, she did."

"Talamh na Sithe is dying. The reasons are complicated yet very simple. We do not have any of the magic you have here, and my magic there is not half as strong there as it is here, and I have hardly tried to use it."

"We have no magic," she laughed.

"You have cars and televisions. There are boxes that make music and paintings on the walls that are lifelike. Your lights never need lit, and the water is hot without fires. We have none of this," I said.

"That's not magic; it's technology. Those things are advances in science, not magic. We have none of the magic you have. My grandmother said that time passes differently there. She was gone from here for many years, but it was only a few seasons to her in your land. It seems to go more slowly there, but it also goes more quickly. It took her a long while to get acclimated when she came back. She said the place was wild and beautiful.

"But you have children," I whispered. "And they are safe," I said in a half-whisper. "I can't be gone for months; my mother will not be pleased. Her punishments are legendary." I sighed, absently petting the head of one of the large beasts that had come to sit by me. Paulina, Devin, and the others just sat in silence.

"Who is your mother, Ari?" Devin asked.

"Her name is Aramea." I ran my hand over my face, pausing to rest my forehead on my palm. Devin's sharp intake of breath let me know she knew exactly who my mother was.

"You're the Queen's daughter. My grandmother said her cruelty is well known. Your mother is the one who finally sent her home. She pushed her through old ways."

"I am nothing like her, my word to you," I said, meeting her eyes.

"You could stay here and be safe."

"If she can manipulate the old ways, I will not be safe. I have husbands at home; I need to go back." I sat fingering the ring on my finger. I missed them. "Someday, I am going to challenge her for the throne, and then we will have television and magic lights."

That got a chuckle out of them all.

"Your grandmother did not come home alone, did she?" I asked.

"No. She didn't. She was carrying my mother in her womb," she answered. Devin looked more Fae than I. I had known the answer before I asked.

"Perhaps we are cousins then," I said. "Well met, cousin."

"It's doubtful, my Lady, she fell for a humble man, and the Queen pushed her out of Talamh na Sithe because of it," she answered, inclining her head slightly.

"Then it's likely she didn't know your grandmother was bred, and that is a good thing for you all. That is also the reason I need to try and find my way home."

"Yes, of course, but for now, can you tell us about your life?" Paulina asked.

"Do you have eggs and flour? I need to bake for this."

And so I did.

Chapter Forty-Two

Seal

I stalked the woods by the crossroads; I could not rest. I tried. I had laid on Ari's bed, and while the others slept, my magic flowed over me to the point of pain, so I gave in and got up. I could not feel her, and that had fear spiking through me.

I have never tracked someone I did not find. I found Solas where we left her and was glad the mare still lived. I urged her to go, promising I would not stop looking for Ari. She left, limping her way towards our home. She would heal.

Over and over, I followed the line of Ari's descent, and if I could have jumped off the cliff and replicated her fall, I would have. She was nowhere to be found.

I tracked the Troll that left this clearing to the border and found him in his den; Teagan was not with him. I took his head anyway. He bore the wounds of his fight with Ari. No warrior is braver than she.

I tracked Teagan as best I could but lost her trail at yet another border. It was then, I worried in truth. Teagan had been taken into Eregion. The Eruhini were known to work with trolls. The troll carrying Teagan did not stop, not once. He carried her straight through. Crossing the border into the land of the Eruhini would be suicide. I would report my findings and let the Queen decide if one girl was worth the war that would follow.

The Eruhini are a race not unlike ours except their ears curved to a pointed tip, and their complexions are largely the same pale-haired and pale-faced. Even lighter than Saige.

They have the same anatomy as the Fae, and for sure, there are Eruhini and Fae bloodlines across both our borders. They are not known to be cruel, but they are a race of fierce warriors led by the females. If we invaded their borders, the conflict would be long and deadly.

The trolls had been doing their dirty work, and they had likely planned on taking more females than they did but did not plan on being stymied by a magical, red-headed, very angry little pixie.

I did not sense Ari beyond the border, nor anywhere along the route. I turned back and made my way, unseen, back through troll country.

I started thinking about what Quinn said. Maybe Ari had gone through the planes, and by traveling the old ways, was in another realm. I did not know much about the other realms, but I knew they existed. I would ask around discreetly before deciding on my next course of action.

All leads exhausted, I returned home to find Saige up and making breakfast. Never had our house felt so empty. Funny how we had lived together all these years, and all it took was one small woman to make us realize how alone we were.

I sat on the couch without saying a word.

Saige ran his hands over his face, trying to hide his emotions. I felt the lack of her presence, like a piece of myself had been cut away. Had I known I loved her? Maybe not before; it may have just been words tied to a feeling I didn't understand the scope of. Now? Gods. It was a terrible feeling. I wish it on no one.

"What are we going to do?" he asked.

"We're going to find her."

"Seal," he started, stopping himself short. "You need to rest." I know he had planned on saying something else but changed his mind. I didn't want to hear what he had to say anyway. I went to my room and slammed the door.

I bathed and changed clothes, planning on going to talk to the Queen. Only when I came out of my rooms, I found that she was in my home.

"Where is Ari, Huntsman?" she asked, not bothering to sit.

"I do not know. She left no trace, and I cannot track her." I said, bowing my head slightly in her direction. I agreed with Lann; something was off about the entire attack. Why send us so many men away? Why, in that exact moment, did trolls attack the heart of the capital? There are no coincidences, but I kept my thoughts to myself.

"I tracked Teagan to the Eregion border. Ari was not with her."

"The Eruhini have a hand in this?" she asked, not acting as surprised as one would think.

"I think there are many hands in this," I said. "Trolls, Eruhini, and possibly others," I finished, not looking at her.

"That doesn't answer the question of Ari."

"No, It doesn't, your Grace." I walked away from her to the kitchen and grabbed a plate, piling food on it. I didn't feel like eating, but I needed the strength to keep searching. "I will search the lands to the west today; perhaps I will pick up her trace there," I mentioned nothing about my theory, for all I knew, the Queen could travel the planes at will. I did not want her to find Ari before I could. Whatever the Queen was up to, Ari was at the center of it.

"I know you won't believe me, but I love my daughter, and I want her home safe," she said, her eyes following me when I said nothing.

Saige sat at the table and did not even bother to rise in the presence of the Queen. Luckily Lann and Laith still slept. Lann had threatened her yesterday. Now would be a bad time for him to wake up.

"I will let you know my progress, Your Grace," was all I could say. "I cannot sleep until I find her, you know this." I inclined my head to her again and watched as she left our house without another word.

"Do the Elves have Ari?" Saige asked, his voice neutral.

"No. I think she went through the planes to another realm. If I make it through the old ways, I can track her," I answered.

"It was smart not to mention this to the Queen." Laith stood in his doorway, arms crossed and spirit broken.

"Agreed," added Saige. "We need not let her know our thoughts on this."

"I'm packing to leave. I won't be back until I find her." I rose from the table, heading to grab a small pack so I could travel light.

No one said anything. They might doubt my magic, but I never will. I would find Ari. Wherever she was, I would find her and bring her home.

Chapter Forty-Three

Laith

Many days have passed since Ari disappeared. I can't count how many sunrises have come and gone; they've all run together into one endless day. Gods. What a fool I am.

I feel the loss of her acutely. Her bedroom door hangs open, the frame long repaired. Her bed is neat and tidy, and her cat lays on it without interruption. Solas is camped directly outside our garden wall and refuses to leave. Ari haunts us. She left an emptiness far larger than her size. It hangs over the place, threatening to crush us all.

Seal left and has not returned. His magic will kill him. We know this. He will be forced to hunt Ari unless he can let her go, and I doubt he can. None of us can let her go. Not even the cat. Our house is silent. Miserable. Unbearable.

How could I not have seen just how much of my life, and theirs, the diminutive creature had stolen from us? Love her? Absolutely. I didn't understand the word until she was ripped from me.

The relationship I share with Saige, Seal, and Lann is a brotherhood. We care. We would die for one another. But love?

No. That is all Ari's. It belongs only to her. I like it less now than I did before. I'm broken. We are all broken. Saige barely speaks, Lann's eyes have dimmed, and his coltish ways died. We sleep alone.

I stopped going to work until the Queen threatened me to go back. I still don't know what magic she used on me, but I can hardly stand to be in my forge.

I understand what Ari meant when she said she never had a choice in her life. I can't get over the idea that the Queen fucked me against my will. And I think that she did.

I am grateful, at least, that I don't remember it beyond a hazy recollection. I think Ari knew the truth, and it kills me that she will never understand how deeply I need her and that my love is deeper still. I would never disrespect our union willingly.

Her eyes were so sad when she looked at me that night. Like her heart was broken. So, I go to work now, and I rest on the pallet where I took Ari that first day she came to me. I smell her there, although the scent is fading. I am lost.

I repaired her bakery walls and locked the doors so that she will have her space when she comes home. I refuse to imagine a life where she is not in it. I regret so many things. I regret never telling her I loved her. I regret any mistreatment she suffered at my hands. My animal side has been quiet since she left. He is subdued and sad. He has regrets, too, likely.

I blame all this on Aramea. She has made us weak. Her poison has spread so far and so deep into our lands that she has ruined the apex of life and magic. I don't remember Talamh na Sithe being any other way, but others do. There is talk.

I wasn't sure I wanted to be tied to a Queen, and now I am tied to two, but there can be only one. Dissent is spreading, and I will fan the flames from my forge. We will build an Army.

When Ari is ready, we will fight for this place, and we will make it whole again so that no woman must decide whether or not it is worth bearing a child, only to see him die. We will build a place where all are free to choose love over a contract signed by the Queen.

But first, she must come home.

Every day, I try to open the door to some land I have never seen and can't name. A land where, right now, Ari lives. I don't know how to walk the old ways, but I try and fail. Every. Single. Day.

I want Ari home. I will never think twice about sharing her again. I will share her every single time we are together if I can hold her after. I will be like Saige and watch. I don't care. She is all that matters. We are a body without a soul and a house without a hearth. We need her. We will fall apart otherwise. It has already started.

In my forge, the best blades are made, and I am making them at a record pace. I place each finished masterpiece behind a newly built false wall. When the time is right, those swords will be placed into the hands of those that will champion our cause. I have never been a bloodthirsty man, but blood is all I taste now.

I will see this land freed. I will see Aramea's blood cleanse her poison away.

Chapter Forty-Four

Saige

Ari and Seal are gone. He will never come back without her. He will die if he cannot find her; I have accepted that. We have not seen him since he packed a small bag and left the morning after she disappeared over that cliff, and that was many days ago. Many.

Laith spends all his time at the forge, and he will not say what he is doing.

Lann just sits. He hasn't reported to the Queen since he threatened to take her head. When he isn't sitting, he is pacing. I don't know which is worse.

I go to work and keep my ears open. I know that betrayal has brought us five to the lonely place we are. I know this. I can't prove it, though. So, I keep my head down and my ears open.

I have compiled a long list of men that hate the Queen. I will go to them, and we will make a strong enough force to overthrow her, but I need Ari to be home to take her rightful place. It may take eons. I don't know, but it will happen. That bitch has done this, and it will not go unpunished. I simply can't believe she is not complicit. Immortality is a long time, but hers is coming to an end.

The Goddess told Ari that we would make a great sacrifice but that we would all survive and that the world would be better. Maybe this is it. Maybe Ari is someplace honing her power, and our sacrifice is not having her with us. I don't trust it. The Gods are always talking about great sacrifices and rewards, but it means nothing if the price is too high. At least not to me.

There has been no news. Not for days and days. Ari has been gone for twelve now. I know because I mark each sunrise with a stone on our garden wall. We don't keep a calendar, and time doesn't matter here, but I want to know. I need to know.

I miss her so much. I miss the scent of vanilla and sugar on my pillow. I miss the sight of her in my brother's arms. I miss the feel of her under, around, and through me. I can't believe we had her for such a short time, and now she is gone. I refuse to accept that it is forever. I refuse.

I pray to the Goddess daily that she will return. I may not trust her on this, but she is the only Goddess I have, so there's that.

The other girls have settled back into their homes. Teagan has never been found. Keena has healed from her injuries, and Arlie was uninjured during her abduction. Our troops march through the town daily.

Ari is the only one that is unaccounted for. Why her? I can only wonder. She is the strongest of us. She has more power than her mates together. Is this why she is now gone from us? I surmise it is, but if she had the power to leave, she surely has the power to return.

Only what if she doesn't want to? What if she never loved us? What if wherever she is is better than where she came from? Aramea's entire bloodline can lie with ease; the rest of us cannot.

Maybe it was all a lie.

Then I remember her body underneath mine, and how she gives everything of herself, how she never balks. Once she is in, she is in all the way; she does nothing halfheartedly. I remember her hands on mine and the way her green eyes follow us through the room. I remember the predatory glances and the way she loved to bake for us. I remember the soft sounds of her pleasure and how she manages the worst parts of us with ease.

I remember the pride and joy she showed in us at the Consummation Ball. How she reveled in our day at the lake and gave us all exactly what we never knew we needed. Even Laith, how she must have handled him in his darkest moment with her, even though I wasn't there to see it, I can guess. You can't fake that. You cannot lie your way through it. There is no way. That is love. It is real.

I rode home alone from the Capital on the sixteenth day of Ari's disappearance. Even my stallion was dull; Solas was listless and no longer played with him. I suspected she was bred and perhaps lost her foal due to her wild run through the land; time would tell.

I came to the crossroads, and just like every other night, I went to the cliff. I have tried and tried to walk the old ways. I imagine we all have, but I don't know how, and despite wanting to, I can't. Seal's stallion is standing just shy of the stone that tripped our dear Ari.

Seal was standing there, looking over the edge. His clothes were dirty, torn, and they hang off him in tatters. His pack hung empty on his back. His hair was long and tangled. I could smell him from where I stood. I called his name, but he did not answer. I dismounted my horse and started his way. This madness had to end. He needed to come home.

I watched as he raised his arms from his sides and let himself fall over the edge without a backward glance. He did not scream or cry out. I rushed to the edge, but he was gone.

Chapter Forty-Five

Ari

They tell me I have been here for five weeks. The days pass from one to the other. I do not know how to keep time, but they are teaching me. I have a magic band on my arm that they call a watch. It lets me know the hour and the day.

Every morning I get up, and I walk to the place I landed and try to walk the old ways home, but it doesn't work. I go most evenings too and try again.

Paulina and Devin say that our realm and the mortal realm lie hand in hand with only a thin veil between them. They say that I should be able to go home when I want to and that I just have to believe that. Maybe I don't. Maybe I don't want to go home badly enough. I want my mates here and hope they will walk the ways and find me. We could be free here in this beautiful place.

Then I realize how selfish that is. What of the other Eight? What about any children they may have? My potions will have worn off by now. Their children could come in time, and they will suffer because I wasn't brave enough to leave this place. Only I can't seem to make it happen.

I bake for them daily in payment for their kindness. The debt between us stays equal. I tell them everything I know of our history, and they take me to places called restaurants where food is ordered from menus. I am nearly fluent in their language now. I have become friends with Remi. She is just eighteen years old. She is a baby by Fae standards, yet she is old enough to have a child of her own in their realm.

She takes me shopping, and I make her grandmother potions as payment. Paulina doesn't need to use her walking stick anymore, her eyesight has improved, and her back is no longer hunched. I have made them enough potions to last her a lifetime, for their lifetimes are short, they tell me. Usually, less than one hundred years. I would be almost middle-aged, were I mortal. There is nothing I have not tried to learn of this place. I have read their books and watched their television.

Their friends come to talk to me over dinner, and I answer every question I can, even the intimate ones. They are fascinated with my mates, as well they should be. For so am I.

I work my magic, and it comes like breathing. That is the wonder of this land. None of the mortals have magic, not like I do. Even Devin, who is part Fae. Her plants grow well, and she has a way with animals that I do not, but she can do no magic, I have tried to teach her. There is no debt between us. Should I find a way home, I do not want to leave a balance.

They say that I am always welcome and that if I should ever need to come back, I can. They have shown me their maps, and their world is one hundred times the size of mine. They encourage me to stay and be safe, but I am more desperate than ever to get home.

I am missing four very large pieces of my soul, and without them, I feel myself changing, and it is not for the better. I do not want to be like my mother.

I need a good fight. No one here can use a sword, and I find that horrifying. I have ridden their horses, but they are not the same as Solas.

I have found that I love the food called a hamburger and that beef is delicious. We do not have beef at home. When I am Queen, we will have all the beef taken to Talamh na Sithe. All of it. Mortal food is so tasty and varied, and I find that I cannot get enough. For the first time in my life, I want to eat.

I wonder if it is the sickness over the land that has made the food there so plain. I stuff great amounts of beef into my face, and my waist has gotten nothing but smaller even though my ass is unchanged. I do not understand this.

Remi says she has gained twelve kilos since I arrived, and she blames my cakes. I'm not sure what a kilo is, but her pants do ride a bit snugger than they used to. Everyone in the house wears tight pants now.

I love blue jeans. Talamh na Sithe will also have all of those under my rule. I put my favorite pair in my pack every time I go to try to open the old way, just in case. I will not be separated from them.

Dogs are not as bad a creature as I originally thought. Though they are still very wet.

They have taken me by car to the top of the nearest cliff many times. I can't bring myself to jump off of it. Surely that is not the only way.

I was in the garden one twilight, throwing balls of light with the children. Paulina and Remi watched from the porch with soft smiles. I had just gotten back from the base of the cliff, and my nightly attempt to return home when the soft little boy I hold often stopped me and held up his arms. I popped him on my hip and lobbed pink balls of light to an older girl with long blond hair and bright green eyes wearing a cute little frock. She reminds me of Arlie when first I met her. Arlie, whom the trolls took.

Trolls will never take this child. Those things don't happen here.

I felt a sting in my chest that I had never felt before but recognized immediately.

Seal.

How I knew it was him, I can't say.

I saw him at the top of the hill with sword in hand, watching me, his body silhouetted by the setting sun looked gaunt.

I set the boy down.

Paulina and Remi stood, shielding their eyes against the glare.

He looked like a wraith. A shell of the Seal I knew. I took off, running toward him. I stopped just short of his arms. He hadn't moved. His usual scruff had grown long and wild. His eyes were feral, and the planes of his face sharp. He looked starved. His eyes never left mine, but he was not behind them.

"Seal," I said, breaking the silence. He grabbed me then, pulling me to him. His body shook, and I could feel his bones moving beneath my hands as I wrapped them around him. He smelled of Earth, Pine, and old blood.

And then I remembered his magic. He said I would do well to remember that he could track me anywhere. Saige said that he could not rest when he was tracking, that it drove him mad until he found his quarry.

I believed it. I had been gone a long time, and he had suffered horribly.

"Ari," he croaked, barely getting the word out.

"Seal, you aren't well. Come, let me take care of you, and then we can go home. I've been trying to walk the old ways; how did you manage?" I cried and clutched him to me. Goddess had I missed him. Missed them all.

"I took a leap of faith," he said into my hair. When he pulled away from me, he was calm, his eyes less wild. He was there again. He kissed me, wrapping himself around me. "Goddess, I missed you."

"I love you, Seal."

"I love you too, Ari. I love you."

"Thank you for coming for me."

"I will always come for you."

I held him to me until I felt each muscle relax in him. When he was still, I pulled back.

"Laith?" I asked, afraid of hearing his answer.

"Was alive and healing the last time I saw him," he said, swallowing hard.

I closed my eyes and took a deep breath. "I thought he died and that his death was the last I would see of any of you."

"No, Ari. Solas came to the border; we followed her back and found him in time."

"Thank the Goddess." He pulled me to him again, holding me tight.

"Arlie?" I asked.

"She is home safe."

"Teagan?"

"Is lost."

I cried then. I cried for all that we had been through. I cried because Seal looked haunted, and my friend was lost, but I also cried because I was in his arms, and Laith survived.

There is good and bad in every day we live; I know that now. Life is never one thing. Never all good, and never all bad. He held me while I cried. Once I started, I couldn't stop. I couldn't remember the last time I cried like this. Maybe I never had. Maybe I had needed to.

When I was done and clean on the inside, I pulled away. "Come, I have cupcakes cooling, and there are people that would like to meet you. I will grab my pack, and then we can go home." I met his light brown eyes with my green ones. I knew he wanted to leave this place, and so did I, but I must say goodbye first.

He nodded silently and allowed me to take his hand and lead him down the hill. "You can relax your hand; you don't need your sword here, Love," I said, noting the way he watched everything around him and kept his hand hovering above his blade.

"What kind of place is this?" he asked.

"A place where children roam in packs and dogs give wet kisses."

"Packs of children?"

"Just wait."

At the bottom of the hill and the very edge of the village known as Clifden, packs of children huddled in wait. Seal's steps slowed, then faltered as he approached them. I kept steady pressure on his hand, not wanting to let him go. Despite his wild appearance, they walked, toddled, and crawled up to us. I plopped the little Humanling back on my hip and lobbed colored balls at the others for them to play with.

"Ari! Ari! Throw me one!" They cried in their language, and I answered in kind. Seal's face locked on mine when he heard me use their strange tongue. I smiled at him, wrapping my free arm around his waist.

"One day, Talamh na Sithe will be this way. I swear it." I felt the promise settle over me in a binding and knew the Goddess had accepted my word. "And it will have all the beef," I added for good measure.

Seal reached a tentative hand toward the little boy I held, then let it fall. His eyes watched the easy way I held him on my hip and smiled.

"Would you like to hold him? He is squishy."

"Squishy?"

"Yes." I foisted the child on him then walked to where Paulina and Remi waited. We were followed by a pack of children, all yelling for more magic balls. Paulina shooed them away, taking the little boy from Seal even as he fought her for him. She set the boy down, and he toddled after his older sister.

"Paulina and Remi of Clifden, meet Sealgair, Master Huntsman of Talamh na Sithe," I said first in their language and then in mine. "You may call him Seal." He bowed slightly to them, keeping a concerned eye on everything that was going on around him.

I imagined this was how I looked on that first day, scared, worried, threatened, hostile, and wild. Children rode their bicycles in the road, dogs barked, cars passed, and poor Seal took it all in. I had been there too. I knew, now, that it wasn't magic. I would explain it to him later- to all of them.

"May I allow him to use the shower?" I asked.

"Of course," Paulina whispered, not taking her eyes off Seal. I couldn't blame her. He was a bit of a mess. "My husband was about his size; I will get him some clean things."

I saw him as she must, furs hanging off of him in tatters, his moleskin riding pants covered in old blood, poor Paulina. I felt the debt between us grow and knew I'd be baking more or telling tales in a bit. First, though, I guided Seal through the house, around the television and radio that happened to both be on. I saw him staring, his eyes never staying on one thing for long. I knew it was a shock.

In the bathroom, I stripped him naked, reveling in the feel of his skin on mine. I ran my hands over the hard planes of his muscle and the sharp edges of his bones where they had lost their flesh. I turned the water on and made it hot for him before placing the soaps out and explaining what each one did.

I pulled out Collin's scissors and trimmed his beard while we waited for the water to heat. He let me take care of him. I kissed along his jawline and gloried in having him in front of me. Then,

I pushed him under the hard stream of hot water and laughed at his startled cry.

"We are so getting a magic waterfall when we get home." I picked up his dirty clothes and placed the ones Paulina had laid outside the door for him on the toilet. It took me almost a week to stop peeing in the yard and use it. Ours at home was functional but much simpler in style. I bet Seal would love to try it.

I left him to enjoy his shower and placed his clothes in the trash to be burned. There was no saving them.

In the kitchen, I started baking a cake. Paulina had made a beef tenderloin that she knew was my favorite, and dinner had already been almost finished when we went to the base of the cliff. I placed the beef, potatoes, beans, and salad on the table while waiting for the others. Paulina and Remi sat quietly.

"Your Huntsman is rather wild," Remi said, waggling her eyebrows at me.

"It's his magic. I feel terrible. He probably hasn't slept since I've been gone."

"He'll be better now," Paulina said. They knew the stories. I had told them everything about my men. All of it, there was nothing they didn't know; that was the deal we had made. When I made it, I didn't think I would be here long enough to have to tell them much. In fact, I had told them everything down to the smallest detail.

Seal walked around down the hall, his eyes finding mine immediately and his body relaxing. He looked amazing, his dark blond hair slicked back and dripping down his back. The different browns in his eyes glittered as he took in the kitchen, not missing a single detail. I put the cake in the oven that required no fire and went to him.

"He is so pretty," Remi said. "He doesn't understand me, right?" she said, glancing sidelong at the half-wild Faeman in her kitchen.

"No, he doesn't," I laughed.

"Perfect." "Now, he was the first one, yes?"

"Remi," Paulina shushed her with a twinkle in her eye.

"You speak their language well," Seal said, eyeing me.

I piled a plate high with everything on the table and set it down for him.

"Eat, Seal. Paulina speaks our language," I say, letting him know she understands him. "They taught me theirs. How long have I been gone?" I asked.

"Do you not know?" he asked, curious. "I see they have been good to you. I will not have to kill them."

"They have been very kind, yes. They are very good people." I laughed. "Time passes differently here. They say I have been here over thirty-seven days, but I do not know. Their calendar is hard to learn."

"You disappeared sixteen days ago, Ari," he said, taking a forkful of beef in his mouth and then stopped. I watched, fascinated. "What creature is this?" he said with his eyes closed.

"It is a beef," I answered proudly.

"A cow," Paulina corrected at the same time.

There was no more conversation. Seal cleaned his plate. Three times. It was a good thing they always made extra because he ate the extra too. He ate the entire bowl of salad, so I got up to make more.

I iced my cake as he ate and added four trays of cookies to the mix. He ate half the cake and an entire tray of cookies before he spoke again.

Paulina, Collin, Remi, and I chatted while we ate. We switched languages enough so he could hear most of our conversation. Seal did not miss that I shoved two plates of food down my throat, too. His eyes narrowed in speculation. My heart was light that I had not been gone in Talamh na Sithe as long as I had been here. Sixteen days sounds so much better than five weeks. The way Seal looked on that hillside, he would be dead if I had been gone five true weeks.

He reached for my hand under the table, and I gave it to him. Surrounded by warmth and friendly conversation, his head found the table, and he slept. My poor, brave Seal. My heart bled for him, but I could not wake him now.

Chapter Forty-Six

Seal

I saw her holding a child, the sunlight glinting off her red hair, and I almost turned around and went home. This place was good for her. She wore her hair long and loose and was surrounded by more children than Talamh na Sithe had ever seen at one time. I have never seen her more relaxed; she did not even carry her sword. Her smile was real, and her laugh tantalized me, even from this distance. She tossed balls of light to the children, and they ran with them, throwing them about until the light died, and they had to return for another.

I was speechless.

I should have left her, but I did not. Then she saw me. I felt her relief through the link I used to track her, and I wondered if I had read the scene wrong. Maybe she was a captive here. She raced to me, and no one stopped her, so that must be wrong too. I was confused. Weary. Nearly dead, but I had found Ari.

I stood on the edge of that cliff when I could take no more and let myself fall. Either way. I would get relief.

I had never seen her look more magnificent. Her magic swirled around her like water between the banks of a river. She was glorious. This place swelled with magic, and Ari had soaked it all in. All of it was hers. She stopped short, staring at me. I couldn't move, couldn't speak, or breathe. I was lost to her.

"Seal," she said my name like a prayer, and I was done. I wrapped her in my arms and would have taken her then, but I was weak from the hunt. I needed to just feel her. My magic calmed, and I felt peace for the first time since that awful day.

Until she cried.

Once upon a time, I thought I saw a tear on Ari's face, and I wanted to kill the tear for falling. When Ari fell apart in my arms, it was the end of my world. Her heart broke, and I felt it, but then it came together again, and I felt that too. She is so strong and so brave, but maybe bravery and strength aren't always enough. She cleansed herself of every emotion she had ever bottled up at that moment. I held her tight and let sobs rack her tiny body until she was lighter in my arms.

When she had calmed, she dragged me down the hill and tossed a child into my arms, and I honestly didn't know what was happening. Hands reached for her, and voices called her name. Maybe she had become their Queen, and this was her kingdom now. It was hard to say. Magic surrounded us, and great metal beasts stalked the roads.

Insanity.

Then she showed me the magic waterfall, and she is right; we will have one of those in our home immediately upon our arrival. I don't know how, but it will be done.

Ari spoke their language, often forgetting to speak ours at all. I didn't care. The sound of her voice in any tongue was music to my ears. I had been so wrong. About everything. I hadn't wanted to apply for her, but now I knew that I was nothing without her in my life. Maybe that was the insanity.

I had never seen an old woman. Ari said she was mortal and not a Goddess, but I am not sure I believe her. Three females sitting at one table is such an oddity, their sparkle and shine so distracting that I thought they all had to be Goddesses. The children outside had been equally numbered boys to girls. I couldn't wrap my head around it, but it didn't matter because Ari gave me a beef.

Great Goddess, I will learn that creature's realm and hunt it to extinction. I couldn't think anymore after that. All I could do was eat. I couldn't remember the last time I had. Then the oddest thing happened.

Ari ate too.

Plates of food.

Her eyes rolled back in her head, and she ate and ate with pleasure that I had never seen her take in food. Her backside was round and her waist just as tiny as ever, and she glowed luminescent in the light of their magic torches.

These people had fed her and cared for her when we could not. I owed them a debt that must be paid before leaving this place, regardless of what they say. I would find them a stag that would feed them for all the days they had cared for her.

I shoved Ari's cake in my mouth with my bare hands, moaning at the taste of her magic. Goddess. I had missed her cakes.

Then I ate the cookies.

My head hit the table, and I knew no more. Exhaustion took me, and I couldn't stop it. I felt Ari pat my hand and her fingers twine in my hair. I was lulled by the warm feel of her and the soft sound of their conversation in a language I did not know.

I reached for my sword only to find it gone.

Someone had placed a pillow under my head where I still sat at the table. I felt better than I had in many, many moons.

I rose, stretching, and followed the tracking link to Ari and found her sitting in the garden with a glass of something amber in her hands. She was talking softly to the other women. The moon hung heavy over the treeline like it was either just coming up or getting ready to set. As the horizon was dark, I guessed the former.

The sad tone of the conversation struck my heart. I went to her and bent my knee.

"If you want to stay, my Queen, say the word, and I will go." I bowed my head, not meeting her eyes. She placed her hand in my hair and fisted it with a deep sigh.

"I wish we could stay here, Seal. I wish we could all stay, but I know we can't. My mother can travel the ways, and that she hasn't already is a small miracle. If she found us? I don't want to find out what she would do. My magic is much stronger here, and no doubt hers would be too. I'm not ready to take her on. I'm certainly not ready to endanger innocent lives," she said, gently caressing my hair. She handed me her glass, and I rose, taking a drink. It was an ale of some sort, light and pleasant. I drank it down.

"I was just saying goodbye, Seal. I'm ready when you are." She held up her pack and mine; my sword was with hers, strapped across her back. She was speaking the truth then; you can't always trust that with Ari. It's one of the things I love most about her.

"I owe them a stag for feeding you," I said, bending my knee to the old Goddess.

"You owe us nothing, Seal," she said to me in my language. "Ari has more than paid any debt she might have felt she owed." She patted my head, and her warmth seeped into me. "Ari is a special girl, Seal. I have tried to tell her this, but she doesn't understand. Some of your histories have already been written as you are our past. Our roads didn't diverge all that long ago.

Airmed's name is in those history books, as is some of your story. You have a way to go but know this. Should you ever need help or a place to hide, come here. We will see that you are far away and safe until you can make your claim and keep the promises you made. It will happen soon enough. I may be an old woman, but I read well."

"Thank you for your prophecy, Great Goddess of the Mortal Lands; it will not go unheeded," I said.

She laughed at me, but it was not an unkind laugh, more of an amused chuckle. Then she mussed my hair and pulled me up into a hug. I was quite taken by that.

They all stood and hugged while Ari held them to her for a long time. She said words I didn't understand, and she didn't repeat so that I could. They were her words; I would not ask her to. Then she grabbed my hand and walked with me into the night.

"Where to, my Lord," she said with a wink.

"To the base of the cliff, my Lady."

"Don't call me that," She chuckled and pushed me away from her. I grabbed her tight to me, and together we walked up the hill and the short distance to the base of the cliff.

"Do you trust me?" I asked.

"With my life," she said, training her glittering green eyes on mine. I saw the absolute seriousness with which she said it. She could have stayed here and been safe forever, but she would not. She would trust me to keep her that way, and I would. I watched her for a moment, letting that understanding fill my eyes for her to see.

"Close your eyes, take my hand, and believe we will walk out in Talamh na Sithe."

And she did.

I took her hand and walked us straight into the rocks at the base of the cliff; only the rocks rippled and gave way.

We were home.

Ari said nothing as the oppressive weight of Talamh na Sithe settled over us. I knew she felt it. I had only been gone a few hours, and I felt it. I couldn't imagine how it felt to her after so long an absence, but she didn't complain.

She kept my hand in hers and waited quietly, her pack slung over her shoulders looked heavy, and I wondered what magic she brought home with her. I whistled for my stallion.

We didn't wait long. Solas and Cloch came running together, Solas screaming and pawing the entire way even though Ari didn't call her, she knew. She ran up to Ari, nearly knocking the girl over. Ari bent her nose to the mare and exchanged breaths with her.

"I never dreamed you survived, old girl," she said, feathering her nose with soft kisses. She wrapped her arms around the mare, who stilled at her touch.

"We dared not let her die, love," I whispered, enjoying the sight of her. Every sight of her.

"Come, let's go before we are spotted. I don't know what may have happened in my absence. I've not been home since that day."

"Oh, Seal, I'm so sorry," she reached for me, and I pulled her in to kiss her forehead.

"Do not apologize, just don't ever fight Trolls on your own again, please."

"I will try not to," she said in all seriousness.

We mounted our horses and rode home as fast as we could.

Chapter Forty-Seven

Lann

Goddess, it had all fallen apart. How had it happened that quickly? One moment, I was surrounded by the greatest joy ever, and the next, nothing but sorrow. Laith and Saige were ghosts in my life. The brotherhood we had was gone.

Seal was missing, probably dead, and Ari disappeared. I had no one to even raise my sword with. I refused to go back to the barracks, not yet. When I could see the Queen without putting my blade to her neck, I would go. That wasn't today. That likely wasn't tomorrow either.

I had just gone for another cup of Ale when the sound of hooves clattering in the yard stopped me short. I caught a glimpse of a white wraith and dropped my ale. I was out the door before I understood what I was doing. Ari was home.

Ari was home.

I heard doors opening and voices calling, but I only had eyes for one person.

She stood in the garden wearing the oddest blue pants and a black shirt. Her hair was long and loose about her face. She looked whole- safe, whole, and completely Ari. I grabbed her up and spun her in a circle; her laughter thrilled through me, and my lips crashed into hers. She kissed me, gripping my neck in her hand until I was breathless. She was ripped away from me, and I growled, never wanting her to be ripped away from me again.

I reached for her, but Laith had her in his clutches, and you know how that goes, there would be no getting her back. They kissed, and he cried, sobbing into her hair and messing it all up. The simple act of seeing her had us back together. All of us. She truly is our center, and without her, we frayed. Badly.

Saige stepped up, and like the warrior he is, he grabbed her from the giant sobbing man, wrapping her in his arms, and crushed her to him. He pulled her onto his lap and sat on the couch, rocking her like a baby. He kissed her, and our world shifted, settling back into a place of peace.

Seal just watched through satisfied eyes. He had done it. I don't know how, but he had. The magic is strong in that one. He looked gaunt and exhausted but happy. I had never been so glad to see him.

We passed her around, taking turns hugging and kissing her, and she let us, our desperation, was that obvious. When we settled down, and the tears stopped, she stood, taking in the place like she had never seen it before. She walked around the room, touching things, just like she had the very first day she came to us.

I watched her. We all did. Not knowing her thoughts, not knowing what had happened to her was killing me, but I wouldn't rush her. She moved almost too slow, and I worried for her. She didn't move to the kitchen to bake, and that meant something. She plucked the damn cat off the table and held her tight, pushing their noses together until Isa let out a strangled meow. She took the cat to the couch and sat. Maybe our exuberance was too much, I don't know. We sat quietly, waiting her out.

"I missed you all so much," she said, her voice barely above a whisper. "I honestly didn't think I would ever come back, yet the way home was so simple. I don't understand why I couldn't come back the instant I left," she said, her voice cracking. "I put us all through so much when it should have been so simple," she added, a tear falling from her lashes and undoing me.

"Ari," Seal said. "It wasn't that easy, I swear. Do you know how many times I tried and failed? Maybe it is part of being a Huntsman that finally allowed me to do it. Don't beat yourself up about that."

"I just," she started.

"No," Laith said. "No, Ari. We all tried to walk the ways and couldn't. It's not your fault, and it may have felt like forever, but it wasn't that long."

"It was there. It was a long time there."

Then she told us. It fell from her lips in half sobs and halted starts. She told us everything that had happened from the start of that day to the end of this one. She filled in our gaps, and we filled in hers until there was one solid story.

She told us of the family that had taken her in and of the wildness of the mortal realm. She talked a lot about magic waterfalls and beef and how they must all belong to her. I didn't even know what those things were, but I believed her when she said she would have them all. Seal nodded his head in agreement, and I wonder what kind of place they had been to.

In the end, we sat four across, as close as we could get, with her on our laps in the middle. Our need to touch her was so great. Seal dozed on and off as he hadn't slept in truth since that day.

We decided that action must be taken. We no longer felt secure in the fact that Ari was safe in our home. We would be more vigilant. We would not allow the Queen to get her hands on Ari at any cost. Sometime during the night, we slept. We hadn't meant to, but exhaustion and emotion had other ideas. We ended up on Ari's bed. Crushed together and fully clothed, which wasn't exactly how any of us wanted the night to end but was the end to the night we needed.

Chapter Forty-Eight

Ari

I awoke under the crush of four men, a slow smile spreading on my face. After the weeks I had spent alone in a bed, it was nice to have this bit of normalcy back. I wiggled my leg loose from whoever had it pinned, setting off a cascade of movements around me.

A nose nuzzled into my neck, a hand drifted across my waist, and a leg twined with mine. I moved my hand up the back of the man on top of that arm and turned my head into the chest of another, inhaling the scent of iron and smoke. Their scents drifted around me in the air, and I could pick out each one of them by that alone.

A hand drifted over my breast, and I arched against it.

A mouth found mine in the dark, and I sank into it.

Soon, the clothes were gone. They were one thing, and I was all. I didn't know where they began, and I ended. It was a rush of tongues, lips, and teeth. It was fevered, uncontrolled, and fierce.

I couldn't get my hands on them fast enough, and I was covered with bodies and filled in every way. I didn't know who was who in those moments and didn't care. It was smooth and seamless. Lips clashed, and hands twined. They took each other and me.

In the haze that surrounded us, it all flowed together, one body into the next, into the next. I came, again and again, yelling their names to the Goddess and not caring that she might be listening.

Where one cock left me, another one entered: my mouth, my hands, everywhere. There are no details about which one did what; there were just endless waves of pleasure.

The first man came, pulsing inside of me and sending me over the edge. It had been too long since I held them in this most intimate of ways. Then the next one came as if each one set off a cascade for the next.

When the waves of one finished, the next one took his place because they all needed to be in me at that moment, and I needed it too. I needed that core of them as deep as it would go. I needed them in me to be whole again.

Their grunts signaled their final pleasure, and the night was filled with them. When the last man slid between my thighs, I caught a whiff of citrus and oak, surprised that Lann would have the patience to wait. Maybe he hadn't, and he needed more to be satisfied; I lost count of their orgasms and mine.

I rolled my hips into him in welcome. I could do this all night, and it was wonderful to have them all together, just as wonderful as I always knew it would be, should it happen. Hands touched my breasts, and fingers rubbed my core until I was all but writing under him. Hands fisted in my hair, and lips kissed mine, while others traced their way down my neck and teeth grazed my nipples. We were frenzied for each other.

I felt the beginnings of the thing before I saw it. Threads of purple wove around us like cloth, wrapping us in a delicate spell.

Weaving. Knotting. Binding.

And as Lann moved his hips with mine, sending me over the edge with one final cry that joined his, I felt the magic snap into place.

And I knew.

I knew then what gift the Goddess would give me.

A gift I had not wanted but now wanted more than anything.

A gift that would require the greatest sacrifice, and that is no understatement.

From four seeds came one child, and her magic is legion. It has no beginning and no end. It just is, and I knew in an instant, as all Fae do.

The Goddess had taken the best from the five of us and created something the world has not seen before. That knowledge settled with certainty into my soul, and I froze under Lann as the waves of his final orgasm ebbed.

We saw. We all saw the purple threads binding us, and they knew, too. There was no doubt.

We spent the night silent in each other's arms, no one knowing what to say.

They wanted children. This had been their job in the beginning, but it became something else in the end. We fell in love. The Goddess, in her infinite wisdom, had chosen us. I cannot say why.

The next morning, I climbed from beneath the arms and legs that held me and went to the garden to watch the sunrise, the cup of tea I brewed cold in my hands. The sky was heavy with pink clouds, yet behind them, there were lavender skies. I had never seen a more beautiful sunrise.

"Pink sky in morning, warriors take warning," I said to whichever of my mates had sneaked up behind me to wrap their arms around my waist, placing a protective hand over my flat stomach.

"Yet there is lavender too, and that is the color of the Goddess. We will get through this, Ari, she promised you." I turned into Saige and buried my nose in his chest to try to keep from crying. He held me tight to him.

"When will you leave?" Laith said from behind him.

"I'm not leaving. I can never leave you again," I said, losing the fight with my tears.

"Ari," Laith said, taking me gently into his arms. "You can't stay. Even I can feel our Faeling's magic, and I am the weakest of you all."

"No. There has to be another way. I won't go."

"It's not forever. Just until you can face the Queen and win, or all of us together can face her. We must build armies and make plans. You aren't close to safe here, and our baby certainly isn't," Lann came, arms crossing around me too.

"She will take you, Ari. She will take you, and when this child is born, she will kill you and take our child. She will take her, Ari. You know this. Our child will have no equal. Imagine her in Aramea's hands." Saige leaned into me, and I grasped him tight.

"She will kill her too," I whimpered, unable to stop myself.

"Or worse."

"She never wanted a powerful child; imagine what she would do with this Goddess Blessed child with infinite power."

"She will kill us both before we can save ourselves."

"She will."

"I don't want to leave you. I swore if I came back, I would never miss you again. I love you all too much for that." I broke down then, sobs racked my body.

"This is the sacrifice, love. The reward will come," Seal said. He was suddenly beside me, his face filling my vision. "The Goddess made you a promise. She will not break it."

I nodded into him. I knew they were right. I couldn't stay. I wanted this child more than anything. The love I had felt for a Squishy mortal boy whose name I didn't even know was nothing compared to what I already felt for this spot in my womb that leaked strange magics. I would die protecting her, but I would not die in vain.

"We have time. A few days. We will make this as right as we can, Ari." Laith moved to my side, leaning in to kiss my hair.

"What if you don't want me when she's old enough for me to return. What if I give up everything for her and lose you anyway?" I asked, voicing my real fear.

"Never, Ari," Saige swore, and I felt the truth of his words settle over me in a promise. "We are yours and you ours. We are a family, all of us. Nothing is more important."

"We waited for you from the beginning. We made a choice, and we chose you. Maybe you didn't choose us, but you choose us now. You must do this for all of us."

"Your daughter will grow up and not know you. How can that be right?" The tears fell for real then. I didn't want to face this alone.

"Our daughter will live and grow in the mortal world. She won't be allowed to do that here, Ari. You will tell her about us, and we will be together again under a better Queen," Laith said, kneeling in front of me. "That Queen will be you, and if you don't want the job, it will be our child who will bring us all peace. Our very powerful girl child. If left here, she will be a short-lived pawn."

"Seal can walk the ways. You'll go together, and he can bring us to visit when it's safe. You won't be alone." Lann knelt beside Laith, begging me to see it.

In the end, all four men knelt at my feet, and I cradled them to me as best I could. I knew there was no choice, but I didn't have to like it. They were my heart, but then so was our child.

We spent the next few days planning, making love, and planning some more. I spent hours with them alone and together. We made love until we were sore and spent and then we danced. Chest to chest and skin to skin, shirts off in the moonlight, we danced and talked until there was nothing left to say.

We did not sleep in those days. Not much. Our bond tightened, and even I felt the solidity of it. It was unbreakable. In those moments, our speck of a child knew nothing but love if she knew anything at all. We ate only cakes and cookies. I baked so much that they thought my cakes would last to the end of time. It was all I could do. We did not leave the house.

We poured over the encyclopedias I had borrowed from Paulina and learned everything we could. I began to teach Seal some simple English and spoke in English when I could. The men soaked it up.

We had no money for the mortal world, but we had what they valued in spades. Diamonds, gemstones, gold, and silver filled our pouches. We would not be poor there. We could live well and be safe. It was a small comfort. After looking at maps and charts, we decided to travel to America. Clifden was too easy a target, and the Queen would find us there eventually. I let Lann, Saige, and Laith decide where we would go and pick their daughter's name. I needed them to be involved. They thought on that until the day we knew we could wait no longer.

We burned the encyclopedias.

Whether it was their blood in mine or a gift from the Goddess, my four learned to lie and lie well. We developed a story, and they could tell it to perfection.

Seal and I had fallen in love, and I would not share, and neither could he; we only had room for each other. His small bit of human DNA was like a curse to my mother, and she would believe that it had tainted him.

He had disappeared right after I did and had not been seen since. It was a coincidence none could deny, not with his Huntsman magic. They would play that up and be angry so that she would not doubt them or suspect their duplicity.

We ran away. The note I left hidden from them in my room said that we went to Tir fo Thuinn and that I was sorry, but they should not worry.

In their anger, my mates will share this note with the Queen when the time is appropriate.

They will keep her close, as she is the greatest enemy we have.

I did not say goodbye to The Eight, who are now Six. They may know, and they may surmise, but I could never lie to them, so it was best to say nothing.

I said Goodbye to Solas, for that is what it was. I would never see her again. I cried into her mane and begged her forgiveness. I know she knew of the child, as her magic could be felt by the stone wall in the garden. I knew she understood, as well as she could, for she would be a mother soon too. I cried anyway, for I loved that mare.

On the fifth day after her conception, I shoved Isa in my pack. I would at least take my cat. The five of us took one last ride together, following the winding game trails so we would not be seen. Seal knew them by heart, and we went to the crossroads and just a hint north.

At the edge of the cliff, we clung to each other as the dawn broke over the horizon. We all cried. We smiled too because we knew it was not forever. We had been made a promise and had faith in our Goddess. She surrounded us that morning in love and lavender light, but she did not intrude on our farewell. Like she said, what is thirty or forty years in the natural span of a nearly immortal lifetime? It would pass quickly.

Before Seal and I held hands and walked over the cliff into the world beyond. We were given a name. It came from the women that the three left behind had been influenced by the most. Lara after Laith's mother, Liann, after Lann's Grandmother, and Hennessey after Saige's aunt, who had raised him.

She would be Lara Liann Hennessey.

Epilogue

We watch her play in the waves on her second birthday. She is a child of the Sea, and the Goddess visits her there, I believe this. She is a beautiful thing: fierce, brave, beautiful, protective, and magnificent. She outshines us, as children should.

She looks the most like all of them and very little like me, which is also as it should be, for they are beautiful men. They visit often, not always together so as not to raise suspicion, but we six unite as often as we can.

On her first birthday, they all came. We wove a spell that covered our home in Pawley's Island, South Carolina, because Lara's magic is too wild to contain. We feared it would reach out to the Queen in Talamh Na Sithe. Just as it took the five of us to make her, it took the five of us to make a spell strong enough to protect her.

After finding our daughter had turned herself into a tiny white pony with a rainbow-colored mane and tail. She was running around her room, bucking. I begged Seal to go to the Goddess for help with her power.

During his absence, the neighbor's cat was hit by a car on the street near our house, and Lara healed the thing. From near death came a spry cat that will not leave her side and spends its nights curled with Isa at her feet.

I knew what she was then, and it terrified me. A true Healer had power like no other Fae, and it would be a death sentence for her if any found out before she could protect herself.

I could not explain any of this to the neighbor, so the cat stayed with us.

Seal returned with Lann, Saige, Laith, and a stone.

I made them explain to me why I should let their baby eat rocks.

They told me that the Goddess had made the magic we needed into a stone that, when swallowed, would build the wall that would keep our daughter safe.

When she was old enough to control her power, the wall would crumble away slowly, giving her time to learn.

Should her life ever be in real danger, the wall would break, and the magic save her life. The consequences of this could be severe, and we were encouraged to not let it happen that way.

We fed our daughter the stone with her cake.

It helped immediately, and we spent a week loving her and each other.

Time does pass quickly, and it will be okay. The sacrifice is worth it to see her live and grow.

They soak up her love, and she calls them all Da-Da. She knows. In her glorious heart, she knows we are not complete unless we are all together. Where once I was their center, now she is ours.

Someday we will go home. One of us will be Queen, and we will bring the mortal lands' prosperity with us. For all of our People.

I know this.

I have an unbreakable promise from those I love most and the Mother of us all. I believe in happily ever after and live the fairy tale, which has no end.

Sharilyn spent most of her early years on the Grand Strand of South Carolina, annoying local police officers and probably pretty much everyone else. She graduated from the University of South Carolina and now lives on a small farm outside of Morgantown, WV, with various farm animals, her husband, and three kids who love to annoy her. (Karma is a bitch). She writes Urban Fantasy, Reverse Harem, and Omegaverse. She loves showing Quarter horses, trail riding, reading, and being annoyed by her kids. If she is missing, check for her horse trailer. If it is missing, no worries, she'll be back. Probably.

Healer Series: Series Complete

Cerridwen's Tears

Healer

House of Fire

The Scarlet Heron

The Flame Keeper

Goddess Bound

The Eight Series:

Airmed

Ravena

Teagan

Omegas of The New South:

The Omega Rule

The Omega Challenge

An Alpha's Grace

Trauma- Spring 2021

Follow me on Facebook, Instagram, Twitter, Goodreads, and my plain old website.

www.sharilynskye.com